BETROTHAL OF DUTY

by
Francis Davison

JOHN 20:27

In loving memory of Josephine Davison
February 29, 1932 to January 25, 2008
I wish you here to read this Gramma, I love you and I
miss you. See you there…

The Author would like to thank Mike Foley for his
invaluable help and advice.
Visit his website at http://writers-review.com/ and sign
up for his newsletter.

Special thanks to my beta readers;
Debbie & Dave, Bruce & Jessica, Lanette, Sharon,
Andrew, and Chris.
To my mother Jo Lynn, who read the first *unedited*
concept draft.

Cover Art by Delaney V. G.
www.deeevgart.tumblr.com

Prologue

Captain Victor Rostov hid in the shadow of a tall pine tree. The bitter cold of the Splinterwood Forest reddened his cheeks. The winter had been a harsh one. In the west, he could see snow lingering on the peaks of the Granitespine Mountains reminding him that spring was still months away.

He held the reins of his horse as he stood out of sight, peering into the forest with all-seeing eyes. Waiting.

Scattered around him, crouched against the ground among the low-lying shrubs and hiding behind trees, his soldiers watched. All of them wore boiled leather armor reinforced with steel studs. Each bore a dark-green tabard, emblazoned with a single pine tree on the chest. They clutched weapons as they looked to their Captain, waiting for his signal.

Rostov's blood ran swiftly in his veins. Against the excitement in his heart, doubt gnawed at his mind. He feared that he guessed wrong about where his enemies, the ogon, would appear. If he did, those he pursued would escape into the forest and evade the punishment that awaited them as they had twice before.

Just as he felt the nagging doubt would swallow his heart, he heard the hollow thud of hoofbeats, growing louder.

He raised a hand and his men stirred. He could sense their eyes fixed on him and felt their readiness to follow his commands.

The Captain glanced at two of them hiding on

either side of the trail ahead of his position. Both gripped a rope that strung along the ground, ready to be pulled taut at his command.

Mixed in among the approaching clamor, came the sound of heavy breathing and snorting beasts.

The sounds grew louder. They were close, and getting closer. He smiled as satisfaction swelled in his mind knowing his quarry was within reach. He had chosen wisely. This time, there was no escape.

The low bushes moved. Branches snapped under the weight of the mounts that carried the fugitives, giving away their position.

Rostov dropped his arm with a snap, signaling his men to action.

The soldiers gripping the rope pulled their ends, drawing it taut across the trail, hovering a foot off the ground.

His prey came into view, appearing from between the bushes and trees. The mounted beasts began tripping over the line as the men struggled to hold it tight. Their riders flew forward, surprised and confused, toward the waiting swords of Rostov's unit. Without hesitation, the soldiers soared into action, hacking and slashing at their enemies.

Rostov stepped out from his hiding place. He observed the ogon. Around their wrists, they wore strips of red cloth. Stolen teeth of both men and beasts decorated their ears and necks. There was no doubt in his mind. These ogon were from the Shattered-Tooth clan.

"I want the bald one alive!" he commanded,

pushing aside his cloak and loosening his sword in its scabbard. His raiment matched those of his men, but instead of a tabard, he wore a green sash across his chest with the pine tree device embroidered in gold at his shoulder, marking him as the Captain.

The beasts the hunted rode regained their footing and flew into a rage. Some of them entered the fight, attacking anyone near them, adding to the confusion before fleeing into the forest. The men killed many enemies before they could rise to their feet. The most savage of the lot, gained their footing and engaged their enemies in bitter combat.

Defiantly, the bald-ogon stood and faced one of the charging soldiers. His countenance was bold. Fearless. He was tall and intimidating. His face bore scars where the claws of a beast had raked him. His hair was gray and thick, but with a bald pate. He was their leader, and the most dangerous of the gang.

Rostov strutted toward him. He trusted his men to secure the others, but this one, he would tend to himself. The Captain watched his soldier as he charged. Alone, the bald-ogon posed a great challenge, and he doubted the young man possessed the skill to defeat him.

The soldier lunged, swinging his sword as if to kill and end the fight quickly. He was either afraid, or did not hear Rostov's command among the din of the fighting.

The bald-ogon dodged and countered with an elbow hard against the soldier's nose. The sudden impact stunned him and he reeled, grunting under the pain.

Suddenly, he was vulnerable! The Captain quickened his pace to a charge fearing his curiosity would get the young man killed.

The bald ogon, using the tip of his foot, scooped up a shorten spear off the ground, flipping it upward into the air and catching it. He reared, preparing to thrust its point into the heart of his opponent.

Rostov leaped ahead to close the distance, drew his sword and intercepted the spear, forcing it up and away from the reeling soldier. Using his opposite hand, he struck his enemy on his upturned nose.

The bald-ogon grimaced. He gripped his spear tightly. The punch to the nose angered him and rage filled his gold eyes.

Rostov held the point of his sword toward him, ready to engage the scowling monster.

The soldier whom he defended stood at his side. He collected himself as he wiped blood from his crushed nose on his glove.

The ogon gave an ear-piercing war cry then attacked. Rostov first, then the other bleeding soldier. Both men retreated a step away from the thrusting point of the spear.

Behind his opponent, Rostov glanced at his gathering men. They defeated the gang, and turned to see their Captain and one wounded man fighting the leader.

Rostov attacked to keep his opponent's attention fixed on him and away from his unit. With a clever step, he maneuvered his unsuspecting enemy to turn his back on the balance of his men.

Rising like a wave, the soldiers tackled the bald-ogon as a group.

After a vicious struggle, amid a cloud of grunts, cursing and threats the men tied his hands, subduing him. Afterward they lifted the prisoner to his feet, presenting him to their leader.

Rostov put his sword back to its scabbard and turned to the young man putting a hand on his shoulder. "Are you ok, lad?"

"Aye, Captain," he answered, still fidgeting with his nose. It was obviously broken and painful.

Without speaking, Rostov nodded and patted him on the back. Afterward he stepped up to the bald-ogon. "Ghronn Mak'Nabb. You are under arrest in the name of Baron Manfred Raddlif."

"Baron who?" hissed the ogon sarcastically. "Shattered-Tooth ogon don't know your Baron, invader." His speech was laced with a heavy accent of his native tongue.

"You are a thief and murderer," responded the Captain, "and so is your brother. Now you will face punishment for your crimes."

"Captain," came a voice from behind. He turned, seeing his soldiers holding other ogon only injured in the brawl. "What of these two?"

"Well done Sergeant," he replied.

Rostov approached the captives. He looked at their faces, burning them into his memory. They were ugly. Their skin, green tinted and bearing the bold facial features typical of the ogon in the Splinterwood. Their eyes were bloodshot, and their hair long and coarse.

"Hang this one," said Rostov as he turned to the second captive.

"Newcomer kopike–" hissed the condemned ogon before being clubbed from behind. They drug him away towards the trees, tying his hands, and wrapping a scarf around his eyes to blind him as he struggled to escape.

"You," continued the Captain, stepping up to the second wounded prisoner, "return to your clan. Tell them what happens when they bring their chaos to Raddlif lands. The pact is in force. The Raddlif family is the law south of the gorge and wish no further bloodshed, but we will not abide thieves and murderers. Go now! Stay on your side of the bridge!"

As he finished, he took the frowning ogon by the shoulder and pushed him away. He stumbled a few feet then paused, his hands bound behind his back. He glared defiantly at Rostov. The two held each other's gaze. Each refused to back down. The Captain noticed he looked different from the rest of his dead cohorts. His hair was lighter, and his features softer as was his complexion. His frame was smaller, but he possessed the same strength as his companions.

'Go I said! Before I change my mind and hang you as well!"

After a long moment of a glare that dripped with hatred, the fair-haired ogon ran, and disappeared into the trees.

Rostov approached the bald-ogon. The soldiers bound him, forcing him to his knees. He was dangerous and they took no chances.

'You are coming with us. First, those you have hurt will identify you. The Baron will convict you and decide your punishment."

The men gathered their horses and headed south, towing their prisoner running behind them. Rostov kept him exhausted knowing to do so made him less dangerous.

Away in the distance to the north, shrouded in a gray haze, Castle Raddlif overlooked the forest. Soon, they arrived in the flatlands to a small hamlet that rested outside the protection of the walls, but not its soldiers. The group rode between rows of vines that waited for spring to grow its fruit. On the opposite side of the community, tall bramble covered shrubs grew in lines soon to bud in bright purple flowers and yield baskets of savory bracken berries. The Captain's favorite.

Centered in the field, hidden among the vines and hedges, sat numerous small houses. They were simple in their construction, with walls of wood and sod. Old creepers, woven with reeds from the banks of a nearby narrow river made the thatched roofs proof against the rain.

Rostov and his clutch of men approached a group of waiting townsfolk dressed in simple clothes. The women wore white bonnets tied at their chins. Their children surrounded them clinging to their skirts and weeping while their mothers tried to comfort them.

Among the houses, four corpses laid on beds of leaves and vines. They were battered and beaten, their lives lost in a vicious fight. Two were farmers, dressed in the same simple clothes of the other townsfolk waiting for Rostov and his men. The remaining two were soldiers from the castle in the distance. The green beds on which they laid were stained crimson by the still running blood from their broken bodies.

"That's him!" shrieked a woman, pointing an accusing finger at the prisoner. "That is the ogon who attacked us. Him and his brigands! I will never forget his face and those scars!"

Waiting with the townspeople, were two men on sturdy horses. One rode a black horse, tall and strong. He was older with a short beard and wearing a cloak as a shield against the weather with fur-lined gauntlets. He sat tall on his steed with a noble bearing.

The second rider's horse was black as well, but his bore a white blaze between its eyes. He was hooded and cloaked, quietly watching the unfolding drama. His warm breath was a mist, dancing on the cold air.

Rostov approached the mounted men and saluted them.

"Baron Manfred," said the Captain, "we have the fugitive."

As he finished, his Sergeant brought the captive forward. The rest of the platoon formed into a triangle behind their leaders.

Rostov waited for a response while Manfred inspected the prisoner. He looked down on him from his horse with a grim and angry expression.

"Well done Captain," he said. "We meet at last, Mak'Nabb. Do you enjoy the wailing of my people? Listen closely. You will never hear it again."

The ogon wheezed from his forced march. His black trousers torn. His knees and elbows were skinned and bleeding. He dripped with sweat, even in the cold of the winter's day.

"Hang me if you will, but do not speak to me," said the prisoner defiantly.

"Not only do I speak to you, but I will pass judgement on you for what you have done to these people and the tradesman you have accosted on the road. You will pay for your crimes. The charge is murder and theft."

The ogon said nothing. He cleared his throat with a ghastly hacking sound and spat on the ground at the feet of the Baron's horse, smiling a sinister grin.

"You see, Son," said Manfred in a disappointed tone, "there is no respect among these beings. Never forget that."

"Shall I ride with Rostov and find a suitable place to stretch his neck?" asked the hooded man on the white blazed horse.

The Baron stayed silent as he pondered the question, shifting in his saddle as if his authority and judgment were a weight on his shoulders.

"No," he answered at last. "It would give these people great satisfaction to see you hang. However, for now it is to the dungeon with you. You may be more valuable alive. Captain, get the filth out of my sight."

Rostov snapped his fingers and one of is soldiers struck the prisoner in the gut, doubling him over and softening him up to move. He wanted to hang the ogon and be done with him, but he would never disobey a command from his baron, and always trusted in his wisdom without hesitation.

Chapter 1

There was a thunderous rumble. Like one I had never heard before, or wish to hear again. Then in the sky the rocks shimmered red, white and orange. Bolting across the blackened sky like sling-stones from the gods...

-From the History of House Raddlif by Baron Fredon Raddlif

Drawn behind two flat horned wooly beasts, a pear-shaped carriage ambled along a coarse earthen road, leading a caravan so long it vanished into the distance. Their journey carried them south from their home in Trodenheim. Two days ago, the caravan left the main road and turned west, entering the ancient Splinterwood Forest. Tall pine trees now edged the road once trimmed by gentle rolling hills. Overhead, thin rows of white clouds lined the azure sky on a pleasant day.

A crimson carriage led the caravan, trimmed in shining gold, and flanked by a retinue of soldiers armed with spears and shields. Two poles sprouted from the front of the carriage bearing gold-frilled crimson flags emblazoned with a token of two crossed war hammers set below a single, five-pointed star. The spearmen wore chain mail shirts over black trousers. Over their armor, the soldiers bore a crimson tabard adorned with the hammers and star of the family they served. Ribbons fluttered in the gentle breeze from the tops of their spears, and each soldier bore their weapon

11

with a flat, solemn countenance.

Inside the carriage was Lady Veronica Moresten, younger of the two Moresten children along with her handmaiden Amma and a sulking old hag of a woman named Elga Von Triss, Veronica's teacher.

Shifting on a thinly padded wooden bench, Veronica did her best to be comfortable. For days on end, the carriage, and its massive entourage of guards, tradesman, other royal families and soldiers, bounced its way toward its destination, the Castle of Raddlif, deep in the Splinterwood Forest.

Moving a drape away from the window, Veronica peered outside to see her father, Count Olan Moresten, riding alongside the coach upon a grand black Stallion. As she watched him, she thought about her elder brother Donal, whom she adored. He resembled Olan, and she thought about how much she missed him. He remained in Trodenheim, to tend the Frozen-Throne in the absence of the Count. He wanted to journey south with his family, but their laws called for a member of royal blood to sit the throne, or surrender it, and hold a moot. Olan would not have that, so Donal stayed behind.

Before leaving, her Brother hugged her in his strong arms. He said nothing. Once in his warm embrace, she burst into tears, knowing it would be years before they would see each other again, if at all. She hung out the carriage window, watching him grow smaller and smaller as he waved his good-bye with one hand and cradled her newborn niece in the other. The bittersweet memory still brought tears to her eyes when she reflected on it.

She eyed her Father as he rode alongside, hearing the clip-clop of the horseshoes, and squeaking of the carriage axles. Away in the distance, she could hear singing as the travelers entertained themselves on the long road. Looking around, she did not see her mother among the caravan. She was a skilled rider and a proud woman, preferring to ride on her own horse.

The carriage rides were always lonely. Her mother seldom rode in it, and the Count only once that she remembered. She was a young child at the time and he was injured, suffering from broken ribs after falling from his horse in an accident during the yearly tournament at the Moresten home at Icekeep.

She turned her attention to the passing scenery on either side of the carriage as it traveled the road deeper and deeper into the forest. Tall and majestic pine trees stood over various smaller gnarled ones, recently in bloom, marking the early months of spring. The trees grew along the road like an enormous curtain, so dense in places she could only see a few yards into the forest. She felt an eerie feeling when she looked at them, as if the trees themselves were watching her.

"Is it much further?" she asked at last, holding on to the window as the carriage jostled along the ruts of the road.

"We'll be there soon enough," Olan answered, "and your next adventure will soon begin."

Veronica felt excitement in her heart at hearing the journey was nearly complete, but the emotion mixed with frustration at her father's mention of the "next adventure." She knew what he meant, so she decided to change the subject.

"Why is the road so rough here? It was smooth till we entered the forest," asked Veronica.

"We are not on the Mournway anymore," answered Olan. "Some miles back we left it to turn onto this rugged path leading to the castle. Raddlifs' home is several miles in the interior of the woods."

"But why is it so much rougher? My back is killing me, and poor Elga, I don't think she will ever be able to move again once we arrive."

"Because, my dear, the Mournmen laid this road we are on now, but they did not lay the Mournway. No one knows who laid it, or where its builders found the flat stones they used. It is called 'the Mournway' because it connects the Mournlands to the south, named by our people who crossed the Maelstrom and landed in Tharrin when they fled the old world. If the road had a name before our people found it, I don't know what it was. Doesn't that old hag teach you any history?"

"History is boring!" snapped Veronica in a haughty tone, closing the drape to keep out the glaring sunlight. She picked up a large piece of linen next to her and ran a needle and thread through it. The needlepoint occupied her mind and hands during the long days riding inside the uncomfortable carriage, or sometimes when she needed to clear her mind of troubles.

Veronica was an attractive young woman of

fifteen years. Her hair was brown and when the light caught it just right, it had the hints of red that marked most of the people who had settled in Icemarch. Her eyes were small but bright, green in color, sitting over a scrawny beak-of-a-nose with full lips and straight teeth.

"M'lady, would you care for some food? You don't look well. Are you all right?"

"No, Amma, I do not wish to eat, and yes, I'm fine, just bored out of my mind," responded Veronica, still focusing on her needlework. Amma was slight of build and fair of hair. Back home in Trodenheim, her family worked as servants in the Icekeep. The Count noticed her pleasant disposition and spark for life that showed while she served the Morestens in their dining hall as well as the stables, tending the horses. As such, she had proven herself to be an excellent servant and Olan chose her to be Veronica's hand-maiden on the journey. Over the long road, she was the only one Veronica's age to keep her company. She appreciated her constant presence and attention.

"You should eat something, My Lady," said Veronica's teacher, sitting in the front of the carriage and reading a book. "You must keep your strength up."

"I said I'm fine. Please don't nag me," whined Veronica, glaring impatiently at the old woman.

Elga's haggard face was lined with age. Her wiry, gray hair was tied into a loose ponytail that hung down her back. She wore a long black gown, trimmed in gray. In her hands, she clutched her book with

15

skeletal fingers, pained with arthritis.

"It is best that you remove that tone from your voice before you reach the castle, young lady. You would not want to make a bad impression with your future in-laws or your suitor," Elga retorted, not bothering to look up from her reading.

Suddenly, Amma exclaimed, "I can see the castle!" She held back the drapes from the window. "It is there," she said, pointing into the distance, "at the top of the hill. Tonight you will sleep in a warmed chamber, with a bed of feathers and a hot meal."

"You paint a cozy image, dear Amma. But I will believe it when I'm out of this rocky carriage on this hell-sent pile of rocks these Mournmen call a road," Veronica responded in a cynical tone.

"Are you sure you will not have something to eat or maybe some water?" Amma asked, "It isn't like you to sound so bitter."

As she listened to Amma's pleads, Veronica stole a glance out of the carriage window. On top of a hill, in the distance, she could see the castle against the blue sky and it made her feel better. "Perhaps you're right, I will take an orange. A small one. The journey is almost over, and if nothing else, I will be out of this bouncy carriage."

"It has been many years coming, Lady Veronica," Amma replied. "I hoped that you would be of a better mind when the day came."

Veronica knew Elga was listening though she maintained the facade that she was still reading her book.

"I will never be of a '*better mind*', about this Amma," said Veronica. "My family will not give in on this marriage, on that you are correct. I have never wanted this, but it appears I have no choice. My Brother didn't either, when he married Kellon. The Baron-Apparent will find that I will not melt under his charming presence as easily as he might have envisioned."

Amma carried on peeling the orange, placed the slices onto a small silver plate, and handed it to Veronica. Setting aside her needlepoint, she took it and looked back out to the passing scenery outside the carriage window.

As they turned a curve, she could see down into a small meadow covered in bright purple flowers. It struck her how the trees gave way to this oblong clearing where flowers grew as if someone had laid them like a rug in the center of a great room. Veronica admired the beauty of the glade as she bit into a wedge of orange. The well-ripened fruit exploded with flavor. The sweet taste excited her senses and she was glad she decided to eat.

Then, a swift movement outside the carriage caught her eye. "Amma! Look at that!" she called as they both peered out of the window. There they saw a strange form. It was a rider, but he did not ride a horse. It was a squat, fast creature that looked more like a boar. It moved quickly, riding alongside the caravan for a short distance, staying among the trees. The rider looked like a large man but with strange features. She could only catch a quick glimpse before it turned, disappearing into the woods as the guards turned their horses to chase.

"What was that? Did you see it?" asked Veronica, excited and unsure how to react.

"I did!" answered Amma. "Was it a man? It didn't look like one."

"It was an Ogon, my dear," Elga said, looking over the top of her book. "Calm yourselves. They are native to these woods. The Count will deal with any bold ones who think they can waylay our royal caravan."

"I have never seen an ogon," said Veronica. "Have you?"

"Not in many, many years. The beasts seldom travel outside the Splinterwood because this is their ancestral land, but they will occasionally travel to the Mournlands north of the forest."

"Isn't it strange that he should draw so near to us?"

"Just a passerby," replied Elga returning her attention to her book. "You have other things to be concerned about than a passing ogon. Now eat your orange and rest all you can. Soon, you will meet the Raddlif boy, and you will need to make that impression I have cautioned you about."

***

After riding through the day, stopping only for brief rests, Veronica held open the drapes and craned her head out the carriage window, looking up to the castle of wood and stone that perched proudly at the summit of a solitary hill rising above the tops of the

18

trees. She found its modesty surprising. It consisted of a main, rectangular central keep, with several tall towers some of which were round with others square.

A giant wall surrounded the lower grounds of the fortress, composed of large stones in the lower portion and graduating to smaller ones along the top of the wall. Battlements lined the top, reinforced with sharpened iron spikes where the archers of the guard could stand and shoot from relative safety.

Outside the walls and below the castle, surrounded by a palisade of enormous fallen trees, the towne of Raddlif laid down the side of the hill like a vast wool tapestry. A nearby tributary of the mighty Duola Voda River ran swiftly, wrapping around and behind the bottom of the hill, providing water to its people and fields.

Veronica had grown up learning the history of the family of her betrothed. Looking up to the castle, she knew it had been the seat of the Raddlif house for the past two generations since their arrival in Splinterwood Forest.

She heard the booming voice of the Caravan Master bellowing a long, "Hollllld!"

The carriage stopped. Peeking outside, she saw three men sitting on horseback at the gate of the imposing wall of wood that protected the structures within.

Armed lookouts walked along the crest of the palisade, surveying the forest beyond. Some guards had stopped and were watching as their caravan approached. On the ground near the group waiting on horseback, a detachment of men, leaning lazily on spears, stood sentinel.

The gates of the towne opened under the efforts of a group of soldiers led by a tall, coarse-looking man clad head to toe in brown studded-leather armor. Over his shoulder was a sash of dark-green stripes, and a sword hung at his waist. The men worked in unison as their leader organized their efforts shouting, "Pull! Pull!"

The first of the waiting trio wore a fine brocade tunic of brown embroidered with green sprigs of ivy about the chest, over matching trousers, and calf-high riding boots. He was the oldest of the three, wearing a closely cropped, gray-flecked beard. His eyes were bright against a handsome, yet aging face. He sat on a large and spirited black horse that danced about impatiently beneath him, moving his head and his legs constantly and puffing with an occasional impatient snort.

Next to the older man was a much younger one, dressed in the same colors, except for his boots that rose to his knees. His hair was long and brown, hanging freely just short of his shoulders. His eyes were crisp, and he wore a thin and patchy stubble on his face. He too, sat on a black horse with a white blaze, but his mount stood at ease near the others, moving its large head side to side, as if making its own observations of the approaching party. The rider sat with his back straight, and his hands folded over the pommel of his saddle, clutching a riding crop capped in silver.

The third waiting man wore a much simpler green cotton tunic belted at the waist. His worn trousers were modest and his boots were scuffed and scratched. Hanging over his left shoulder and down to his waist, was a tan colored sash with wide orange stripes. Well-built but not tall, he was young, also wearing his hair long.

Veronica watched as her father, flanked by four spearmen, broke away from the caravan. He rode his stallion at a brisk trot toward the waiting group, pulling his horse to a stop a few feet from them.

A mop of frizzy red hair hung from the Count's head. His bushy beard was graying with age and grew all the way up his cheeks nearly to his eyes. Under it, he bore a tattoo of runic writings, running from the top of his forehead, down the right side of his face and onto his neck, disappearing under his dark colored-tunic. A war-hammer hung by a loop from the pommel of his saddle. Over his back hung a kite-shaped shield on a leather strap.

The four spearmen crowded him as they rode closely behind. When he halted, one of the soldiers bumped into the rump of his horse. The Count's stallion kicked at him in response, swinging his head around and fidgeting beneath its rider.

"Leave off, you!" shouted Olan in a gruff voice. "Intend to mount me, do you? Give a man his space! These three woodsmen couldn't best me in a drinking contest, much less a fight!" He paused before speaking again, and then said, "go tend to the women."

Veronica watched as the two men at the front

21

of the trio, glanced at each other, grinning at Olan's antics. Finally, both her father and the older stranger broke out into laughter together. Both leaped from their beasts and embraced, pounding each other hard on the back.

As the two friends separated, each placed their right hand on the left shoulder of the other, and squeezed.

"Baron Manfred Raddlif, you old codger! Look at your face; you have grown old on me."

"It is what happens when you take so long to come see your friends. You don't look so smooth of face either as I remember." Manfred laughed good-naturedly. "I see your runes have grown longer beneath that beard of yours. They were at your cheek the last time we met."

Veronica and Amma, leaning out of the carriage, looked on with interest. Elga sat quietly reading her book, ignoring everything else as she often did.

"Tournaments to win. Battles to fight. The runes grow longer. See here," said Olan pointing to a line of runic writing below his cheek bone, tracing it with his finger. "This is where your family is mentioned. While I am here I'll teach you to read runic. Your sword grip is still strong I see," he continued. "Can you say the same for that manhood of yours, or has it grown old too?" The Count finished with a deep and powerful belly laugh, leaning forward and slapping his knee with self-amusement.

"It's fine if it's any business of yours you nosey

old boggett!" Manfred answered before laughing with his old friend.

"Nosey?" responded Olan, "I'm not asking because I intend to propose to you. I want that boy of yours to give me more grandchildren, and if yours still works, that bodes well for my future son-in-law!" He laughed again and turned his attention to the nearest young man sitting on his horse.

"You lad, you must be Fredrick," said Olan, "is your sword grip as strong as this old man of yours? Once you're married, I hope you intend to get right on the job of making me a grandfather once again. Are you up to the task?"

"Father!" Veronica shouted in embarrassment as she pulled back from the draped window, pulling Amma with her. The young handmaiden's head bumped against the top of the sill with a hollow sounding thud as she withdrew inside. Blushing and embarrassed, Veronica pulled her knees up to her chest covering her face with both hands, hiding behind a tent of hair, while Amma rubbed her throbbing head.

Fredrick smiled nervously at the Count.

"Quiet down little-girl!" snapped Olan in a stern but loving tone. He turned his attention back to the still silent Fredrick.

"Well lad, cat got your tongue?" he asked, then slapped Manfred on the back in affection.

There was a brief pause as the question hung in the air. The Baron remained quiet as he peered up at his son.

"As long as the cat left his cock, eh Manfred?"

exclaimed Olan, followed by his deep and jolly belly laugh that seemed like it could shake the trees. "He will need it!"

After finishing, he swung himself adroitly back up into his saddle with the grace of a younger man. There he sat on his horse, laughing so hard at his own words that tears were forming in his eyes.

Riding up from the caravan, a woman stopped alongside the still laughing Count. "Olan," she said in a sultry voice, "stop embarrassing this young man. Don't you understand you're making this harder on our future son then it needs to be?"

"Oh come now, I was just having a spot of fun." Olan wiped the moisture from his eyes. "You will forgive me, won't you young Fredrick?" he asked, not expecting an answer.

The Countess Mary Moresten was clad in a tan riding gown. A blue corset held her amble breasts tightly. Over her raiment, she wore a light-colored cape trimmed in fur that draped over the rump of her tall white stallion. Despite being middle-aged, her features were smooth with eyes like crystals and straight, golden hair. She was graceful and bold, always armed with a sword at her saddle.

Manfred returned to his beast and mounted it. He put his right arm out to his side and lowered his head. Fredrick imitated the movement, and Veronica thought about how awkward he looked trying to be polite.

"Countess Mary, it has been too long," said Manfred in greeting. "You are as stunning as I remember. I see you have no problem managing this old coot of yours."

"Thank you. The years have been kind to you too. Your son is handsome. I'm pleased."

Mary turned her eyes on Fredrick. She studied him with a penetrating stare.

"Are you nervous?" she asked at last, guiding her mare near to him as if to get a closer look.

"No, Countess," he answered, trying to sound confident and bold.

"You are a poor liar. You are, and you should be. If you were not, you would be little more than a handsome fool," she stated calmly, not averting her relentless, incisive gaze. She flashed a fleeting smile, then turned and rode back to the caravan. Inside, Lady Veronica hid from view, watching out the corner of the window while her handmaiden hovered over the top of her. Elga continued reading and ignored the entire exchange.

"He is handsome, M'lady," Amma whispered, "Maybe things are not as bad as you have convinced yourself."

"Be quiet!" Veronica commanded, still blushing with embarrassment.

From the rear of the caravan, a fat man in a gray doublet appeared wearing tight-fitting pants and a plumed purple hat. He rode a white speckled horse that strained under the weight of his rider. He was clean-shaven and the absence of a beard showed his doubled chin and low hanging jowls on both sides of his large, round face. His eyes were small, making his nose look enormous between ears that stuck straight out off the side of his head.

"What's all this?" said the man in a grating voice as he pulled his horse to a stop behind the group.

"Quiet, Krell! I'm talking to my friends," answered Olan, turning his face away from him.

"Do not speak to me that way," responded the fat man. "The Krell house is invited just as you are, Moresten. We have a right to be here, just as you do." He turned up his nose, speaking in a matter-of-fact tone.

"No one said you didn't. I simply told you to quiet down," snorted Olan. His disdain for Krell was obvious.

"Lord Krell," said Manfred, "so glad you could make it. This is my son. The last time you saw him he was still an infant."

"Yes. You have grown well lad," he replied, raising his hand in greeting.

"Behind him, my friends, is his steward, Lamar Atmore," continued the Baron gesturing toward the young man waiting quietly behind Fredrick.

"And how is your Lady Wife, Lord Krell?"

"She is flourishing, but has decided not to make the journey. She does not travel well you know."

"Oh?" responded the Old Baron. "A pity. We shall miss her."

"I haven't missed her at all. On the road, she is a terrible nag. In fact, I shall enjoy the quiet with her in Krellton and me here. I hope you have good musicians in your court. I will be able to listen them without the constant prattle of her in my ears the whole time."

There was a hushed reaction as the group responded to Krell's words, each in their own way. Olan, true to form, laughed aloud at him, while the rest snickered or rolled their eyes.

"We best be getting on with it, Manfred," Krell said. "Nightfall is coming soon and I wish my people and stores to be within your walls before then. What with all the blasted ogon in these lands, they will steal all the wine I brought for the feast."

"You'll find there are few problems with the ogon these days."

"Good to know."

"Captain Rostov!" commanded Manfred.

"Aye, Lord," responded the leather-clad soldier wearing the green-striped sash, turning from his team of men.

"These carts and goods are to be moved within the walls. There is much to be done. See to it."

Rostov saluted, then sounded off with a loud whistle and walked a brisk pace through the gate and into the towne, signaling to his men with his arms as he went; pointing, waving and shouting.

Through the night under a bright moon, and late into the next day, the soldiers brought the wains within the walls. The travelers helped, busied themselves making camps and securing their stores. Once inside, there were so many wagons and supplies it became difficult to move around on the main roads of the towne.

Chapter 2

It was clear we could no longer stay. It was then my Baron sent me out to find as many ships and families as I could for our perilous flight west. We all knew, for those of us who survived, there would be no returning, and for those who stayed in Annan, only slow death.

-Journal of Gavyn Wellbrown

Fredrick's ears rang as the report of his pistol echoed through the fields of the towne of Raddlif. Downrange, several burlap sacks, sewn into the shape of a plump man, swung from a gibbet against a light afternoon breeze.

"Squeeze," said Rostov patiently. "Squeeze the trigger. You are pulling it too hard. That is why you are missing the target. You're twisting the pistol."

Standing behind his Captain, Lamar finished loading another weapon, and handed the firearm to Fredrick.

"Try again," said Rostov. "This time use only the tip of your finger. Squeeze, do not pull."

He took a deep breath and extended his arm, aimed the pistol and fired. Straw flew from the target and frustration filled his mind as his shot found its mark low and right once more.

Rostov shook his head in disappointment before speaking. "You're distracted. Nerves for this evening's event?"

Lamar smirked as he listened, pouring powder into another firearm, loading it for the next shot.

"If I must admit it then it will be to you,"

responded Fredrick as he laid the spent pistol on the table between the three of them. "Yes, I am nervous. I thought I would not be, but I am. Her father is jovial enough. An odd chap he is. He's different than the other Lords I have met."

"Count Olan is a brave and decent man, though I would not want to meet him angry, and with a hammer in his hand."

Rostov gestured to Lamar for one of the loaded pistols. He took the gun, turned, and aimed, firing the weapon deftly. Downrange, Fredrick saw straw leap from the target over the painted red heart.

"Calm your mind. Squeeze the trigger," he stated, handing the pistol back to the steward. "She is just a woman. It is not as if you haven't crawled out a lancet, or lied about going hunting to see one before, is it?"

The boldness of the question took him by surprise. "Of course it is! I'm to marry her, and we have not even met."

"How many times do you need to meet them? They are all the same down there you know?" Rostov grinned mischievously. Both he and Lamar laughed, but Fredrick did not join them in their mirth.

"I would thank you not to encourage our dear Captain Rostov," he said, pretending to be annoyed while smiling brightly from embarrassment.

"I'm sorry, My Lord." Lamar responded, feigning contriteness and turning his attention back to loading the pistols.

Despite his joke, Rostov's demeanor was

always grave and morose. He trained Fredrick in blade, bow, and pistol. He was the family's personal guard, trusted by both the baron and baroness as a confidant and councilor. Both he and Lamar studied not only the art of combat with him, but also the skills of a woodsman and survivalist. The three of them spent many a night in the forest, learning the land and growing with it. His respect for the Captain was endless.

Lamar handed the freshly loaded pistol to Fredrick. It was still warm from the prior shots.

"Remember," demanded Rostov, "relax. Control your breath and squeeze the trigger."

He gripped the gun, looking to the target swinging in the distance. He breathed deeply, calming himself with his arms at his side, drawing back the hammer with his thumb. In a brisk movement, he lifted the firearm and looked down the barrel. He held his breath, aimed, and squeezed the trigger. The report of the pistol left a ringing in his ears but this time he saw the straw fly from the heart of the burlap man downrange.

"A fine shot. Well done," said Rostov encouragingly.

Fredrick smiled and nodded his acceptance of the compliment.

The Captain then addressed Lamar. "Do you wish to try?"

"No thank you, sir. I will wait for archery practice."

"Archery it is then," said Rostov. "I'll bet

neither of you scoundrels can outrun me to the arsenal!"

The Captain turned on his heels and bolted back toward the castle just as he finished issuing his challenge.

"We'll see about that!" said Fredrick as he waved at his friend to follow. The two gave chase as Lamar lagged, trying not to drop the brace of pistols weighing him down.

***

Veronica leaned against the wall of her guest-chamber with crossed arms, looking out over the grounds toward the main road of the towne below. Away in the distance, she could see gathering clouds on the horizon, but so far, the day was bright and calm.

Once arriving and guided to her chambers, the elegance of the furniture surprised her, but the room itself was modest and cramped. The bed was comfortable and inviting, with four carved posts holding a canopy. Dark green drapes covered the gray stone-walls and several iron lamps hung from hooks in the ceiling to brighten the space. A wide lancet overlooked the town, and across from it, a small balcony faced the forest. The fireplace nearly consumed the entire wall. At night, servants tended to the hearth. It was early in the spring, and the nights brought with them a chilling wind.

Elga and Mary, or sometimes one or the other, escorted her everywhere since the group arrived at Raddlif. Both took great pains to keep the betrothed from meeting each other before the upcoming feast of

31

celebration and introduction. The constant attention and enthusiasm for the wedding that everyone but she was feeling, left her crestfallen.

"Come away from the lancet, dear," said Elga in her raspy voice. "I do not want you to catch a foul draft. Let us return to the review. What was Baron Manfred's Father's name?"

"Elga please," whined Veronica, "I have been in this room all day, can we not go out?"

"No, we cannot! We have already been through this once today. We will finish your lesson and afterward prepare you for the feast. Be of good cheer though, once the introduction has taken place, you can move around the castle freely. Now, again, his name?"

Veronica did not stir. She gazed into the bright day wishing she could be outside. If even only for a while.

Then, on the grounds below, three men crossed the yard, running as if being chased by brigands. The first was an older man, then two younger ones. The one at the rear juggled something in his arms awkwardly as he moved. She realized, from her quick glimpse of him on her arrival, the runner in the middle was Fredrick, her betrothed.

Astonished by the unexpected sight, she lunged forward, placing her hands on either side of the slit in the stone, leaning her head out to get a better look. She watched as the three moved quickly through the bailey. Fredrick stopped, as if he sensed someone watching him. He looked up at her, and their eyes met for that brief second at a distance before she pulled back inside, turning away from the lancet and hiding. Her pulse raced with a mixture of surprise and confusion. She found him attractive, and his family kind, but she did not know this man nor did she wish to. She wanted to choose her own love and stay near her brother at her home in Trodenheim. But she was no longer there, and moving toward to a marriage she resented.

Elga looked up from the pile of books scattered on the table before her, "What is it, Veronica?"

"Nothing."

"What did you see?"

"I didn't see anything," said Veronica. "Alfred is the answer."

"Superb. And what was *Alfred's* Father's name?"

"Fredon. Also called 'The Bold One.'"

"Yes. Yes." Elga paused pursing her lips, then asked, "What ship did he command when he led his people west from Annan after Rockfall?"

"He commanded the Exeter."

"Good. You have been listening. Our review is finished. Next, we shall–"

The door opened with a shrill squeaking noise, interrupting Elga. Amma skipped in happily, carrying food and a flagon. She smiled as she entered and sat the tray on a small table near the fireplace. Afterward, Mary followed.

"Well," said Mary as she approached. "Are you keeping our young Lady entertained?"

"I'm doing my best, Countess," answered Elga,

in her usual pessimistic tone. "She is distracted and still walking the room pouting."

Mary paused, saying nothing. She turned to Amma who stood waiting for instructions. She pointed at the flagon, and the servant filled a cup.

"Come here, Veronica," she said pulling a chair from under the table. "Sit."

She sat and folded her hands in her lap looking toward the floor at Amma's feet.

"Drink," Mary demanded, presenting her the cup.

She obeyed and took a swallow. A heady and bitter taste attacked her tongue. She looked inside to find it filled with a wine as dark as blood.

"Finish it."

Elga moved aside taking a position next to the door, holding her hands together at her chest, watching quietly and staying out of the way.

Veronica took a deep breath then drained the remaining wine, swallowing it with a gulp. She disliked the bitter tang. Even after she finished drinking, the tart flavor lingered on her tongue. She returned the cup to the table, and Amma refilled it.

The Countess looked at her with an impatient expression. For a long and torturous moment, her mother stared at her with daggers in her eyes. Mary swept the cup up to her lips and with two loud gulps downed it herself, slamming it back down on the tray.

"Still sulking as if you will have a tooth pulled I see," she scoffed pacing, with her hands behind her back. "Why are you being so stubborn?"

She did not expect and answer and Veronica knew it so she remained quiet, as if waiting for a storm to pass.

"Elga and I have spent years preparing you for this wedding, yet you still behave this way," Mary continued. "Did you see the Raddlif boy when you were hanging out the carriage window? He is handsome. Your father has chosen well for you."

A frown of cynicism washed across Veronica's face. "Chosen well for me?" she asked. "We have dinner tonight, and then we marry. How can I know him, much less love him after one night?" She tried to retain her composure, but her voice wavered as she struggled to stand her ground against her mother's intimidating presence. Veronica loved her father. But, as a girl growing to womanhood, she admired Mary. She revered not only her strength, but also her unwavering resilience. She had seen her mother strike men who insulted her, stare down Olan's detractors in council sessions, and practice with her sword with the men-at-arms in Trodenheim. She wanted that for herself, but she was scared. Afraid she would never be as strong as her mother was.

"And so it was when I met Olan. I was just as fearful as you are, maybe even more so. Here was a man ten years my elder. His engagement was to my sister. When Leonedes died, I inherited her betrothal. Do you think that I had time to get to know him? You have spent your life knowing your future; I learned of mine the day after she perished. I was twelve. Olan had to wait for me to reach flower-age. For a man like your father, I'm sure that was a long three years."

"But I do not love him. How could I?"

"Maybe you're right," said Mary turning away and approaching Elga. The silence was torturous. Veronica hoped that her mother had some sort of sudden change of heart, but deep down she knew that would never happen.

"We should let you choose. We should let you take your time and find this man of your dreams. Meanwhile, childless Lords such as that stooge Bertrum Krell can suggest to the others we offer you to a southerner to keep the Blackfeathers in the south. Would that suit you?"

Mary carried on, turning on her heels to meet Veronica's eyes. "From here we will travel to Cliffside. It's only another four-hundred miles south on the Mournway. You can marry a southern noble at the gates of the Mourn-Fort, or, if you wish, we will have it on their side of Blackfeather Pass in Southgate. Is that what you want?"

"No," she responded contritely.

"Then put a smile on your face and warm up your heart," said Mary. "The feast begins at sunset, and you will have your introduction to the Baron-Apparent. He will want to see a pretty, young woman. Not a sulking, miserable little girl."

Veronica did not respond. She looked at Amma who peered back at her with a silent and sympathetic expression.

"It is and important night for the Lady. See

needs to look her best. I will return to fetch her at sunset."

After finishing, Mary stood near her daughter, lifted her chin, and pressed her face close.

"Please trust me," she said in a softer tone. "Olan has chosen well for you with these Raddlifs. Their holding is more modest than you are accustomed to, I understand, but these woodsmen are honorable and just. The lad Fredrick is handsome, and you and he will have many children and you know your father wants this very much."

As she finished speaking, they embraced. Veronica wanted to resist and keep her hands at her sides but found she could not. She loved her family, and even through her intense frustration, she felt the love burning warm inside.

Mary smiled, but Veronica refused to return it knowing it was what her mother wanted. She was still unhappy about the betrothal. She did not want to smile and give her the impression she had changed her mind on the topic.

The Countess exited the chamber stopping in the threshold. "At sunset, I shall return," she said before closing the door.

***

Fredrick stood before a polished bronze mirror inspecting his own blurred reflection. Over a slim fitting tunic, he wore a brown leather gambeson, matching bracers on his wrists, and black gloves. His trousers were a coarse cotton hanging over boots that buckled at the ankle. At his left shoulder, three green braids wrapped around under his arm. One braid for each generation of Raddlif who dwelled in the Splinterwood Forest bearing the title of Baron. One day, he would wear a gold braid among the others. Visible behind him in the mirror's image, he could see Lamar, holding a belt and waiting for his queue.

"I'll never be as good as you with the bow," said Fredrick as the two carried on talking about their practice session earlier.

"It should not surprise you. You spend most of your time practicing with pistols. You were just having a bad day. I have seen how well you shoot and I am not the one meeting my future bride tonight. It is no wonder I can hit a target and you cannot."

Lamar wrapped the belt around Fredrick's waist and stepped back. He stood as if he were at attention, looking at the Baron-Apparent through the mirror. "I would be nervous too if I were you. Did you see the women when they were hanging out of the carriage window?"

"Of course."

"I would say then you cannot go wrong. They were both quite lovely."

"Do you think so?"

"Yes," said Lamar. "But maybe that is the difference between the eye of a Baron and a Steward."

They laughed together as Fredrick turned from the mirror satisfied with his raiment at last. He looked at Lamar and straightened his tunic, inspecting him.

"Is this not your job?" he asked as he plucked and fidgeted with Lamar's clothing. The steward dressed to match his master but with subtle differences. In place of the gambeson, Lamar wore a modest leather vest. His thick canvas trousers were wear-worn at the knees, but the tall, knee-high riding boots that covered his feet helped to obscure the abrasions. Over his left shoulder, he wore his orange striped sash.

Fredrick thought about what his Steward, and future apothecary, meant to him as he straightened the sash around his chest. His mind drifted back to how he and Lamar grew up together as boys and were now on their way to being men-grown. The two spoke as equals. Friendship had replaced the station of lord to servant long ago.

A knock came at his bed-chamber door. It opened, and he watched as in strode an old man clad neck to foot in a faded, baggy robe. A wiry beard grew from his chin and cheeks. The top of his head was bald, giving way to a ring of long gray hair.

"Gavyn!" greeted Fredrick in an exuberant tone. "It is good you have come. We're always happy to see you."

"Yes, yes my boy," said the old man. As he approached, he threw his arms open wide and invited both to a long and pleasant embrace. He patted the boys on the back before they separated.

"I'm sorry I have seen little of you recently," said Gavyn, "but as you know I'm a busy man."

"What brings you here," asked Fredrick. "A last few words of wisdom?"

"Oh no, no. Your Mother will be here shortly

and I wanted to wish you well in person. I shall not be attending the feast. My hearing you know," he said, gesturing to his ears. "It isn't so good in loud rooms."

Gavyn beamed a yellowed smile, excited by something on his mind. He motioned to Fredrick to come closer and spoke in a feigned whisper. "I met your betrothed yesterday while she walked the bailey. Oh the beauty of a young woman for old eyes, my boy. I think you shall be pleased."

"What did she say?" asked Fredrick. He was bursting with curiosity about his fiancé.

"Countess Mary did most of the talking when we spoke. Veronica is pleasant and pretty, but she is quiet and reserved. I am so happy for you, lad."

He took Fredrick's hand in his own and patted it with affection.

Next, the old man addressed Lamar. "When you're finished tonight, we have more to do in your final training and tests. See to it you do not forget your place. A steward of the baron-apparent has always succeeded the apothecary in the family of Raddlif. I will not allow it to change."

Lamar bowed as the three men heard the sound of heels on the wooden floor outside growing louder.

"Your mother comes now," said Gavyn. "I just wanted to wish you well before your party, My Lord. Good night." With that, he turned and left, bowing to the Baroness as she appeared in the threshold.

Kaery glided into the room followed by Manfred. Both were richly dressed. The green of Kaery's eyes, amplified by her gown, sparkled in the light of the chamber. Her hair was pinned up, and two curled golden ribbons hung down either side of her face, cascading stylishly onto her chest. She approached Fredrick and Lamar, while the Baron waited behind.

"How handsome you both are. You make a mother proud. Everyone is gathering, and the sun will soon be setting."

"You look lovely."

"We have not had guests at the castle in many moons. It is nice to get dressed for others for a change. I shall not miss the opportunity. Are you ready?"

"I 'am," answered Fredrick.

"Lamar, it is up to you to not let him say anything to embarrass himself," said Kaery with a waggish smile.

"I will do that, My Lady."

"Tonight we have the feast, and introduction and soon, the wedding. Those days in between will be your time to get to know each other. Veronica is lovely, I don't mind saying."

"So I heard."

Kaery's eyes narrowed as she feigned frustration. "Is that what Gavyn was doing here then? Letting the cat out of the sack?"

"He came to offer his best wishes."

"Kaery," said the Baron. "I will speak to our son."

She leaned forward and kissed him on the cheek then wiped away the rouge left behind with her thumb. "I leave you to your father now. Do not be late for your own party!" she commanded before moving to exit the chamber.

As she passed Manfred, she smiled and touched his hand, pecking his cheek as she had Fredrick's before leaving him. The Baron stepped forward, staying silent. He looked at both as if he were inspecting them. At last he spoke. "My boy, you are on your way to becoming a man. Today begins a life I have wanted for you since you were a baby. Do you know that?"

"I do," said Fredrick.

"Our house is secluded in the Splinterwood, but that does not lessen our duty to protect our friends from our enemies."

"I wish only to make you proud, Father. To be as strong as those before us. To carry on the name of Raddlif to my son, and my grandson."

"*I am* proud of you. But there is still much to be done. We must not falter, or the Blackfeathers will put their boot on our necks as they did our ancestors in Annan. That must never happen."

Fredrick choked on his own words and found himself unable to speak. The two stood in silence looking at each other. He felt the pride radiating from his father like heat from an open flame. For the first time, he thought he might see a tear fall from his eyes. Manfred reached forward and snapped him into a hard embrace. As they separated, Fredrick saw his father discretely drag a finger along his eye to dry it before he turned to Lamar.

"And you, young steward. Atmore's have ever

dwelled in the home of Raddlif, ere it continues in you. I remember your father though he has long been gone. You need to find your woman and bear a child that another Atmore will live here. You are as much a son to me as you are a brother to Fredrick. I desire grandchildren as Olan does. I am proud of you too. Soon you will pick up where Gavyn leaves off. He is a jolly man, but he is tired and nearing the end of his service."

"I have always hoped to please both you and Fredrick, My Baron."

"And so you have, young man." He grabbed his shoulder and squeezed it tightly in affection. "And so you shall continue. I will hold you to that pledge. I leave you both now. See you at the feast."

He turned and left the chamber closing the door behind him.

"One last item to put on," said Fredrick as he stepped up to a wooden armoire next to his bed. He opened the doors and took from it a long-sword. At the bottom of the grip, it bore a disk-shaped pommel into which a single leaf was etched. At its base, the blade was wide, tapering to a fine point with a length of just under three feet. Its edge was keen, and along its center ran a deep and cruel fuller.

"A sword forged in the south," said Fredrick. "Taken in the beginning, present at the end."

With that, he put the weapon to its scabbard. Not speaking, he stepped toward the small loophole in his chamber. He breathed deeply while he settled his nerves and calmed his mind. He looked out to an angry red sunset with golden streaks of light cutting their way through gathering black rain clouds.

"You heard the Baroness. Let's not be late."

***

The Castle's refectory was the largest chamber of the manor. At one end sat a warm hearth, alive with a great fire, warming the room and providing a bright light by which the guests could enjoy the evening. Flanking it on both sides, carved into pillars of stone, stood the likenesses of long dead members of the Raddlif family. The statues guarded the fireplace as a tribute to their lost loved ones. The refectory was as modest as the rest of this forest castle. The stonewalls were supported by an exposed assembly of large timbers. Its peaked ceiling was tall and held fast by evenly spaced trusses. An elaborate network of chains allowed the chandeliers arranged along the center to be lowered for lighting the tallow candles nestled into the ironwork.

Several ornate tapestries decorated the walls. They depicted not only the Raddlifs, but members of those families with whom they shared an alliance for many years, including long dead heroes of the Moresten house, among others.

Baron Raddlif waited with his family dressed in a black leather tunic and trousers. He wore a green cape over his left shoulder, fastened with a clasp in the shape of an oak tree. Two polished iron chains looped under his arm, with a third golden braid marking him as Lord of the manor. Kaery stood next to her husband. Her gown held no specific marks of station, but around her neck, she donned a chain of silver with an emerald pendant. She greeted each guest with a warm and inviting smile while Manfred bore a more authoritative bearing.

Fredrick stood between his mother and father. Behind and to the left of the Baron's family, the balance of the court watched the guests arrive responding to each with a polite nod. Everyone wore happy expressions except for Rostov. His countenance was always gloomy. His eyes were ever watchful, discreetly surveying even the trustworthy visitors in the refectory.

The Young Baron found most of the faces unfamiliar. Others elicited vague and shadowed childhood memories. Some of them he knew only from the stories that Manfred or Rostov shared while out on the range or over a meal. The guests clustered in small groups and engaged in conversation. The din of the overlapping discussions, the musician's tune, coupled with the roaring fire in the hearth was deafening. Fredrick wondered how anyone could hear anything over the noise. He had never seen so many people in the dining hall at once.

In one corner, he saw the gray and gaunt form of Davtiln Whitefawn with his wife Cainda. They arrived to the castle from Greenwake, northeast of the Splinterwood, shortly after the Morestens. Davtlin was laughing and drinking with Bertrum Krell. As the two men carried on with each other, Cainda stood behind her husband, arms at her sides. She looked bored, and not amused.

With a booming voice to overcome the clamor, the crier called out, "Lords and Ladies, Count Reginar Archibald and Countess Murial of the city-state of Roscommon."

Fredrick watched them stop in the threshold. The man and his wife held out their hands together bent at the elbow, with the Count's hand above the Countess's flat against each other. Both stood with their heads high, stopping and taking a conceited pose. They ignored the crier where the others would at least nod politely. It appeared as if they only stopped to give the rest of the guests a chance to look at them. Reginar and Murial wore matching ankle length white robes. A "V" shaped patterned embroidery adorned the front of both garments.

After their moment of gracious recognition, they glided into the hall, mingled briefly with other nearby guests, and then approached the greeting family.

"May I extend my congratulations to you Master Fredrick of Splinterwood?" said Reginar placing his hand on Fredrick's shoulder. "You have grown into a handsome young man. I doubt you will remember me. We rarely come south from our lands, and the last time I was here, you were just starting to walk. I regret we do not see more of your family, but the journey is long, and there is much to do in Roscommon."

"Thank you, Count Archibald," said Fredrick surprised by how much younger he was compared to the other nobles. The Count's rich brown oiled hair was pushed straight back on his head. The crow's feet that sprouted from his narrow-set eyes only showed themselves when he smiled. His teeth gleamed white through a thin beard.

Reginar shifted his attention to Manfred and Kaery. "Good evening and thank you for inviting us. May I present my wife, Murial?"

"Welcome to Splinterwood Forest," said the Baron, "it's nice to meet you at last. Is this your first time in the woods?"

"It is," she answered, "though I have seen it from a distance."

"Kaery and I hope you enjoy your stay. Thank you both for coming."

"I could not miss it.," said Reginar. "Our families have been through much together. It would be a sin to not see this fine lad married to such an honorable family."

As they moved on, Fredrick watched them merge into the crowd of nobles. Suddenly, the dining hall grew quiet. The silence cascaded like a wave, starting at the entryway, and sweeping through the chamber as people turned their attention to the new arrivals standing in the open door. The many expressions of the guests, once happy and entertained, morphed to a mixture of surprise, curiosity and disdain.

Two mountainous and threatening looking individuals approached the awestruck crier. Fredrick knew the forms, squinting his eyes as he tried to recall their names. He fought an urge to put his hand on his sword-hilt at the sight of these menacing new arrivals. He forced himself to remember that these were not enemies of his family.

Drawing himself up, then clearing a lump in his throat, the young crier called out, "Lords and Ladies, I present Chieftain Rak Gan'Sann of the Ogon clan of the Red-Hand, and his guardian Torgk Ant'Togin. Friends of the Raddlif–"

The crier's loud voice died off as the two new arrivals walked by him, ignoring the announcement and not interested in a formal introduction.

Rak donned a patchwork jerkin of many colors that dropped to his knees over a short black trouser with banded sandals. He wore a crown made from the head of a great striped cat, plumed with bright colored feathers, and braids of different hempen ropes that extended like a loose cape down his back. Both ogon towered over other men in the room. Rak himself, immense in height, stooped as he entered through the wide threshold. His nose was broad and flat, with yellow eyes and a high grizzled forehead. Fredrick found his face to be hideous.

Torgk Ant'Togin wore a jerkin reinforced with rings of rusted steel. His black trousers where strengthened in the same manner at the hem and knees. As he walked, the rings moved and made a peculiar clinking noise. A leather cap from under which his dark, oily hair hung to the center of his back covered his head. He wore an altered pair of boots crafted by men and well-worn. Fredrick found it strange that boots of men were on the feet of an ogon. He wondered where he had acquired them, and under what circumstances.

The sight of these people, though friends of the Raddlifs, always made Fredrick uneasy.

The Captain moved closer to take a stance between the ogon and his Baron. Manfred discreetly took him by the wrist; stopping him and steering him to a less threatening position behind, silently commanding Rostov to stand-down. The hall was eerily quiet, except for the musicians who continued to play, though slightly out of tune, trying to keep the atmosphere in the chamber festive.

As Rak and his guardian walked the dining room, the guests they passed along the way stepped back in confusion and fear. Some fanned at their noses, turning away from the stench of them. Others watched in silence, enthralled by the drama of the strange arriving visitors.

At last, they stood before Fredrick and Manfred. He could tell why some of the guests were turning away as they passed. The odor of them was stifling, but he must ignore it. He must keep his place and welcome these two visitors as he had done the other sweet smelling aristocrats that he had greeted this evening. He must not offend these unusual guests. It had taken many years after settling in the Splinterwood for the Raddlifs to form a pact with these beings whose ways differed greatly from their own. The Red-Hand clan were the first ogon to treat with house Raddlif. Without their help, the "Newcomers" as they would later be called, might never have gained acceptance in the forest.

Baron Manfred took a step forward and placed his right fist against his left shoulder. "Chieftain, it is well you have joined us. I bid you welcome to Castle Raddlif."

Gan'Sann returned the Baron's gesture. He stood before him forebodingly, with his gaze shifting between the members of the family. He looked at them as if he were inspecting them.

Fredrick's heart raced as he waited to hear what the Ogon had to say.

"Raddlif," Rak said at last, in a coarse voice through a foreign accent, "the pact between us is strong. We will honor it, as long as you honor us."

He paused, looking around the hall, drinking in the sounds, sights and faces. Presently, he fixed his piercing yellow eyes on Fredrick, and then turned back to the Baron.

"Our clan bids you well on this union. Fredrick is a strong lad, and he rides well. He is accepted by ogon of the Red-Hand."

"Thank you," responded Manfred. "Will you join us for dinner?"

"No. We will not. But we will stay near your castle and attend the young man's wedding once you send word of its time."

Baron Manfred turned his head and gave his son a quick glance. He recognized it as a queue, and stepped forward to stand next to his father.

"Chieftain Gan'Sann," said Fredrick. "It is an honor to have you, and your people, here at our castle.

Thank you for your words and acceptance of our invitation."

The grizzled old ogon looked confused. Then he asked, "What is it you Newcomers say? 'You're Welcome.'"

With that, turning on his heels, he stepped back out of the hall the way he came.

Before following Rak, Torgk snapped his hand to his left shoulder to return their salutes.

Fredrick looked at Torgk and their eyes met. They were strange. His gaze unsettled him. It was lifeless and cold. His eyes were a colorless leaden gray where Rak's shined like gold. He looked much older than his Chieftain did. The glance chilled his heart, sending a shiver along his spine. Torgk stepped away, following Rak as the two departed the chamber.

It did not surprise Fredrick they declined the invitation to stay. Though sincere, there was little they would find toothsome. In addition, he felt sympathy for anyone who sat next to them, forced to endure their stink while trying to eat their meal.

The pact with the Red-Hand was vital for the safety of the towne and the roads to and from it. It was important, diplomatically, to invite Gan'Sann to any events at the castle, despite what the other guests would think or prefer.

Gradually, the roar of conversation rose in the chamber with the ogons' departure.

After a time, the voice of the crier rang out as a single figure appeared in the threshold. "Lords and Ladies, Count Olan Moresten of the City-State of

51

Trodenheim, in the territory of Icemarch. Guardian of the northern Mournway. Father to Lady Veronica."

Olan passed through the door slapping him hard on the back rocking him forward. "Enough with the introduction lad!" he said as the crier collected himself while blushing. "These noble snobs know one another so quiet down and fetch us ale!"

Fredrick grinned as he looked to his father standing stiffly next to him. Manfred shook his head, grinning at Olan's antics, giving way to the three folds of skin on either side of his face that only appeared when he smiled.

Olan strutted toward them. He wore a button-down dark tunic secured at the waist with a crimson leather belt and a silver buckle. His trousers were black and trimmed in red. Well-fitted boots shod Olan's feet, fixed with a set of riding spurs. Around his neck hung a sturdy gold chain with a pendant formed to the sigil of his house.

"Gentlemen," he said in greeting, "you grin as if you had just stolen the last whore. Surely you can make some decent conversation tonight for one who has come so far to give up his most prized possession."

"Indeed we can. It is good to be in the company of old friends," responded Manfred.

Olan turned his attention to Fredrick. "And you lad, I see you smirking, bearing that southern-forged butter-knife at your hip. You should be ashamed of yourself! Where did you get a dulled-out trophy such as that?"

"It was taken from a dead southern hero," he answered. Fredrick had grown fond of the Count in the days since his arrival. He felt comfortable around him.

"That it was! Make sure it stays in its scabbard," Olan demanded. "I don't know how many more times I can stand to be close enough to fight with those Southgate sons-a-bitches. As much as I enjoy killing them, I've become bored with the game."

Then he turned to Kaery. She smiled at him as he bowed, returning the gesture with a graceful curtsey.

"My dear, you look younger each time we meet. I am so proud of this lad. He gets his good looks from you. I was afraid when I arrived that he'd favor Manfred."

Kaery giggled at the Count's jape. "We are proud of him too. We are so happy to join our families."

"As are Mary and I." Olan kissed her hand and looked back at Fredrick as he drew himself up straight. "Are you ready for your introduction, lad?"

"I am," he said, sounding bold and feeling nervous.

Olan stood next to Manfred as he took his position with the host family.

Across the room, the crier cleared his throat, then called out, "Lords and Ladies, Countess Mary Moresten with Lady Veronica, betrothed to Master Fredrick!"

As the crier announced their names, the women stepped together into the threshold. The tune played by

53

the minstrels changed to a song that Fredrick recognized as "The Victorious Hammer", the traditional refrain of the Moresten house. They marched ahead slowly as they approached. Fredrick immediately noticed the disparity in the expressions of the two women. Mary was clad in an off-white, crimson trimmed gown with tight-fitting sleeves and a wide bell skirt. Her bearing was noble, proud and happy.

Veronica's demeanor, however, caused him to be more nervous than ever. Her green eyes were bright, but stony and emotionless. She neither smiled nor frowned, walking arm in arm with her mother to her left. She wore a crimson veil lined with flowers flowing down her back against her red tinted hair. Her gown matched the veil, with golden embroidery adorning the cuffs of the trumpeted sleeves.

Behind them, Amma and Elga entered the room and followed at a respectful distance.

Fredrick regarded her as she approached, smiling brightly. He could read nothing in her lovely, but reticent and expressionless eyes. As the two stopped a few paces in front of the family, he stepped forward, taking Veronica's hand in his own. She did not clutch it, nor respond. His smile slowly faded under the coldness of Veronica's expression.

"Baron-Apparent Fredrick Raddlif," said Mary, "may I present to you Lady Veronica Moresten."

At the mention of her name, Veronica curtseyed gracefully.

"It is a pleasure to meet you at last," said

Fredrick. Just as he finished, he lifted her hand and kissed it.

Veronica nodded, but she did not speak.

Together the two of them shared an uncomfortable silence that spread through the room. Watching them with Olan at his side, Manfred spoke to loosen the mood.

"Friends from distant lands, thank you for coming. Let us now be seated and refresh ourselves. To the table!" he exclaimed, holding his hands in the air. "I do not want an empty cup in this hall!"

"I'll drink to that!" Olan bellowed.

The guests filtered toward the giant table sitting off-centered in the chamber. Several smaller ones sat scattered around the refectory. The servants scrambled through the dining hall with large flagons filling cups as the celebrators took their places.

Manfred pulled a carved wooden chair lined with green velvet from under the table and seated the Baroness Kaery. Rostov sat quietly, his cup filled with water instead of wine, ever vigilant, even in a room of friendly nobles.

At the smaller tables were the servants and counselors for the families. Lamar had found his way to Amma and there he took the seat next to her, displacing Elga and she moved, grumbling all the while.

Fredrick took in the sights around the hall. Across the way, he saw Lamar, and a wry smile crossed his lips. He watched Amma giggling as he filled her cup from a clay flagon. It was hard to miss the spark between the two of them as they carried on together.

Looking at the bounty of food, his hunger grew. One platter bore a massive goose, roasted and golden, basted in cranberry sauce. There were cuts of fine venison from a stag taken from outside their gates in the Splinterwood. Down the way was a bowl stacked high with whole chickens turned on a spit. Trenchers of gravy sat within everyone's reach. Platters filled with rolls, fresh butter and vegetables and fruits of many varieties littered the table. There were decanters of a dark and strong wine brought south from Krellton, and small brass vessels of tobacco grown in nearby fields. Servants chased goblets as the guests lifted them, filling them with ale.

Fredrick and the guests filled their plates amid the roar of the overlapping conversations. Veronica sat next to him quietly. She took only a few vegetables and a cut of goose. After doing so, she ate slowly, avoiding the eyes of the other celebrators. Veronica's stony, detached bearing did not dampen the spirits of the other people who carried on in mirth despite her mood.

Baron Manfred waited a while for his guests to enjoy their meal, then stood and held out his goblet. The chamber grew quiet as everyone turned their attention to him. "My friends, the day Fredrick was born, I learned the Blackfeather, Cyrus Crowe, had marched north out of his nest in Southgate. To keep him, and his nobles, out of our lands, we would have to fight. With Captain Rostov, we gathered what men we had and prepared for the battle to come.

"Count Olan, we met at the Mournway and together the Army of the North marched south. You spoke of the pregnancy of your lovely wife. I will never forget how that made me feel. Both of us feared we would never know the children we were leaving behind. We found the Blackfeather near Cliffside and from there we sent him, and his army, back to its nest. My son wears the sword I claimed in that battle from a Southgate noble. Judging by the token on its pommel, I believe he was of the Grayfall house. I fought him, and the rogue nearly killed me. He would have put that very blade into my throat if it were not for you, my friend. Mighty your hammer fell heavy against that southern mongrel. Afterward, I gathered his blade and carried on. Tonight, that sword serves in remembrance of that struggle, and our victory—"

"He never saw me coming!" Olan roared, interrupting the speech. "He was too busy kicking your arse!" He laughed boisterously as he finished while slapping the table and entertaining himself, holding up the flagon of ale from which he was drinking to the cheers of the men. He drank from it as the wave of laughter he started passed through the room.

The Baron smiled uncomfortably, embarrassed by his friend's words but knowing the truth of it. Drawing himself up he continued to speak. "As the battle ended, Rostov, Olan and I walked among the dead, thankful for both victory and life, a Marked Rider arrived on the field. Do you remember what news he brought?"

57

"I do," said Olan, standing and holding out the ale flagon. "He brought the news my wife had birthed a fat daughter. My son Donal had a sister. I cannot describe how it feels to learn, victorious on a field of battle, standing among so much pain and death, that your child is born and healthy. To know I will live to see this new child and she is waiting for me to return home. I was so happy I hugged this scrawny Baron so hard I thought he might break. Now Manfred, do you remember my words?"

"You said your daughter's birth heralded the binding of our families forever in blood as well as victory. I bound my son, to your daughter. That day has led to tonight and the pledge will be fulfilled."

Fredrick looked on as Veronica squirmed in her seat. She kept her eyes down and her hands in her lap. Her manner made him insecure. Frustration with her welled up in his mind. For his entire life, he knew this day was coming, and suspected she did too. He wondered what it was about him she found so undesirable. Olan and Manfred turned their drinking vessels in his direction. It was his turn to speak and sweat formed on his forehead as his nervousness grew. He had given lots of thought of what to say when this moment came. He had hoped that Veronica would be happy and embrace their union, but it was obvious she had not, and now he faltered. Fredrick stood and held out his cup, but with not even a glimmer of a smile to work with from his fiancé, the words did not come easy.

"Ladies and Gentlemen. I am happy to be

among you. I give you my word that I will be a dutiful husband to Lady Veronica. We will honor that for which many men have died. The Raddlifs are Mournmen, and the Morestens are of the ice. Together we defend the north from the scourge in the south. We shall never forget that duty. Our children will learn it, and one day the two of us will be the parents at a union such as this."

The guests applauded Fredrick's short speech. Afterward, Manfred and Olan turned their attention to Veronica. Still, she did not stir. She merely sat her place in a sullen pose, eyes down and her hands clasped together. In the silence that followed, Mary nudged her with her shoulder but she did not respond.

"Isn't there something you would like to say, Veronica?"

Fredrick could hear the subtle sternness in Mary's tone.

"No, Mother," she responded.

"No Mother?" repeated Mary, her impatience now growing more obvious.

"I have nothing to say. I will not lie to Fredrick."

A wave of emotions ran through the room like an icy draft of wind. The guests muttered to each other, mesmerized by the unexpected drama playing out at the table.

Fredrick felt the tension twisting in his gut, finding himself in a state of inward panic. He must be firm, strong and patient, if not for himself, but for this girl who would soon be his woman and wife. He sensed her fear and reservations although he did not understand it.

Mary took a deep breath to calm herself. "Lie? Why do you put it so?"

"Because I do not love Fredrick and I do not want to marry him," she responded. "I will not tell him that I want this, or speak eloquent words." Her eyes stay fixed on the plate still in front of her, refusing to move as a wave of muttering ran through the hall.

When Olan finally spoke, his tone dripped with disappointment. "Love is a choice, Little Girl. One you will soon have to make."

Fredrick viewed the Countess Mary Moresten, wife of Olan, sovereign of Trodenheim, as she grew red faced in silent anger. At the same time, he could see his own father stunned to silence amid the growing drama. Her honesty and bravery, speaking out as she had, somehow had impressed him despite his frustration. It left him with a strange sympathy for this young woman mixed in with the confusion and ire at her rejection of their marriage. He did not wish for this unfortunate scene, one that started so pleasantly with a hearty meal and good company of friends, to go any further.

"Veronica," said Fredrick. "I do not wish you to lie to me or anyone else. If I must earn your respect to do our duty, then I shall earn it. Later, we can learn to love each other."

Hearing the words, she finally looked up at him. He saw, for the first time, emotion in her grim face. Her eyes were uncompromising, but he could sense that even the slightest breeze would collapse them like a pile of leaves stacked under an autumn tree. They looked at each other for what seemed to him like a long time. Then she nodded subtly, and then resumed her sullen pose.

"Well spoken, lad," said Olan. "For a young woman she has the stubbornness of an old one."

Fredrick could tell the Count wanted to say more, but with the people in the room looking on, muttering to each other and drawing their own conclusions, he knew it was not the time.

The awkward silence that settled over the table faded, and the noise of conversation resumed. Servant-girls surrounded them, removed the platters of food, and replaced them with a variety of pastries and desserts. The chamber filled with the sweet-scented aroma of tobacco as many of them enjoyed a smoke.

Fredrick heard a knock at the table. Davtlin Whitefawn stood and held out his goblet. "Young Man, may I extend my best wishes to you and your fiancé. I remember the celebration the night Kaery and Manfred wed here in this very castle. At the time, it was little more than a large fort. I too marched to battle with the Army of the North to face the Blackfeathers. Let us toast the victorious dead."

With that, the rest of the men of the group stood and lifted their cups and goblets shouting "Here Here!" Some of them blowing rings of smoke.

"Mother," said Veronica meekly, "may I return to my chambers?"

Mary had hardly a chance to respond before

Olan spoke with a booming voice, "No you may not!"

Fredrick's gaze turned toward Olan and he could see the fire in his eyes.

"You will sit in your chair. You will listen to the history of our families." He reached up and pushed the servant standing near to him. "Fill her goblet! She does not seem as though she can relax and understand her self-worth or duty. Maybe more wine will loosen her spirits."

For what seemed like hours, the voices of Fredrick's friends and family rang in his ears. He heard them, but he was distracted, and not listening to the words. Discreetly, he surveyed Veronica and wondered what was going through her mind as she sat there so sullen and detached.

***

Brooding and embarrassed by the rebuke from her father, Veronica sat with her hands folded in her lap. The guests were standing and toasting with Davtlin Whitefawn as he went on about best wishes for her union, and ancient victories. His toast annoyed her.

She listened as the nobles shared stories of their family's service in the wars of ages past. Not only since their arrival in Tharrin, but also in the old lands of Annan before the tragedy that sent them fleeing from the east through the Maelstrom in the Great East Sea.

Fredrick's words about earning her trust intrigued her. Before she arrived at the castle, she expected Fredrick would be an unattractive clod. A man raised among a group of back-wood outcasts choosing to live in an eerie forest, miles from any other city-state in the Mournlands. She was convinced that she would be trapped in a rundown, haunted fort far away from Trodenheim, never to see her brother or her family again.

Curiosity, however, was now getting the better of her. Despite herself, she found him to be handsome, charming and nothing she had expected. The castle was not the mud-hut she imagined though it was more modest than her own home at Icekeep. The forest frightened her, and seemed just as dark and foreboding as the stories she had heard, but so far no ghosts of the past visited while she laid in her bed.

Bored with the proceedings, and growing more interested in Fredrick, she wanted to look at him. Hiding behind her hair, she rolled her eyes slowly, attempting to steal a peek at him unnoticed. She found him speaking across the table to Count Archibald. The two of them were deep in conversation. Occasionally they would stop, and roll back in laughter.

Suddenly, as she watched him, his head moved, looking toward her as he continued listening to Archibald. She could not divert her eyes quick enough before the two had a fleeting moment of eye contact. Butterflies churned in her belly as she retreated into her defensive posture and wondered what he must be thinking. She was honest with him earlier when she said she did not want to lie, but now she questioned if stealing this glance sent him the wrong message.

A sly smile came to the lips of the Young

Baron and he held his gaze on Veronica. She could feel his eyes on her, and she fought against the urge to look at him again.

Fredrick excused himself from Archibald, and then said, "Lord Olan, may I make a request of you?"

The other discussions around the table paused as the guests turned their attention to Fredrick with curious expressions.

"Yes lad, what is it you need?"

The nervousness in Fredrick's voice was obvious. He swallowed to moisten his throat with a gulp and said, "it has been a difficult night for Veronica. Might I have her to walk with me? I would like to take her to a favorite spot of mine in the castle. The high-tower offers a splendid view of the forest. The night is cloudy, but the moon is bright and it isn't raining yet. The tops of the trees sway with the evening breeze. I think the Lady will enjoy it."

Olan turned the request over in his mind. Finally, he smiled through his bushy beard. "A fine idea. A breath of fresh air will do her good. Surely all this talk of heroism and politics is boring you near to tears."

"Yes, Father," answered Veronica, "I mean, yes I would like the walk, but your stories are not dull."

"Don't flatter an old man, Little Girl; most of it is horse-shit! These nobles only listen because they have nothing else to do!" he responded, finishing with a jolly laugh and pointing at his cup so a servant would refill it.

Fredrick stood and took Veronica's chair, holding it as she rose to her feet. She sensed the eyes of the guests on her. She felt as if the two of them were actors, the main characters in a drama playing out for the night's entertainment.

Veronica walked slowly. Every so often, Fredrick stopped and looked back to make sure she was still there. The couple soon ascended a narrow spiral staircase. Once at the top, Fredrick flung open a door built into the roof overhead. He stepped through and offered his hand. She smiled, feeling the warmth of his touch as he helped her up and onto the tower.

The clouds gathering throughout the day now loomed low in the sky. The light of the bright moon diffused across them casting an eerie blue glow over the woods. From this high vantage point, Veronica admired the spectacular view of the forest laid out below her like a living carpet of trees.

Fredrick remained quiet while she walked the tower, dragging her hand along the coarse stone of the battlements while looking out over the Splinterwood. He gave her a moment to take in the forest's majesty, then spoke, trying to break the silence between them. "My family and our allies have protected this forest since we arrived after the crossing. I love it, but it isn't without its dangers."

Fredrick waited hoping Veronica would speak, but she did not.

"You know that I'm in the same place as you. We don't know each other, I understand. But am I this distasteful for you?" he asked, keeping his distance.

She pondered the question before she answered. The confusion she felt was like a perfume, detectable, but invisible. "No Fredrick, you're not. In fact, you are much different from what I expected. I am lost in the duties I never asked for and don't want. I do not want to marry you, and I don't want to live here so far from my brother and family."

"We were born into nobility," he answered. "We have duties; we will never be like those who serve us."

"I would thank you not to sound like my mother," she responded with a cynical tone. She turned away from him and stood between the battlements looking out into the dim light over the forest.

Veronica sensed Fredrick reeled under her rebuke. She waited while he remained quiet. He crossed the tower and stopped near her. She noticed the change in his countenance. His soft and comforting face was morphing into a sterner, bolder bearing.

Their eyes locked, and Veronica knew the two of them studied each other in that passing moment. He was doing his best to read her, and she fought hard to make sure he could not. She turned away from him again, afraid of her mixed feelings, hiding behind her long hair. She sensed his rising frustration. Part of her was happy with his impatience. She hoped that he would be angry enough to call off the wedding. However, nagging at her mind was the unescapable sense of duty. Doing so would break her father's heart. How could she face him afterward? How would he treat her after something he would surely take as a betrayal?

She stood with her back to Fredrick, looking out over the tops of the trees. The air was becoming colder beneath the swirling, angry clouds. "You will be a baron; men will follow you. A host of them. This forest is yours. Would you not rather choose a woman? Doesn't it bother you that our families are forcing us to do this against our wills?"

Fredrick took her by the shoulder. He spun her around to see her face. He was gentle, but she could sense the assertiveness of his touch. Their eyes met. His countenance, once compassionate, was now cross.

"Naïve girl!" said Fredrick harshly. "Do those men who go to fight and keep those southern dogs south of their mountains whine about what they want?" His tone was blunt. Angry. She was seeing a different side of him. A side fiercely loyal, duty bound, and unwilling to fail.

"Of course there are women who have caught my eye and who I would like to see, or perhaps love. Do you think I have not climbed out of a balcony late at night to be with a woman? There are many, if that makes you feel better!"

Fredrick waited. He held Veronica's eyes with his own. She could not turn away. His confession about other women shocked her and he knew it. She suddenly regretted taking the walk, for things were not going as she had hoped. Now, lurking in the back of her mind, excitement grew at his sudden passion. She was beginning to respect this man, but she would not put off her emotions. She did not want to be married and live isolated in this forest for the rest of her life. But his words left her mind speechless and her heart raging in confusion.

He reached forward and held her arms in a firm grip below the shoulders. He pulled her close.

Is he going to kiss me? she thought.

"If you mean what you say, renounce your claim," Fredrick commanded. "You will be free to tend sheep, till a field, or serve ale. You will live in exile, but be relieved of your burdensome duty of marrying me. You could go where you want and marry whatever handsome suitor steals your heart."

She could say nothing. Hearing it put that way removed all the romance she associated with liberation from her duty. With great effort, she found the strength to turn from Fredrick's magnetic gaze.

"What is it?" asked Fredrick.

"I wish I could run away. Just simply disappear, and solve both our problems."

"Don't be silly," he responded. "Where would you go? What would you do? Deep down you know that your family loves you, and you love them. You are scared. It's natural you should be. If you want the truth, so am I. I ask only you give me a chance to earn what you are not willing to surrender freely. Your heart." Fredrick's tone softened as he released his grip on her, but she could still sense his frustration.

A streak of lightning appeared in the distance followed by the rolling thunder against the dark clouds. Raindrops fell from the sky, splashing here and there in large drops growing steadier.

"The rain has come," Fredrick said as he descended into the trapdoor holding out his hand.

She felt comforted by his touch. It excited her when he put his hands on her and she could not deny it even to herself.

They retraced their steps to the dining chamber where the partygoers were still making merry.

The two of them again became the center of attention as they rejoined the feast.

As sullen and forlorn as she was earlier, Veronica took her seat, but now, with the brooding feelings she already harbored, she had confusion to go along with them. Fredrick impressed her, and she wondered to herself, if she could come to love him.

NO! she thought, as she resisted the notion. She sat in her seat, sullen as before repeating in her mind, *No. No. No.*

Chapter 3

After the rocks fell from the sky, the days were like unto night. The air we breathed was poison…

-Excerpt from the Journal of Baron Fredon Raddlif, the Bold One

Veronica could barely rest with the swirl of emotions raging in her heart. Occasionally she snoozed, but never slept deeply, only dozing between frightening dreams. The rain faded late in the night leaving a musty smell of drenched earth throughout the soaked forest.

Presently, she stood near the balcony of her bed-chamber looking out into the brisk morning. She wore a white nightgown with her long hair tied into a ponytail. She could sense her father's anger. Earlier, he flung open her door with a crash. She was not sleeping when he entered, but she did not move hoping that if he found her asleep, he would leave her be.

"Get up!" he roared while kicking the framework of the bed.

Mary followed and remained silent, standing in a corner of the chamber where she regarded Veronica with an anxious expression.

"What's wrong with you? Why are you behaving like this?"

"Father..." was all she could muster before her voice gave out.

"You will marry that young man," commanded Olan. "You will stop acting as you are toward him! 'I won't lie to Fredrick,' Indeed. There is nothing to lie about! No one expects you to love him! We expect you to do your duty. There is more happening here than your selfish romantic visions of choosing your one love. The Army of the North must remain strong. Women do not fight in wars. You and the Raddlif heir must seal our alliance for the future by uniting our families. He understands what he must do, why is it you cannot?"

The Count fell silent, wandering in a small circle with his arms behind his back, trying to control his frustration.

Mary glided to her husband and placed her hand on his shoulder to soothe him, finally breaking her silence. "Fredrick is a handsome young man, and their towne is peaceful and happy. I know Castle Raddlif is modest compared to Icekeep, but it is milder in the winter, and well kept. He said himself that he is willing to earn your trust. Why are you so resistant?"

"I don't want to leave Trodenheim," she answered. "I don't want to be away from Donal. My friends. My home."

Olan's wandering brought him close and they looked together out to the morning. The storm that had soaked the forest overnight was little more than shattered remnants of clouds high in the sky.

"In two nights you will marry Fredrick. You will get to know each other. I have arranged a tour for you today to see your new home. Wear something you can ride in and come down when you are ready."

He turned to leave the chamber, passing by Mary silently and stopping at the threshold. He turned his head but kept his back to her, showing only his bearded profile and wild hair.

"I will hear no more of this. It is done, and it has been since you were a baby. Two nights," he said in conclusion. Then he was gone, and Mary followed him leaving Veronica alone in the chamber with only her thoughts.

As the loneliness closed in, she put her face in her hands and wept. Her stomach roiled with fear and insecurity, but after a couple deep breaths of the fresh air, the emotions calmed. She drew herself up, wiping the tears from her eyes.

"Lady Veronica?" said an expected but familiar voice.

Amma stood in the room, holding a covered tray and flagon, clad in a simple gray frock with a stained apron. In her weeping, she did not notice her enter. She felt embarrassed, wondering how much her servant had seen.

"Put it on the table," she said, looking at Amma's smiling face. She appeared blissfully unaware of the unpleasant confrontation only a few moments ago.

Not having ate at the feast the night before, Veronica's stomach growled with hunger. She spread butter over the still warm bread sitting amongst the bacon and hard-boiled eggs. The flagon contained a thick red wine. It was rich and its aroma was pungent and hung heavy about the small table. She did not care for the bitter flavor, but its strong spirit helped to calm her frayed nerves. She drank it sparingly.

"Join me, Amma. Be seated," said Veronica.

Visibly delighted by the invitation, she sat at the table.

"Have you ate this morning, or have you been too busy?"

"Very busy," she answered.

"There is too much food for me alone. Eat some."

With that, in silence, they sat together eating breakfast.

"What will you be wearing today?"

"The green gown. Father said to prepare for a ride."

The servant turned aside to the wardrobe of carved oak against the wall near the bed. From it, she took the requested clothing and a matching bodice.

The two of them were both quiet as she helped her Lady into the dress and buttoned it up the back. The short-sleeved garment extended to her ankles covering the laced boots that shod her feet. Over the whole, she drew the bodice around Veronica and tied it tightly.

As she put on the final trimmings of Veronica's gown, her eyes wandered. Veronica knew that a question loitered there, waiting to get out.

"What is it," asked Veronica. "I know those eyes, is something bothering you?"

"Well, your walk with Fredrick, last night, what did you talk about?"

"Duty. That is all there is for me I'm afraid," she responded in a downcast tone.

"Did he kiss you?" Amma asked sheepishly.

"Kiss me? Don't be silly. We had only just met. Do you think he would just walk up and kiss me?"

"No, I guess not," said Amma, blushing. "He is handsome though M'lady. I expected these forest-dwelling Mournmen to be a band of dirty, swaggering oafs. It surprised me to find they were not."

"As was I, but that still does not mean I want to live here or marry him," snapped Veronica.

After that, Amma remained quiet. She knew when to speak and when not to, always keeping her station. She knew her place and earned Veronica's trust. That is how she, among all the other servants, became handmaid to Veronica, and was chosen to remain with her after her marriage to Fredrick. There were other friends in Trodenheim, but none of them made the treacherous journey south to attend the wedding.

"Let's go. I am tired of these dreary walls. Remove your apron," said Veronica.

"Where are we going?"

"We are getting a breath of air. If I'm going riding this morning, I want my favorite horse. Not some other clumsy beast chosen by the stable-hands."

Veronica led the way. She and Amma left the guest chambers and walked down to the gallery where she found Baron Manfred, along with Fredrick and an elderly man. The three sat at a small table enjoying a cup of hot tea and eating breakfast.

"Lady Veronica, hello," said Manfred as the

two of them stood and greeted the women. "I hope you slept well. You remember our apothecary, Gavyn Wellbrown?"

Gavyn did not stand or speak, but smiled his jolly grin and nodded.

"Join us for breakfast?"

"No thank you, Baron."

"Good Morning," said Fredrick at last, bowing and taking her hand gently and kissing it.

"And to you," she responded. "I thought I might walk the grounds and breathe the fresh air. Father mentioned something about a tour, so I have dressed for the occasion and go to ready my favorite horse."

"It is as you say, Lady Veronica," said Manfred. "We have agreed that you should take a ride with Fredrick as your guide. What better way for you to get to know each other and experience the woods? However, be wary! The Splinterwood is angry this morning. It always is after a rain."

"The woods are angry?" she responded curiously.

"This isn't any ordinary forest," he said, beaming a bright smile.

Veronica listened, secretly admiring the Old Baron's distinguished handsomeness, wondering if Fredrick would age as gracefully.

"Some would call it haunted, but that is not so. It is enchanted. This forest lives and breathes just as you do. When it exhales, it gives off the air we breathe. It produces life and takes it. The trees are its citizens, speaking to one another, recalling tales of people who battle against themselves beneath their branches. Not only men, but of the ogon here before us."

Manfred gestured with his hands to make his point, as if he were telling the story to small children. "It isn't just Raddlifs' who live in this forest. Some who live here are no longer alive. The Restless move when the fog covers the land. You must not ride when it's foggy, especially if the moon is full. Remember that."

"Father," said Fredrick putting a hand on Manfred's shoulder, "the Lady has heard enough. Let's not alarm Veronica before she has had a chance to come to love the forest as much as we have."

"Oh yes, yes, quite so," said Manfred standing up straight holding his head in a noble manner. "Once you are among us as family you will learn these woods as we have. My son is the most gifted woodsman in the Splinterwood. He knows practically every tree and root. Some of them by name, eh Fredrick?"

Fredrick smiled in response.

"By name? How do you mean?" asked Veronica, frowning in her confusion and bristling with curiosity.

"You'll see. There is much to learn and experience in the Splinterwood. And so you shall." As Manfred finished, he returned to his breakfast, smiling widely at Gavyn who beamed his aging, yet still warm grin at both Veronica and Amma.

"We leave shortly," said Fredrick. "Count Olan

had a few things he wanted to do before we set off."

"My Father? Will he be joining us?" asked Veronica, surprised to find that he was going on the excursion with them. After what happened earlier, she did not look forward to spending the day with him.

"Yes. He wishes to tour the forest with us," Fredrick said, "though I half-think it is more that he does not want to leave me alone with you."

Veronica shined a shy smile at Fredrick. "If you'll excuse me, I am off to prepare my horse. If I do not do it myself, it is never to my liking."

"I look forward to our ride."

Veronica turned toward the main entryway to the castle and Amma followed. The doors were open to allow the many guests to come and go as they pleased to enjoy the morning.

As she stepped out into the sunlight, she paused at the top of the bank of steps leading to the yard. Not knowing the way to the stables, she walked the stone footpath that cut through the finely trimmed turf laying at the foot of the stairs just to see where it led.

She passed by many sorts of folks milling about on her way. The number of people, and activity amazed her. Scattered around the grounds stood large gardens and rows of corn and vegetables tended by women in blue dresses, their heads covered in bonnets. Men moved carts back and forth filled with casks, sacks of food, and other supplies for the castle's occupants.

As she walked the curved path along the round

outer wall, Veronica noticed a group of well-armed soldiers guarding an unsavory lot of men bound by a sturdy chain. They wore matching sackcloth tunics and trousers. Their feet were bare, and their bodies reeked of perspiration and filth.

Drawing near to them, she looked closer at the foreboding group in chains suddenly realizing that not all of them were men. Two of them were ogon, but all three were dirty and downtrodden from their labor. If it were not for the sturdy guards glowering over the prisoners, she would have fled in fear at the sight of them.

She passed by, trying to hold her head high and maintain a regal manner. Amma, not skilled in the manners of the nobility, gawked shamelessly at the grim threesome. The taller of the ogon then turned and looked toward Veronica and she could not help meeting his eyes with her own. His bearing was cross. His eyes were large and yellow, shining in the light of the sun. His skin was a sickly green color with an upturned nose. Long gray hair extended from the back of his head with a baldpate. Scars marred his ugly face. His stare bore such a weight, that she turned away, focusing on the path and picking up her pace, thankful for the chain that held him.

She could not see the face of the other ogon. The third prisoner, the only man in the group, carried on with his grim work in silence.

The two soon found their way to the stable. The stables were huge, consisting of several buildings all of which could easily house several animals. Still more beasts could graze in the field that lay beyond the wall. Veronica entered to find a young boy tending to the horses.

The boy wore a simple tan shirt with a brown vest, trousers and bare feet. An apron of brown leather covered his clothes. The mud and waste of the stables mashed up between his toes as he moved, brushing a tall horse carefully as it munched from a sackcloth feedbag strung over its snout.

"You, boy!" commanded Veronica. "Ready two of the Moresten horses. The brown gelding with a white blaze for me and suitable mount for my maidservant."

"Certainly M'lady," he said surprised by the sudden appearance of the two girls, "Yes, M'lady." He tripped over a bucket sitting next to the horse he was tending, falling forward to the ground. The boy picked himself up, cleaning off his hands by beating them together. He bowed quickly and smiled at them. Veronica and Amma exchanged glances, trying to stifle the laughter they both felt welling up inside.

"We will wait outside for the horses," Veronica shouted to the boy who had vanished deep into the stable to fetch the beast she described.

"Yes M'lady," she heard return, the sound of his boyish voice muffled through the wooden half-walls.

Veronica turned and looked at Amma and they faced each other. For a moment, they remained silent. Then, both burst into laughter, joining hands in their mirth at the stable-boy. She hoped he could not hear them. She did not want to embarrass him, but she found his reaction to her amusing and welcomed the laugh afterward, having been so miserable in the past few days.

As they waited outside, the boy returned leading two horses. One of them was the brown gelding with the blaze that Veronica had sought. The second was a docile white horse, smaller than Veronica's beast.

"Thank you, boy," said Amma as he backed away from them, bowing repeatedly as they took the reins of the horses.

"Yes, M'lady," he said once again.

"This is Dago," said Veronica petting the horse's neck. The beast brushed his nose against her face in affectionate recognition. "And who is this?"

"We call him Snow," answered the boy.

The women mounted their horses and smiled again at each other as the stable-hand stood staring at them. His hands were at his sides, still restless and unsure, regarding Veronica and her handmaiden with wide eyes.

"You're dismissed, young man," said Veronica, trying to quell his obvious apprehension.

"Yes, M'lady."

"Can you say nothing else?" mocked Amma.

"Yes, M'lady. I mean, no M'lady, I mean..." his cheeks turned bright red as he stammered in embarrassment. He backed away, still bowing repeatedly until finally turning and dashing into the stable out of sight.

Veronica heeled her horse to a walk. They took the long way around to the courtyard, taking their time. The two rode past more fields and small houses with thatched roofs that housed servants and helpers of the noble's family.

When they returned to the castle, they arrived to find her father sitting on his stallion.

"Ah, there you are lass," said Olan. "I went to meet you in your chambers but you were not there. Went to get Dago, eh?"

"Since it's my first ride in the Splinterwood, I didn't want to go without him."

"Very well," he responded, shorter on words than usual. Veronica had trouble reading his mood. She had never been at odds with him before. The feeling was awkward and unpleasant.

"Amma, you have a horse, do you intend to ride with us?" Olan asked.

"With your permission M'lord, Yes. Lady Veronica requested I go along. I'm sure I can keep up."

The Count regarded her with an uncomfortable glare, pausing for a while before he answered. Veronica was afraid that he would deny their request and was relieved when he gave her a cold affirmation with a wave of his hand.

With Olan leading the way, the trio passed through the gate of the castle walls, leaving the grounds, and soon followed the main cobblestone thoroughfare that divided the towne in half. The road meandered down the hill lined with wooden buildings stacked and stilted along its edges. Far below, she could see the giant palisade of logs. Sharpened trees extended outward at differing lengths strengthening the barricade to keep any intruders at bay. Veronica wondered at how she did not notice the cruel pointed barbican when she first arrived. She realized that inside the carriage, with the curtains closed, she had seen little while travelling to the Splinterwood.

In the center of towne, Olan, Veronica and Amma waited. Soon, three men appeared riding tall horses and approached the waiting trio. Two of them wore leather armor and matching tabards with the man who led them wearing a green sash with a gold trim over the top of his garb.

"Count Olan, my name is Victor Rostov. My wardens and I will escort you and Lord Fredrick on your ride in the woods. The Baron-Apparent is preparing his horse. He will be with us shortly. He sent me ahead to meet with you."

"Thank you for your escort though I'm afraid you and your men might be bored today. May I present my daughter, Lady Veronica Moresten, and the small quiet lass is her maid, Amma."

"Ladies, a pleasure," said the Captain, but he did not smile.

Veronica nodded. He impressed her as a man who took his post seriously, though the soldiers behind him appeared disinterested. As the group waited for Fredrick, she continued to inspect the towne laid out around them. The smell of fresh-baked bread filled the air, and it was noisy. Menfolk passed by bearing tools.

Citizens drove carts full of earth, wood and stone to unseen work sites. Women carried baskets of different vegetables and fruits. Others had set their pushcarts on the corners to sell goods. Children ran and played merrily.

The main thoroughfares were wide, but blocked with wains and tumbrils belonging to the royal wedding guests. The side alleys were narrow, and busy with townspeople. A mismatched patchwork of different construction techniques made the towne dissimilar from her own in Trodenheim. Cabins of notched fallen timbers made up many of the houses, but some were built of both stone and wood. Some stood on stilts hovering above the ground while others did not. Many consisted of two stories or more. Some had thatched roofs, others wooden shingles. A few of them even had tiles of sod from the nearby river.

After a time, Veronica saw Fredrick and Lamar appear in the gate of the castle, making their way toward the group on horseback. Fredrick wore a green boiled leather sleeveless tunic over a tan colored shirt, belted at the waist with trousers and tall boots. The leaf-etched sword he bore at the feast dangled from his belt. At his chest, he carried two pistols in a bandolier. She heard about these dangerous weapons from Donal, but before now had never seen one. An iron cap adorned the dark wood butt of the pistols so it may also serve as a cudgel. In a holster at his saddle, was a matching long-gun of similar design to the handguns. Atop his head sat a brown wide-brimmed hat with a black hatband.

Lamar rode to his left. He towed behind him a third horse with bulging saddlebags she presumed to be filled with food and refreshments. He carried a bow in his hand with a quiver of arrows fletched with white feathers strung across his back. His face appeared gloomy as he approached, but lightened when he noticed Amma. She found him to be a hard man to read. He wore his hair tied back with a cord of leather, just as it was the first time she saw him with Fredrick, on the day she arrived in Raddlif.

"Greetings to one and all," hailed Fredrick as he and Lamar joined the group, "A fine morning for a ride."

"Hello lad," said Olan. "The overnight rain has made the air fresh. Let us hope it isn't too muddy for the horses. That is a mighty beast you ride. I have never seen a horse like that before, what sort is it?"

"We call them Striders. Deep in the forest, there are wild horses called the catazon. They are a smaller breed with swift and sure legs. We captured some, and bred them to our war-horses brought from the old world. It makes for a powerful and graceful mount. This is Lady," he stated, patting her on the neck as he finished.

"A magnificent animal to-be-sure. Perhaps before I leave we shall hunt these catazon and capture one. I would like to stud one for my stables. In the meantime, where did you intend to ride?"

"We will keep to the trails around the castle. Lamar and I know them all. We should do well." Fredrick turned his attention to Veronica as he continued, "There are several meadows and small tributaries we can visit I'm sure you will find to be lovely, Lady Veronica."

Olan responded with his deep belly laugh rolling back in his saddle, "Stow that 'Lady' business, and call her Veronica. No need to stand on tradition here. She is to be your wife for grief's sake."

"Indeed, Count Olan. Shall we be off?" said Fredrick. "I look forward to showing you the beauties of the forest. Don't let my Father's words about its being angry trouble you. It will behave itself, if you are with the right guide."

The gates at the entry of the palisade opened. Fredrick led the way as the modest sized group exited the towne riding the main road. Soon, Veronica followed the others down a narrow forest trail lined by majestic trees.

As she moved, she could hear many critters, both large and small, skittering around nearby. Hundreds of ugly rabbits with long black-tipped ears, no tails and huge gold eyes zipped across the path both in front of them, and behind. She heard another strange sound and turn to see what made it, only to find nothing there. Squirrels of both gray and brown dashed out to the ends of limbs before rushing back to their dens in the trees upon seeing the group. Enormous stags grazing near the trail looked up from the grass before prancing away, disappearing into the woods. Except for one. One of them simply held up his head defiantly. He watched the party as they passed as if they were trespassers on a farmer's field. Animals both familiar and unfamiliar surrounded her. Birds flew by so close she felt she could catch them while others soared high overhead, surveying the riders and inspecting them with curiosity.

There swarmed as many varieties of bugs as there were animals. She swatted at them as they landed on her arms, shooing away those buzzing around her face. She was unsure if she was enjoying the trip or not, but she could not deny the forest was a busy place. Much busier than the frozen landscape she grew up in where the rabbits had cottontails, and the elk fled from them by nature.

After a distance, the trail widened, and Veronica noticed that Fredrick had slowed his horse to a pace that would allow her to catch up to him. Soon the two were riding side by side. She remained quiet, and they walked together and neither she nor Fredrick knew what to say to the other. The balance of the group, rode behind. The Captain's voice was proud as he conducted Amma and Count Olan through the journey.

Finally, Fredrick asked, "what do you think so far?"

"I'm amazed at how busy the forest is. There are animals everywhere," answered Veronica

"Did you see the stag?"

"Yes. There were several of them."

"Did you see the one that did not run?"

"Yes."

"He is a Lord Stag. His name is Iagonn. Raddlifs will not hunt him," explained Fredrick as they both continued down the trail. "If a beast is strong enough to live as long as he has, we will grant it its freedom. Iagonn has earned his. I have seen him many times. It is almost as if he and I are old friends now. I once remember hunting him as a boy, before he earned his pardon. I took a shot at him and missed. It was as if he sensed when I would loose my arrow, turning and running right at the proper moment to avoid my shaft. I tracked him for hours, but I sometimes wonder who was tracking who."

Veronica listened to the story, fascinated by Fredrick's words. She was impressed that he could know a single stag among the many she had seen.

"How can you single him out among the others?" she asked.

"Well for one thing how big he is. He is the largest of them, with the tallest antlers. We all know him now. He will often come around to the hunting parties to see who is in the woods."

"And the ogon, what of them? Do they grant him freedom as well?"

"The Red-Hands honor our ways and will not hunt Iagonn, but most of the other curs know no laws at all. Savage they are. Most just deserve the blade or Raddlif justice," answered Fredrick proudly pointing as he spoke, "like those three there beyond the thicket."

Veronica looked in the direction he was pointing. She squinted against the bright morning light and at first saw nothing. Slowly, her eyes focused on a sight that chilled her spine, and sent her heart to racing. Three figures hung from ropes by their necks. They were large men-like creatures. Their hands were tied behind their backs, and she could tell by the distorted, grotesque lines of the bodies they had been dangling there for a long time. Animals had chewed away the hanging limbs below the knees. Around them hovered a black cloud of insects, attracted by the stink of the rotting flesh.

She felt lucky to be far enough away that she could not smell the death on them. Her head swam, and she felt sick to her stomach, putting the back of her hand to her mouth while looking away from the macabre display. Approaching from behind, she heard hooves walking slowly up the path.

"Are you alright, Little Girl?" she heard her Father's voice say.

She remained quiet, took a deep breath and breathed out deeply, trying to be strong in front of a group of people she respected. She resisted mightily the nauseous feeling growing in her guts.

"Amma lass, fetch a waterskin," said Olan, peering out into the thicket in the direction that she was looking.

"Ogon scum hanging there, eh?" he said. "Hanged by Red-Hands, lad?"

"No. Captain Rostov and I captured them on Raddlif land and passed sentence on them," responded Fredrick, with Rostov nodding in agreement.

"I see," said Olan.

Veronica could hear reservation in his voice. She seldom heard him sound anything but confident and in control.

"And you left them there to rot?" asked Olan.

"Aye. We did," answered Fredrick. "These ogon must recognize that the Baron Manfred is the sheriff of this forest. The fiends understand little else than blood."

Olan returned his attention to Veronica as Amma handed over the waterskin. She drank deeply and collected herself. She held up her head, regaining her regal posture seated on the horse.

"Return the skin to the supplies," she said. "I'm quite alright now."

Fredrick regarded her and Veronica refused to look back at him. She was still not altogether well, but better after drinking some water. She did not want him to see her looking so weak. At last, she asked, "what was their crime, these fiends hanging in the trees?"

"They were ogon on Raddlif land."

"Were they poaching?"

"Probably."

Veronica, unsure how to respond to Fredrick's one-word answer, looked down the trail into the forest. It was still beautiful, but now, somehow, the colors seemed muted and dismal, where before they seemed so vibrant

Rostov guided his horse a few steps forward and spoke, "Lady Veronica, if I may. These ogon are savage and brutal. Raddlif women come into the woods to gather berries and other herbs. We must deal harshly with invaders. They must stay on their side of the gorge, clear of Raddlif lands. This is the pact."

"Aye, Captain," said Olan. "We have our problems in Icemarch, but only with local thugs and thieves. There are no indigenous beasts such as these running amok. Veronica will need to learn about these things."

He turned back to her, placing his hand on her shoulder.

"Will you be all right to continue?"

"Yes," said Veronica proudly. She felt as though her insides were twisting themselves into knots and she tried hard to hide it from the others. "I'm fine."

"We are nearing the meadow where I would like us to have lunch," said Fredrick. "There is soft grass that never gets too tall, stumps to sit on, and a small brook with freshwater. It's just up the way."

Reeling from the memory of the three gruesome figures hanging from a tree, Veronica was no longer hungry in the least. Her mind was a swirl of confusion, racing with questions.

How could such a charming man watch while they hanged?

How could he have done that?

What is he capable of?

Lurking beneath her fears, however, she respected his strength. If the ogon were dangerous to his people, he had a responsibility to protect them, just as her father and her brother did in Trodenheim. She understood the duty, but as a Lady of the house, she had little contact with the unpleasant dispensation of justice.

The group soon came to a dense stand of trees beside the trail. Fredrick stopped his horse and looked at her. Still feeling distraught, she smiled thinly back at him. She could not see past the thicket. She was afraid there would be further horrors waiting for her beyond the green veil of the foliage.

"We walk from here. There's a small path among the trees leading to a meadow in the center. The path is narrow and the horses will fit, but not if we ride them," explained Fredrick. He swung his leg over and jumped from his horse then walked to Veronica and helped her down as the others dismounted.

Lamar and the guards tended to the horses as Fredrick led his guests down the path between the trees. Sunlight rarely broke through the dense foliage, making the ground damp and muddy. Veronica held Fredrick's hand. He helped her to balance on the soft muck as they walked the narrow lane. She noticed the pungent smell of soaked trees and decomposing leaves.

Ahead, over Fredrick's shoulder, Veronica could see a light marking the end of the pathway. It shined like a bright beacon, golden and warm, where the darkness ended and the light began anew. As the two stepped out into the meadow, she felt her blood running swiftly from the magnificence flooding her senses. The grass that covered the ground looked as emeralds spun into thin strands, dancing in a gentle breeze. The clearing was oblong in shape and sprawling in size. The splendor of it was so intense it quickly quelled her reeling mind from the horrible visage she beheld earlier. It was as if an unknown force of great power had come and removed the trees twig root and berry from this area and left behind this shard of paradise. She could hear the babbling of water running in a small creek nearby. Here and there, a few fallen trees served as makeshift benches, decorated with floating, graceful butterflies of many colors flying throughout the hollow.

"What a beautiful meadow!" Veronica exclaimed.

"I hoped you'd like it. I have spent a lot of time here with the Captain learning weapons and lore. Father sometimes came along, told us stories, and sang songs of the old world. He said this place reminded his father of Annan. Before the rocks fell and drove us west."

Walking in a circle, and turning as if dancing, Veronica said, "Father has told me stories, but he was born on the journey across the sea. He has no memories of the old world, only legends handed down from our elders. I have never had a place like this to enjoy, or to practice. Father would teach me sword techniques occasionally. I have a rapier, but he made me leave it at home. He said I wouldn't need it."

"Indeed!" exclaimed Fredrick in a surprised tone. "A dangerous lady. All men must fear a woman trained in combat. He never knows when she may try to use her lessons. If you promise not to scratch me with it, I'll have a new one forged for you."

Veronica giggled at his offer.

The others in the party emerged from the small

path and fanned out along the entryway to the field. She heard her Father and Amma gasp in awe as they too entered the area, drinking in the beauty of the glen.

Veronica walked toward the sound of the water, and after several yards found herself at the edge of a stream. She noted that it cut the meadow in half, twisting its way through the glen. She knelt and looked at the swiftly running water. Fredrick knelt next to her, placing his hand on the small of her back. The water was icy. She lifted some to her lips. It was crisp and refreshing.

The two of them walked to the remains of a tree that looked as if it had fallen across the stream centuries in the past. Fredrick jumped onto it and reached out to help her up. Both sat together on the center of the ancient log, dangling their feet, and watching leaves floating in the creek while listening to the sound of the babbling water.

At the edge of the clearing, Olan interacted with the rest of the group. He was keeping his distance and she knew it, but she was never fully out of his sight. The party looked as if they were in a casual discussion. Occasionally, the party laughed together, before resuming the conversation.

"Are you enjoying the meadow?" asked Fredrick after the long stillness between them.

"Yes, it's gorgeous."

"That it is. You can spend as much time as you want here once you are my wife."

Veronica again fell into silence.

Fredrick then jumped to his feet. "Are you

hungry yet? Wait here."

She viewed him as he moved at a jog to the group. The horse with bags stuffed with supplies wandered around the meadow, grazing near the others in the party. Olan approached Fredrick. They stood apart and talked. She wished she could hear the words they shared, but the sound of the running water and the shrill screech of calling birds drowned out their voices. They suddenly broke out into laughter together. Olan slapped him hard on the shoulder affectionately and he turned to the packhorse. Lamar tried to aid him, but Fredrick dismissed him with a smile. He returned to Amma, who was sitting with the Captain and his men. Lamar and Amma had been enjoying each other's company since entering the field. It pleased her to see them getting on as they were.

Can I be happy here? Veronica wondered silently.

Part of her was afraid of Fredrick, having seen what he was capable of with the ogon hanging dead near the road. Nevertheless, deep in her heart, she learned that was the way of it here in the Splinterwood. Despite its enchanting appearance, this was an unforgiving land where the only choice it offered was kill, or be killed.

Fredrick returned bearing a linen cloth bulging with food along with a skin, fat and heavy with drink. He placed the bundle in the grass and helped her off the log lifting her at the waist and spinning her around on the way to the grassy ground. As he unwrapped it, Veronica saw two golden apples, some grapes, and two lengths of jerked venison. The beauty of the glen had distracted her from her earlier fears, and the sight of the food stirred her appetite.

"Let's eat," he said, handing her a cut of the jerky.

Again, an awkward silence plagued the two of them as they enjoyed their snack. The venison was moist and bursting with flavor. After a few bites of meat, Fredrick picked up the skin and took a long drink. Smiling and seemingly refreshed he handed it to Veronica and she drank to quench her growing thirst. As the skin's contents filled her mouth, she realized it did not contain water. The taste of a sweet wine rushed her senses. Shocked at the unexpected tang, she swallowed quickly with a loud gulp and gasped.

Fredrick chortled at her reaction then said, "There is plenty of water in the stream. I didn't think we needed more."

"You surprise me," announced Veronica.

"I hope so. I wouldn't want you to find me to be boring."

"Oh no, you're not boring," Veronica said as she looked at the wineskin, silently asking for another sip and too shy to speak the words.

Fredrick handed it to her smiling, and she sipped from it gently. Among the bundle was a small wooden cup. He stood, filled it with water from the stream, and then brought it back.   "I wouldn't want Count Olan to accuse me of trying to get you drunk. This water is some of the purest in the forest. It runs into the Voda, but from where I am not sure. I have ridden this creek for many miles and have yet to find from where it springs."

She moved on to the grapes in the bundle and tasted their sweetness. There were seeds in them, and she took them from her mouth turning away gracefully so Fredrick would not see her spitting them into her hand.

"What has impressed you about our forest so far? Has anything caught your eye? Something that is your favorite?"

Veronica thought on the question before answering, "When we were travelling, I was in the carriage. As we left the castle today to follow you, I recognized how much I had missed by keeping the drapes closed. I noticed one place though. A field of purple flowers. Those blossoms were everywhere. It was so pretty."

"Did this valley lie to the south of the Raddlif road leading to the Mournway?" asked Fredrick.

"I think so. I saw it shortly before we arrived."

"Would some of those flowers decorating your room tonight make you happy?" Fredrick continued, taking her hand.

Veronica smiled in answer to his question. She was not sure exactly what he meant.

"The place you speak of isn't too far from here if you know the trails as I do. Wait here! I shall return."

Fredrick took the linen cloth that once held their food and stuffed it into his tunic. He leaped up, hurried over to Lamar, and put his hand on his shoulder. Together, they approached Olan. They exchanged words, and he waved to them, as if the two were leaving, and that they did. They disappeared into the entryway leading to the meadow and disappeared, taking their horses with them.

***

Riding swiftly, Fredrick guided his horse through the treacherous forest-maze of fallen trees and hidden obstacles. Lamar's voice called out, "Fredrick! Slow down!"

The Young Baron stopped. Looking behind him, he watched Lamar following through the trees. Fredrick grinned as he reflected about his friend. The Atmore family had served the Raddlifs for many years. Lamar's grandfather, Willem, had been an advisor to Fredon Raddlif, Manfred's grandfather in the old world before the catastrophe that sent everyone who could, fleeing Annan across the Great Sea, and the Maelstrom waiting there. Willem and his wife died during the crossing, leaving only their child Milton. The Raddlifs took the boy and cared for him. He grew to maturity and fathered Lamar, dying shortly afterward. Again, the Raddlif family took an Atmore child. This time Manfred took him, and raised the child to be Steward to the baby Fredrick, born the year before Lamar.

In the old world, a steward to a royal figure was more than someone who brought a sword or brushed out a horse. They functioned as bodyguards and confidants eventually serving a family in their cabinet or council. For the Raddlifs, the appointment was apothecary. Through the set of circumstances that had brought them together, these two men were inseparable. Fredrick's birth was difficult for Kaery. Afterward, she was left barren, and Lamar was the only sibling that Fredrick would ever have.

"Can't slow down!" he shouted back. "Mustn't keep our guests waiting!" As he finished, he spurred the horse to a canter. The duo left the party and followed the network of animal trails that snaked through the woods like an enormous labyrinth. Away in the distance, he could see the castle at the top of the hill, nestled among the trees and shrouded by a light mist. Before long, after crossing the Raddlif road and riding south, they found themselves next to narrow ravine spread out below them.

Since their introduction at the feast, Fredrick's heart had filled with concern and doubt. The prospect of his betrothed refusing to accept their marriage had never occurred to him. It made him feel angry and rejected, but, somehow, he found himself sympathetic to her feelings. He loved his home in the forest and understood how leaving hers to live in a faraway land with strangers would frighten Veronica. While he laid in this bed-chamber trying to rest after the feast, thinking about her, he resolved to do what he could to ease her mind before the wedding.

"Forest Orchids? We rode all this way so you can pick flowers?" asked Lamar.

"That we did," responded Fredrick. He dismounted and slid down to the bottom of a shallow gulley filled with knee-high, bushy plants bursting with purple flowers. He walked around the web of narrow rabbit-trails that separated the buds, choosing the ones with most vibrant colors.

"Why?"

"Veronica mentioned that she saw them on her ride. We must make her feel welcome, or had you not noticed she isn't enthusiastic about our wedding so far?"

"I have, but I'm not sure a linen full of flowers is the answer," responded Lamar inspecting the blossoms.

"Then what do you suggest?" asked Fredrick. "Shall I drag her to the dais in the bailey kicking and screaming? By her hair maybe? Truth is, I feel sorry for her leaving her home, family and friends. I have told her that I mean to earn her respect and I intend to do so."

"You never mentioned what you two talked about on your walk last night."

"Veronica is not of the same mind I am. Let's leave it at that. At one point she was talking about running away."

"Running away? To where? That would be a foolish thing to do," said Lamar, taking a knife from its sheath.

Fredrick continued carefully cutting the flowers, trying to keep the stems the same length. "She is naïve but not stupid, she will learn in time. However, let us speak of other things. Are you enjoying the company of that pretty little handmaiden of hers?"

"Yes," answered Lamar

"Yes? Is that all you're going to say?"

"These orchids, they are the poisonous ones you know?"

Fredrick sensed the deliberate attempt to change the subject and played along. "She will not be making tea with them. My hope is that they will sit in a vase in her room to brighten the young woman's disposition for the day. Let's not forget, I only have two days to win her over."

They laughed as they finished their gathering, wrapping the stalks of the many flowers in Fredrick's linen cloth. Using the string from Lamar's hair, they tightly tied the bundle together to hold it, soaking them in a nearby puddle to keep them wet.

They returned the way they came. As they neared the meadow, Fredrick had a strange and uneasy feeling. He could not place it, but the forest seemed cold and quiet. It was as if he could hear a sound calling to him sibilantly from the woods. As if it whispered a warning to him. The two had started back to rejoin the group at a casual pace, but now, with the foreboding growing in his heart, he rode with rising haste. It was not long before he moved swiftly, with Lamar following as close as he could. Soon, they arrived where they left Veronica and the others, but there was an eerie silence in the forest.

"Something's wrong," he said as he stopped, leaping from his horse. The menacing feeling in his heart was slowly morphing into fear.

Fredrick followed the muddy path with Lamar following. As they both exited the dim tunnel of trees and into the bright light of the clearing, His fear intensified at the sight filling his eyes. He stood at the edge of the glade refusing to turn his gaze away from the terrible scene before him. Out of an instinctive need for his friend, he reached out, clutching Lamar tightly by the shoulder in speechless disbelief.

Chapter 4

The Baron put his hand on my shoulder and said "you shall lead my men. Will you also be my friend?" I wanted to cry his words so moved me, but his strength held me up, and my eyes stayed dry.

–Journal of Victor Rostov

Veronica opened her eyes to find herself strewn across the hardened spine of a hideous beast moving swiftly through the forest with her hands tied, bouncing along a narrow trail. The ache in her ribs was agonizing. Her chin where she had been struck throbbed in pain as her consciousness slowly returned and the horrible memories of what had just happened replayed themselves in her mind.

Earlier, as she cooled her feet in the refreshing water, enjoying the peacefulness of the meadow, she saw Rostov stand. His face, smiling and serene, had suddenly taken on one of concern and apprehension. Something alarmed him but she did not know what it was. He wandered in a circle, looking to the woods and loosening his sword in its sheath. She could not hear him over the din of the forest, but he spoke and his men snapped from a casual bearing, to drawing blades.

An uneasy feeling entered her heart. She stood, her fear growing with each of Rostov's steps as he peered deep into the trees.

Olan took Amma by the arm, pulling her towards his horse where his weapon hung at its saddle. His eyes turned toward Veronica just as a loud clamor rang from outside the edges of the tree-lined meadow.

Rostov bared his sword, and the sun glinted off the sharpened steel. In his other hand, he bore a dagger cocked for battle.

The ogon attacked, cursing and voicing a bloodcurdling scream as they came. Two of them charged Rostov himself! The first took a sword to its head with an overhand slash. The Captain then executed a clever feint, pulling the second attacker off balance. He plunged his dagger through his back, and into his heart, burying it to the hilt.

Olan unleashed his hammer. Experienced in war, he killed more attackers while Veronica reeled in disbelief at the unfolding carnage she was witnessing. She had never seen anyone die in combat or otherwise, and the sight paralyzed her with fear and shock. She recalled her father approaching, stopping to defend himself, killing the brigands that faced him cursing all the while, and then moving toward her again.

Against the backdrop of the chaos, she remembered seeing Amma cowering in terror in the tall grass, surrounded by a group of snarling enemies and screaming. One fiend had taken her roughly by the hair and neck.

Hearing her screams, Rostov ran to Amma. He charged her aggressors, trying to defend her with his blood-soaked sword before disappearing.

One of the Raddlif soldiers laid dead, killed by a trio of villains who savagely hewed at his body with their blades. Blood splashed from the impacts of the weapons as if the ogon were children, playing in the waters of a pond. She had no memory of the fate that befell the other two guards, but expected them dead as well.

Her final sight, before the world went black, was one of the cruel brigands coming up from behind Olan. She could not see his covered face, but he was a hulking figure. The ogon rode upon a hideous monster with a tusked, boar-like face, bearing the body of a huge dog, but with cloven hooves instead of paws.

Seeing the weapon in the hands of the rider, she remembered calling out to him with an outstretched hand. Horror filled her heart as the rider's spear pierced Olan's leg. He cursed from the sudden burst of searing pain and tried to bring his hammer to bear, but he could not move, skewered as he was on the point of the cruel spike.

Then, a strong grip spun her gaze away. For an instant, all she saw was a snarling, ugly face and a clenched fist that snapped forward, striking her on the chin and plummeting her into blackness.

Now, the rider drove his beast hard between the trees. She could hardly bring her mind to believe what was happening, finding it difficult even to breathe. It was easier to pretend that she would soon wake up from a terrible nightmare.

She struggled to lift her head, trying to see where she was going, but the pain and fear was too intense to move, and all she could do was watch the ground passing by.

Her thoughts wandered to Fredrick. He had not been gone long before these brigands arrived and attacked.

What will he do when he finds out what happened? Will he come for me, or return to the castle? How can he find me, hidden in this forest?

All the times she told him she did not want to marry him, and all the times she avoided even looking at his face returned to haunt her.

What reason have I given him to come for me? she thought, filling her heart with dread.

Veronica's captors entered a small clearing and stopped at the edge of a giant gorge that cut through the Splinterwood as if the blade of a giant axe had rent the forest itself. A bridge of ancient white stones extended across the gap. Arched spires reached to the sky, separated by a great distance from which the spans hung suspended from rusted chains. Cracked and aging, a thick blanket of ivy grew upward from the bottom of the chasm, slowly consuming it.

The beast on which they rode began to snort and shift wildly beneath them. The rider struck it and it roared out at him in anger. As he dismounted it, the animal struggled with him, pulling on its reins, swinging its ugly head and snarling. The ogon slapped it again, this time on the nose, calming him as it growled in protest.

Two callused hands clutched her by the shoulders, yanking her from the back of the creature and standing her up in front of him. She had glimpsed this ruffian during the battle in the meadow, only now however, did she realize how frightening he was. He stood before her in silence, breathing deeply from the arduous ride. She smelled the odor from his breath as it wafted on a chill breeze. It was musky and strong. His flesh had a strange greenish hue. The villain's hair was dark brown and balding, exposing a tall pate. He wore a rusted chain mail shirt that barely fit his broad chest with ragged trousers. His feet were bare and at his waist were two short blades tucked into a wide leather belt.

Face-to-face with her captor, Veronica was petrified and nearly unable to breathe. Then she heard a familiar voice screaming. It was Amma, struggling with another of the vicious ruffians. Her aggressor was not so strange or savage looking as the one standing before her. His complexion was the same sickly gray-greenish tint, with soft blonde hair. His frame was smaller than his companions, but he was just as strong. Amma, kicking and shrieking, struggled to free herself and escape. The blonde ogon frowned in annoyance and struck her with the back of his hand. She reeled under the force of the blow and quieted, falling into the arms of her tormentor.

Finally, a third Ogon appeared. Veronica beheld the most frightening sight she had ever seen in her life. His skin was as pale green as the man-thing that held her subdued, but his eyes burned with a terrible fire. His bearing clearly marked him as the leader of these brigands. A crop of shoulder length thick black hair covered the brute's head and face. His shoulders were broad, and covered by a patchwork leather poncho, exposing the taut and defined muscles in his arms.

He paced back and forth in a three-step rhythm. She looked into his eyes. They were gold, and blood-shot. The darker green skin tone of his eye sockets made them brighter and more menacing still. His jaw was square with a bold chin. A thick beard covered the lower portion of his face. In his hand, he held a single red apple. One he had taken during the ambush. He turned it in his clawed hands, cleaning it with a wiping motion of his thumb.

Veronica watched him as he broke his pacing rhythm and approached while still inspecting the fruit. Standing near, he made a disgusting slurping sound as he took a bite from the crisp apple.

At last, after the torturing silence he asked, "Tell me who you are pretty-pretty, and why are you in my forest?" His accent was thick and foreign, made worse by speaking with his mouth full.

Petrified with fear, both women remained silent.

"No answer? Come now, don't be rude," he said turning his rage-filled gaze toward Amma, who would not look at him.

He reached up gently and placed a hooked finger under Amma's chin turning her face toward his, taking another bite of the apple. "Come now, who are you? I must say, we often see you Newcomers in our forest, but rarely do we see fair-haired women this deep in the woods. One or both of you must be someone of importance I'm guessing."

The grim figure stood in silence in front of his two captives waiting for an answer. Veronica averted her gaze from his, looking straight ahead. With great effort, she could feel herself calming, even if only slightly, and realized that she must regain her composure and not appear so afraid.

"Well my pretties, allow me to introduce myself, if you will not," said the leader. "My name is Gnash Mak'Nabb of the Shattered-Tooth, and these are two of my trusted guards, Borhn and the smaller half-breed is Sajj."

This creature surprised Veronica despite her fear. He spoke with a thick accent, that notwithstanding, he spoke well for someone from the tribal society she had pictured in her mind. He struck her as intelligent.

Gnash took the last bite of his apple chomping on it obnoxiously and licked the apple's core with his green tongue.

"Nothing then?" he said. "I see." He turned this back to her and took a few steps forward.

Amma struggled against Sajj in a sudden burst of strength. Fear had overcome her reason, and had morphed into despair. "Please sir," she pleaded at last, "I beg you to free us. We have done nothing to you!"

Gnash turned to her with a blistering expression.

"Haven't you!" he exclaimed.

Veronica could see terrible anger break over Gnash like a wave. He frowned, and his clawed hands clinched to fists as he strode forward with great authority and grabbed Amma by the hair, pulling her away from Sajj. She shrieked in pain as the enraged ogon turned her to face Veronica, holding their faces close.

"Haven't you?" he shouted, still holding Amma by the hair and neck. "My friends hang from trees, to be eaten by vermin, and you say you have done nothing to me? I don't know who you are, but there are many new invaders from the north in my forest! You have had to come here for a reason!"

Gnash's anger raged with terrifying ferocity.

Behind her, Veronica could hear his companions shout furiously, excited by Gnash's emotion. Sajj pumped his fist in the air, chanting. His hideous face distorted into an angry frown as he cheered on his leader. She could not understand Sajj's words, but the intent was clear by the wrath in his raspy voice that all three were enraged. Sajj took a knife from its sheath, flipped it deftly in his hand, and flung it at the ground toward Gnash's feet. The point of the blade sank into the forest floor where it stood with the handle easily reached.

They want him to kill us!

Gnash bent at the knees and took the dark steel blade from the ground, lifting it to Amma's throat. Her eyes went wide with fear. She saw the blade for only an instant before it was below her line of sight. The blade was sharp and cruel, immediately biting the flesh it touched. Veronica saw a trickle of blood run from where he placed the tip of the blade against her throat.

"Lady Veronica Moresten!" bawled Amma, powerless with fear, "Veronica Moresten of Trodenheim! Please sir, please let us go!"

"Stop! Stop, please!" begged Veronica at last, growing frantic at the sight of the blood at Amma's throat. She pulled against Borhn who held her fast, pulling her back in a swift, violent jerk.

"Veronica of Trodenheim. And a 'Lady' at that," said Gnash mockingly, his accent even thicker now in his rage, "whatever that means to you invaders. You are about the same age as the manling Fredrick. Were you to be his bride? Why else would so many come so far?"

"Yes!" confessed Veronica, "Yes I'm to be his wife, please release us!"

Gnash let the confession hang in the air before speaking.

"I will not! Your future husband, along with his father, have something I want back. The Raddlifs hold my brother, and refuse to release him. He languishes in their dungeons even this moment. Now, I mean to return the favor."

"Kill both these kujas, Boss," shouted Sajj enthusiastically.

There was an agonizing pause as Gnash's eyes squinted at Sajj, then flicked back to Veronica.

A furious expression crossed Gnash's face. It sent a shiver up Veronica's spine that rose to horrible terror as the brigand drew the edge of the blade across Amma's throat. A crimson line appeared behind the knife as it cut cleanly through her flesh. Amma screamed, but her voice went silent with a ghastly gurgling sound.

Petrified with fear, Veronica tried to close her

eyes. She opened her mouth to scream, but there was only silence.

As her servant and friend's life ebbed, a strange awakening came over her swathed in a blanket of terror. Since she was a child, she listened to Olan speak of honor, bravery, family and duty. That this beast could perform such an evil act in the name of his duty and his family, and that she resisted something as simple as a marriage, shamed her. She felt she may never see the opportunity to make amends to neither Fredrick, nor to her father. The thought tormented her heart.

She drew up her head, looking into the eyes of Gnash. She stood up straight, her shoulders back, refusing even to blink as he cleaned the blade with a strip of red cloth. For that fleeting instant, the two of them held each other's gaze. It was only a moment, but in Veronica's heart, it seemed like a lifetime.

As she gazed into Gnash's fiery countenance, she sensed something else. She could not place it right away, but it was there. His expression softened, if only for an instant. Something unexplained and unspoken passed between them.

What was that in his eyes just now, she wondered? *Was it sympathy? Was it regret? Was it respect?*

She thought he might release her in that passing moment of empathy. But alas, when he finally spoke she could not understand the words.

At Gnash's command, Borhn scooped her up, and sat her in front of him on his mount. With a cord, he tied her hands, then placed a foul-smelling sackcloth hood over her head plunging Veronica into a world of darkness. The rancid stench of the sack assailed her nose. Its course weave allowed not even a pinhole of light, rendering all but her ears useless.

Holding her around the waist with his clawed hand, the villain kicked his heels and the animal cried out with a loud growl. It reared up on its hind legs, and hastened quickly. The beast did not turn, and Veronica sensed they crossed the bridge, flying deeper into the forest.

***

Fredrick's heart hammered with anger, fear and dread as he surveyed the meadow where he left Veronica and the others. Scattered around the clearing laid the broken and bloodied bodies of the guards nestled among the remains of several dead ogon bodies. Frantically he moved about the field, calling out the names of the women and getting no response in return.

They separated looking for their friends and identify the enemies. They had to determine what had occurred in their absence.

Laying in the emerald grass, Fredrick found his friend, teacher and captain, brought low by two crudely fletched arrows in his back. He knelt on one knee next to him, hoping against hope that he was only wounded and unconscious. Tears welled up in his eyes when Rostov did not stir. Though in his heart he wanted to drop to his knees and weep at his loss, a time for mourning would have to come later. A single tear escaped, running down his cheek before he forced back the impending flood. Now he must find Veronica, or any survivors. His training, from this very man lying dead before him, had taken over his thinking. He would have to return to this place, and bury Rostov after justice was carried out and he knew the whereabouts of his fiancée.

He leaned to Rostov's ear and whispered into it. "I will return, my Captain. I will bury you with the head and hands of your murderer beneath your feet. The rest of the villain will be left to feed the vermin of *our* forest. I promise you that, my friend."

The two continued to search for survivors. Lamar knelt next to the body of a soldier laying in the grass. Looking across the meadow, their eyes met, and Fredrick watched with dismay as Lamar shook his head. It was obvious from his grim expression the guards were dead.

Then, faintly he heard a moaning noise from nearby. The sound was short, and at first, he did not know from where it came, but right away he recognized the voice.

"Count? Count Olan, where are you?" he shouted.

"Here, lad," he wheezed, raising his blood-covered hand.

He could hear the strain in the usually confident and rowdy speech.

A wave of relief washed over him as he ran to Olan. Next to him were the bodies of three more dead ogon. The smell of death was heavy though they were not dead long. The odors emanated from the split skulls of the victims of Olan's well-wielded hammer.

"Count, what happened?" asked Fredrick as he waved to Lamar, while examining Olan's wounds.

"These Ogon bastards attacked us after you left, my boy. They took Veronica and her servant, Amma." Olan gasped with labored breath.

Lamar approached, bringing with him a sheet once intended for the women to sit on in the grass to keep their gowns clean. He tore from it a long strip, wrapping it around the wound on Olan's leg. Worry entered Fredrick's mind as he looked at Olan's face. It had gone pale from blood loss and his usual vibrant features replaced with a sallow color. He could tell from the Count's weary eyes that he was enduring terrible pain.

"Get your horse and ride for the castle. Bring Gavyn back here!" demanded Fredrick.

Lamar stood to obey, but Olan reached out and stopped him by pulling on his arm.

"No!" commanded Olan, asserting his authority through his pain soaked face. "No, Fredrick. You must go after Veronica. There were only three of them left when they took the women! Who knows what those bastards mean to do with my daughter. I cannot pursue them. You must do it while the trail is fresh–"

He cut off his speech as he winced in agony.

"Count, we can't just leave you here. You could die. Your wounds…"

Olan grabbed him by the tunic with a quick

burst of strength, pulling him near and their holding faces inches apart.

"Lad, must I say it again? My life is not important. You must hunt the ogon sons-a-bitches that did this and get Veronica back. You must go through with the wedding. Our houses must continue. Go! Do not tarry! Each word puts your prey further into the forest. Go now. Ride!"

Fredrick felt Olan's sincerity, and his authority, break over him like a wave. His grip was solid. His breathing labored. He respected Olan greatly. He already felt an obligation to his own father to be as strong as the Barons before him. Now, his charge doubled, and he had two fathers to endeavor to make proud.

"Do you understand?" asked Olan, tugging on his tunic sharply as if to snap him out of a confused trance.

An ominous feeling came to him as he reluctantly accepted the words of the Count. He had already lost much blood and was sure if he left Olan, he would die. His future father-in-law would die, alone and in agony, as had Rostov, in one of his favorite places in all the Splinterwood. A place of peace and tranquility, forever made bloody at the hands of his enemies.

Finally, he looked down at the ground. He could no longer meet Olan's sorrowful eyes. "I understand," he answered.

"Good lad, now go! I will be fine," said Olan.

Fredrick stood up and took a deep breath to

calm his fear.

"I will find the ogon who did this, Count Olan," he said as confidently as he could against his hammering heart. "They will pay for what they have done."

***

Travelling deeper into the forest, Lady Veronica Moresten found herself in awe at the strength and stamina of her captors. With the dreaded sack over her head, the world was still one of pitch-blackness. After riding for a long while, they stopped. The riders spoke briefly, though she could not understand them, and she heard feet hitting the ground with a crunch of dried leaves and sticks.

She felt the same coarse hands as before take hold of her, this time by the hair and by the waist of her torn gown. The unseen hooligan threw her to the ground roughly. She could not see it coming, and with her hands bound she could not break her fall. Veronica landed hard on the forest floor, and there she laid in a breathless heap.

"Careful! Stupid lout!" shouted one of them in a scolding tone. She recognized Gnash's voice.

"Kill her too!" shouted another of the thugs, suddenly switching to the common tongue so she could understand him. "Why are you keeping her alive? Those Newcomer kopikes will never release Ghronn. Kill her now, and be done with it."

"Neither of you will harm her, do you understand that?" said Gnash. His tenor surprisingly calm. "Go fetch us some meat. I have had enough nuts

116

and leaves."

She laid prone on the cold forest floor for a long while before a pair of callused hands helped her to her feet. This time, the coarse hands guided her a short distance to a smooth stone where he seated her. He treated her gentler than before. The ride had torn Veronica's garment and she could feel that her gown and bodice had loosened, falling from her shoulders, and exposing much of her breasts. The stone was cold, and Veronica sat quietly, unable to fix her clothes. She felt undignified, embarrassed and helpless as she heard the unseen rogue walking away. Then, the footfalls stopped, paused, and returned. Her mind raced with unease.

What now? What is he up to?

Having ordered the others away, she knew the remaining ogon must be Gnash. She could sense his face near to hers. There was a torturous pause as she pondered what he would do. Then, gently, he pulled the shoulders back up to cover her, tightening her garments as best he could. Even through her burning animosity, she felt surprised and thankful at Gnash fixing her clothing.

Why would he do that? Why would he care if I were uncovered and embarrassed?

His hands were gentle, but he tied the bodice too tight for comfort. As he finished she remained silent, refusing to speak to this rogue and murderer.

Gnash walked away again, the way he had before. As she sat quietly, drowning in the stink and darkness of the sack over her head, she could hear wood cracking. As he went about his chores, he hummed a tune, then sang a song in the ogon's odd, guttural tongue.

He sang well and went on for some time before finally ending his song.

"Your trip taking longer than you expected, is it?" he chided, following with a cruel chortle. "It will be a long night for you, Little One. A shame you did not dress warmer. If you behave yourself, I will allow you to warm yourself by the fire."

It was a long while before the sounds of footsteps announced the presence of the returning hunters.

"Gnash!" called a shrill voice. "See wha' brave Sajj bagged for dinner."

"Just in time, you toads," he scolded. "The coals are ready. We eat good tonight. Better than the scrawny hares you two brought back last night."

As they continued talking, they switched between the common tongue, and their own language. They laughed, and at other times, they pushed and shoved, as if they would fight. They would break out into song together, finish it, and return to shouting obscenities at each other. They ignored Veronica entirely. She could hear them stumbling around while they sang, then fall as they danced around the fire. Their speech became more slurred and vulgar as they drank themselves to drunkenness.

"Sajj! You half-breed," shouted one of them. She was sure it was Borhn, who delighted in tormenting him.

"Gitch'er ass over 'ere and cut that boar. Gnash wants Mo' meat!"

As the heat of the cook-fire grew, the temperature inside the sack over Veronica's head became unbearable. Streams of perspiration ran down into her face, dropping from her nose into the coarse fabric of the hood. The meat was still sizzling over the fire, but she no longer heard them moving and carrying on around it. The villains had grown silent, and now the only sound was that of smacking lips as they ate their meal.

She had nothing to eat since her nosh in the meadow with Fredrick. Her stomach growled at the aroma of the meat. Her back ached from her hard-stone seat. She wanted to stand and stretch, but she was afraid of what her captors may do in reprisal if she did.

Having eaten their fill, one of them stood and approached Veronica. Fear mixed with the hunger in her belly as the footsteps drew closer. The unseen captor lingered there for several agonizing seconds and she wondered which of them it was. The thought of what these thugs could do to her, alone and defenseless in the woods, nearly sent her into a panic. She trembled as she waited to be struck, groped or insulted by these fiends. She forced herself to be brave, and sat quietly, bound and helpless, trying to preserve what she had left of her dignity.

The ogon snatched the hood off Veronica's head and the light of the fire flooded into her eyes, dazzling her. His face was only a blur as he hooked his finger under her face, lifting it and holding her chin with this thumb. Once her vision focused, she stared into Gnash's face.

"Hungry are you?" he asked in a calm voice, putting his face near to hers. In his eyes raged the same fire she had seen in them before. His teeth still had meat in them, and his breath stank of liquor. She said nothing, and stubbornly refused to turn away from him. She heard steel scrape against leather and he held up a cruel blade. She did her best not to show weakness, forcing back her tears and emotions. She tried to be proud and bold, but deep down she wondered silently how long she could maintain the façade. Despite the knife in Gnash's hand, she fixed her gaze on his, and waited for whatever would happen next.

Gnash smiled cruelly. "You wonder what it is I will do with this knife? Well, Little One, rest assured it is not for you. When I wet this blade again, it will be with Raddlif's blood. Do you wonder why?" he asked, looking at his two companions, then back at Veronica.

"I'm not doing this because I wish to. They hold my Brother in their dungeon unjustly and with no intentions of freeing him. They refuse to ransom him. They feel if he is a prisoner, they have me where they want me, and they are wrong. You Little One, are my last chance of getting my brother back without having to kill all of them. Which I would rather not do."

Veronica remained silent, but her mind wandered back to when she saw those three prisoners in chains while walking the castle grounds. It suddenly came to her, the scary one among them, the large one; he bore a likeness to Gnash that she now found obvious.

Could that monster be his brother? It must be, she thought.

"I will not be offering you much in comfort," Gnash announced.

He looked at her for a moment in silence. In that passing instant, his angry countenance softened, "I would rather not kill you, but that remains to be seen. I *will,* have my brother. The Raddlif kopikes will give him back, one way or another."

Finishing his statement, he brought down the keen blade, nimbly severing the bonds around her wrists, freeing them.

As he released her face from his firm grasp, she looked around, for the first time seeing her surroundings. She sat on the base of a fallen smoothed stone statue of a man she did not recognize. The fire roared in front of her in a shallow ringed pit. Skewered on a rusted iron spit, remained the uneaten portion of an animal, still sizzling over the coals. Surrounding her were remnants of what were once small lodges formed of stone. It looked to her like a camp where outriders could have a place to stay through a night to make their travels more comfortable on their lonely road.

Borhn and Sajj sat next to the fire, gnawing away on chunks of meat. They chewed their food with open mouths, watching Gnash with curious expressions.

Gnash took her roughly by the chin, picked up a leather skin and poured a foul tasting, strong alcoholic drink down her throat that made her chest burn like it contained liquid fire. The drink was thick, heady and salty. He walked back to the sizzling spit. With his blade, he took a cut from the animal, and then returned, presenting the meat to her with his filth-covered hand.

In her pride, Veronica hesitated to take the offering. She was hungry, and Gnash knew it. Her belly was howling from hunger. Her captors could hear it, and she felt weak and embarrassed.

"Go on," said Gnash sternly. "Take it, you're hungry. That little swallow of blood-whiskey will keep you warm through the night. There is no way you would have drank it if I didn't poor it down your throat, but you'll be glad I did." With that, he threw another bottle at her feet. "That one is water," he said with a wry smile.

The cord around her wrists had chafed and cut them. She rubbed them with her free hands as they ached and itched. Reluctantly, she took the meat from Gnash. It was still hot, and she juggled it in her hands, waiting for it to cool to keep from burning her mouth.

As she took her first bite, she was surprised by the richly spiced taste of pork.

Could these beasts have packed spices to eat better on their expeditions? she pondered, taking another bite and trying not to make it obvious that she enjoyed the flavor.

"You look terrible," commented Gnash as he

122

lingered, watching her eat. Both of his companions laughed at his observation. "You need the food to keep your strength up. In the morning we ride to the ancient fort beyond the ridge. We didn't arrive tonight, but will be there tomorrow." He then turned away, stumbling back to the fire to sit with his two cohorts.

While eating the cut of pork, a thought crossed her mind. *Should I run? They are all drunk. I might get a head start. Maybe I could lose them?*

As she sat planning her escape, the reality of trying began to set in. *What would I do then? Where would I go? I don't know where I am, or which way to travel.*

The drink that Gnash poured down her throat made her head swoon. She was too exhausted to give any sustained chase. After the thought passed, she simply sat as proudly as she could, hoping someone from the castle would come to her rescue.

As she sat on the hard stone, Gnash glanced over his shoulder as if to check on her, then gestured to Borhn a silent command. With not a word spoken, he stood and strolled toward her menacingly. He picked the hood up and put it back over her head, returning her into the foul-smelling darkness. Taking her hands, she felt him loop the cord around them and tie them tight.

As he finished lashing her wrists together, she heard snapping branches emanate from outside the camp and Borhn stopped. She listened to his steps as he scrambled toward the disturbance.

A groundswell of emotion came over her. A

123

blend of fear and relief as she listened intently. She heard the singing of steel as her captors armed themselves, taking positions around the camp. Veronica, depending only on her sense of hearing, could tell the ogon were waiting for what lurked beyond their sight as well. Expectation grew as she waited for the voices of someone she recognized. The delay was agonizing, but also exciting. She turned her head as if she could see, straining her remaining sense against the darkness in which she found herself trapped, trying to grasp what was unfolding in the woods. Hope welled up in her heart as her mind raced with possibilities.

Who's there? Is it Father, or maybe Fredrick? Oh, I hope it's him. He's come for me!

Then, from a direction that would place the voice well outside the camp, a gruff, and unrecognized voice called out.

In response, she heard Gnash's voice; it was loud but not a shout. The two unseen groups conversed, but she failed to understand what was being said.

With one last word from Gnash, she heard a large group of footsteps and voices emerge from the forest. As the new arrivals joined the camp, they greeted each other merrily. She heard the slapping of flesh as they patted one another in greetings, putting their weapons away. As the trio turned to a horde of these cruel rogues, her hopes of rescue slowly melted, draining from Veronica with their arrival. The thought of the hood coming off again and seeing the now

124

swelled numbers of the gang of these ugly monsters filled her with terror. She lowered herself and laid down on the ground on her side with her back to the statue. There she laid in a fetal position, trembling in fear and hopelessness.

***

As an expert woodsmen and tracker, Fredrick quickly established the general direction the ogon gang travelled. He inferred from the evidence the mob took the women west, toward the ancient bridge. Riding hard, he could see in the distance the top of the arches coming into view, looming large over the tips of the tall trees near the gorge over which the bridge spanned. Leaping over a fallen tree, he looked back to check on Lamar to find him following, right where he expected him to be. The path they followed was little more than a barely discernable rabbit-trail.

The light of the day was fading as Fredrick pulled Lady to an abrupt stop. His eyes grew wide with dread as he spotted a single lonely body lying in the clearing before the bridge of white stone. The gruesome sight shocked not only Fredrick and Lamar, but their horses as well. Both animals snorted, throwing their heads about nervously at the odor of the gelling blood staining the forest floor.

"What have they done?" Lamar exclaimed.

Side by side, against the protests of their restless horses, the two rode forward and slid to a stop near to the body. Fredrick dismounted, kneeling next to the corpse turning it over gently to see Amma's sallow and lifeless face. Her eyes were still open,

125

rolled upward away from the grievous wound inflicted to her throat. Blood soaked the front of her dress. Her once attractive appearance distorted by the terror left frozen there in death. The cut was so deep that Fredrick had to catch her head, finding it clinging grotesquely only by her spine and a sliver of flesh.

His mind reeled, shocked by the gruesome sight. As Fredrick inspected Amma's body, he noticed a red shard of cloth tied to her right arm, fluttering in the chill wind blowing through, sending a shiver down his back.

"Gnash Mak'Nabb did this," Fredrick said desolately as he laid the body on its back with her arms at her sides, in a more dignified manner than the heap in which he found it. He closed her eyes with a gentle touch of his finger and untied the shard of cloth, clutching it in his fist. "That dirty murdering bastard and his band of villains did this to this poor girl."

He stood, turning away from the corpse, no longer able to gaze at the appalling sight.

"We knew ogon were responsible, but this?" he continued, looking at Lamar and gesturing with his hands out to his sides speaking in disbelief, "this seems even beyond them and their evil ways."

Turning Amma over and seeing the gruesome sight of the wound on her throat and terrified expression on her face had shaken him. The grievous gash, her lifeless eyes, and the macabre movement of Amma's head was a memory that would haunt him for the rest of his life. Nearly overcome with loathing, he fought against the nauseous sensation in his gut and

126

swirling in his mind. He leaned over, supporting himself with his hands on his knees, breathing deeply. The world was spinning around him and black spots shown in his vision. He felt as if he were about to collapse. He took a deep breath then stood upright again, trying to preserve his proud posture. He removed his hat, and wiped the sweat from his forehead with his sleeve before replacing it. With great effort, he pulled himself together, remembering his promise to Count Olan and Rostov.

"And Lady Veronica, what of her?" His mind was racing with awful images of what would happen to her in the clutches of the villains.

Fredrick looked at Lamar to find him sitting his horse in silence. He could see the terrible anguish written across his face. A wave of sympathy came to him for his friend and brother. The attraction that he and Amma shared was obvious, and his sad expression revealed his broken heart.

"What horrors do you think she is living, or has she had her throat cut as well?" Fredrick asked rhetorically.

A loud voice boomed from within the forest near them, "No young one, they did not kill the other female."

Fredrick spun on his heels squaring toward the sounds. Lamar pulled the reins of his horse turning and taking a position behind Fredrick. In one nimble move, he drew his bow, set an arrow to the string, and made ready to shoot.

"Show yourself! Who are you?" shouted

Fredrick, placing his hand to the butt of his pistol.

"You will not need your weapons," the voice responded. "And you, Lamar, Steward of Raddlif, put your needle back into its quiver. It will only be wasted if you shoot."

"If there is no need for weapons, there is no need to hide! Come out!" demanded Fredrick sternly.

"I'm not hiding; you just don't see me. Filled with worry indeed you must be to be so distracted. For any other day you would have seen me easily, and greeted me warmly."

Fredrick focused on movement in the woods. There he spotted a mighty figure approaching him from the forest. He could see the giant maple tree, bearing a great green canopy, regarding him through unevenly placed wooden eyes rolling about in their sockets. It walked on two trunk-like legs. His roots clung to the earth, rending the ground as he walked. Birds of many colors and varieties circled the tree as it moved, shaken from their nests fashioned within the tree's boughs. A woodcutter's axe protruded from his trunk-leg, left there after someone's foolish attempt to chop him down. Around the blade were several scars where the axe had struck, and now it wore the embedded rusted axe like a trophy. On his right trunk jutted a maple spout. Sap ran down his leg from the open tap, forming a gummy mess. Once the mighty tree stopped, the circling birds returned to their nests, squawking in protest.

"Lahn!" exclaimed Fredrick. Walking up to him, he looked up to the tree's strange and wandering eyes. "It is good to see you, old friend. I certainly should have seen a Green-Man watching us from the woods, but you are hard to spot even when I am not distracted with concern. Did you see what happened?"

"It is as you suspect, though I did not witness it. My birds told me. An ogon group passed through. With them, they carried two of your females. They killed one, and bound the other before carrying her away, leaving the cloth for you to find. Across the bridge they fled, and rode deep into the forest."

"Do you know where they were going?"

"No, young Fredrick, I do not," responded Lahn. "I cannot hear the trees beyond the gorge. However, the birds suspect they travel toward the ancient fort, past the long ridge. The fort left behind by the Missing Ones."

"If that is true they will not make it there today on boars." said Lamar, finally breaking his ominous silence.

"Yes," Lahn agreed, "it is a long way to the old fort and a dangerous climb in the dark. I have not been there in ages. It is difficult for me to cross the bridge. The stone hurts my roots, and I lose my balance because I cannot cling to it. I nearly fell from it once you know."

"We thank you for your words Lahn," said Fredrick, bowing as he spoke. "You have aided us in the past, and so it is today."

"Good luck to you. Fear not for this poor female they have left behind, I will place her high in my canopy and surround her with branches. She will be peaceful in her long rest and will not be disturbed."

Lahn took her gently in his leaf covered branches and lifted the body from the pool of blood. Small flexible sticks surrounded her, and green leaves bloomed around them as they encased Amma. Slowly and carefully, Lahn lifted her toward his lofty heights and she disappeared into the dense coverage of his canopy. Lamar placed his hand to his heart as Amma vanished from sight. Neither of them spoke, taking comfort only from the silent presence of each other's friendship.

"Thank you, Lahn," Fredrick said at last, once both men regained their composure. "You are a good friend to us."

With that, Fredrick fetched his mount and swung himself into the saddle. The strider danced nervously underneath him as he brought it under control. Then, he spurred the beast toward the bridge with Lamar following closely. He must ride hard. His horse was faster than the waboars the ogon rode, but he knew he would not overtake them against the dimming daylight.

***

Despite her fear, Veronica drifted in and out of a restless sleep. Several times in the night, the snoring mob of ogon sleeping near the fire pit had awakened her. Off and on, the snores of one would rouse another. They pushed and shoved each other while cursing, shifted around, then fell back to sleep. Slowly over time, the snoring would slowly rise, growing louder until they cursed and shifted again.

For the third time during the night, the changing of the guards disturbed her. This time, however, she sensed something was different. A strange feeling filled her mind, driven by the stinking sack over her head depriving her of sight. Where before, the other ogon grumbled about their undesirable post, this brigand was quiet. He sat nearer to her than the others and she could somehow sense him watching her.

Still exhausted, she continued to doze.

A snapping sound startled her, and set her pulse to racing. Deprived of sight with her hands bound, her sense of helplessness intensified. Something was wrong, and at first, she was not sure what it was.

Then it came to her. *Where is the guard? He isn't there!*

The silence of the forest was ominous. One thought repeated, *where is he?*

Her heart pounded in her chest as fear gripped it. She was fully awake now where before she was drowsy and exhausted making this all seem like nothing more than a twisted nightmare. She looked around instinctively, but her eyes were useless in the darkness of the hood. She could only hear, and as she listened she overheard whispering voices blanketed by the snoring of the gang.

Footsteps skulked about above her head and below her feet as she laid prone on the ground. A stalker was near. She sensed his presence, though she could not see nor hear him.

131

Suddenly, several sets of strong hands grabbed her violently! One set took her bound hands and pulled them over her head, holding them against the ground with his great strength. Another hand wrapped around her mouth so she could neither scream nor speak. She could only make muffled sounds as she tried to fight off her attackers. One clutched her ankles, pulling her legs apart.

She struggled, trying in vain to scream as she felt one of her assailants lay on her between her flailing legs. He lifted her clothes as he went, gathering them about her waist. A cold blade cut away her underclothes beneath her gown. She could hear the ripping of the cloth, and feel cold air close in around her exposed midsection and thighs. Though there were only three attackers, in her mind, she pictured the entire gang closing in, watching as if she were in some obscene carnival act.

"Lay still, kuja!" demanded a sinister hissing voice. She could feel the warmth of his body between her thighs as he opened his trousers and pulled them down, freeing himself for her. A sense of indignity, fear and defenselessness overwhelmed her. This was the moment that she feared most. That these vicious beasts would violate her, and that time had finally come. Exhausted and hopeless, she felt herself slowly stop struggling. She laid still, as the wicked voice demanded, fearing what would happen if she did not, and dreading even more what would happen if she did.

Her assailant pinned her shoulders back with this coarse hands. She felt the warmth of his flesh just outside her body, about to enter her.

Then a terrible sound filled her ears! It was hollow and grotesque, as if an axe had just struck wood. Her attacker stopped! A crushing weight landed on top of her and laid deathly still.

The hand across her mouth released her, standing quickly with one foot on each side of her head. Now freed, she cried out with all she had, screaming a long and drawn out, "NOOOOO!"

She heard shouted voices, and the sound of a struggle ensued, followed by another shriek of pain. Someone lifted the heavy deadweight off her chest, then took her by her still-bound hands, pulling her to her feet while the fight she could only hear continued.

The gang of ogon were awake now, and the sounds of shouting, footfalls and chaos was deafening.

As her mind cleared of shock and confusion, she realized that someone had intervened and stopped her attackers, but with the hood still over her head she could not see who her savior was. She could sense him in front of her, hearing his steps amid the clamor of the vicious struggle.

Who is it? Who is here? she wondered as excitement grew at the thought of her imminent rescue.

She yearned to look at Fredrick, or to hear his voice, but only the sounds of the battle met her ears.

Surely, he has not come alone.

"What did I tell you dumb kopikes?" someone shouted as the sounds of the struggle diminished leaving only the moans of the wounded. She

133

recognized it immediately. It was Gnash Mak'Nabb, and her hopes at rescue burned away under the fire of his gruff voice.

"She isn't yours, stay away from her!" he commanded. "Next one of you that touches her will pay like that dead son-of-a-kuja there."

Gnash jerked the hood from off her head, uncovering her eyes. Two ogon laid on the ground. One of them bore a ghastly wound where Gnash's blade had cloven his head in two like a melon. The second was still alive and clutching a grievous slash to his chest. He kicked his legs as he moaned in pain. A few of his companions came and carried him away into the darkness among the others of the band. The third of her attackers disappeared. It left her with an uncomfortable feeling knowing she might never know who among them it was.

After taking off her hood, Gnash took her by the front of her gown. Gore from the ogon he had killed covered her clothes. It was dark and vile, much darker than human blood and reeked a foul stench. He was holding his sword in his other hand and the horde of ogon that he commanded were looking at him with an odd expression of fear and respect as he eyed them back.

"Back to sleep! All of you!" he commanded. "The sun rises soon and we still have a lot of riding to do. I'll take the last watch."

Gnash led her along behind him to his camp, placed away from the main group of his brigands. He sat Veronica down near where he had piled a small bed of green leaves.

"Don't move!" he commanded as he lifted a bottle to her mouth. "Drink."

She was in shock, shaking all over and too scared to protest. She drank, tasting the same vile blood-whiskey from earlier. As the warmth hit her chest, her head swam, and her fear lessened. As Gnash watched her with his burning eyes, she realized the liquor was having its intended effect.

He is trying to calm me. Why does he care?

He took a long quaff from the bottle. He then replaced the stopper and threw it near to a small pile of other belongings. The drink had helped to quell the uncontrollable shakes running throughout her body.

With what energy she had left she muttered with down-turned eyes, "Thank you."

Gnash glared at her. "There are many curses the Raddlifs will call me. Rapist isn't one of them," he said putting the hood back on her head, returning her to the blackness within.

"Stay near to me," he whispered in her ear, being careful not to be overheard. "My ogon have smelled you, and blood. Now they are restless, desiring both. The blood sends us to rage, be still. Do nothing to provoke them. You will ride with me when the sun rises. I shall protect you."

Gnash's words struck Veronica. Her captor was now her protector. His words had given her a strange comfort among the lingering fear that dogged her since her abduction.

He guided her by the shoulders and sat her

down with her back to a tree on the padding of leaves where he laid before the attack. It was still warm from his body heat. There she stayed with her hands in her lap, and the infernal sack on her head marveling at how her abductor had suddenly become her defender, and she waited for a rescuer.

***

In the distance, Fredrick could see the setting sun against the jagged horizon of the tree blanketed rolling hills. He and Lamar had ridden through the day with no sight of their quarry. As the sun's light diminished, he felt as if his hopes of rescuing Veronica were fading with it. Both were exhausted, and with no moon overhead, he knew the night would be black as pitch over the Splinterwood.

The cooling trail was diminishing in the dimming daylight. As darkness fell over the forest, he realized that if he did not stop he risked losing the trail altogether, and decided it was best to camp.

Fredrick and Lamar were unprepared for an overnight stay in the woods. Having no tents, or materials for even a simple lean-to, they found a flat spot under a tree to spend the night. They fed themselves on berries they happened upon, along with the meager rations remaining in their saddlebags. Taking what they could from their packhorse at the meadow, they released it to wander home, knowing their need of haste in the pursuit. With no blankets or shelter save the trunk of the fir, the night would be long and cold.

As the first slivers of light peeked through the

distant hills, the two set out again. Fredrick had established the ogon's general direction of travel. The waboar left a split-hoof print easily mistakable for other faunae of the forest, particularly a stag. The ones he looked for were deep, and broken from their haste and the weight on their backs. The ogon left other signs of their passing due to their carelessness and ferocity. Along their trail, remained the bodies of dead animals and sword-chopped branches where they used their weapons to cut their way through the woods.

Presently, they came to a long ridge, too steep for the horses to ascend while ridden, and too long to go around while trying to make haste. Much of the Splinterwood was a rolling terrain carpeted by trees, but here and there were scattered mountains and foothills like the one on which Castle Raddlif sat. Some were tall and majestic, requiring an arduous vertical climb to reach the top. This one barring their way was a long, tall ridgeline, flat at the top, as if a giant wedge had been driven into the floor of the forest at a sharp angle. A dense, low brush covered the embankment, and large boulders protruded from the face of the ridge. A layer of loose stones made the surface slippery and dangerous, especially for a horse.

Undeterred and driven by concern, the pursuers took their mounts by the reins and began the treacherous climb. The horses protested as they struggled for balance.

Reaching the halfway point of the hike, Fredrick glanced up to see a figure come into view at the top of the ridge. He wore a gray cloak that hid his face and sat on a waboar that tossed his head and snorted.

"Who are you?" shouted Fredrick, balancing himself against the hazardous footing of the slope.

The question was met with an ominous silence as the rider studied him with unseen eyes.

"Pull back your hood if you are not on with ill deeds! Show yourself!" demanded Fredrick, taking his long-gun from its holster in his saddle.

"I mean no harm, Young Baron," responded the stranger.

The rider pulled back his hood as he finished, revealing a familiar face.

"Andrej Bedrich," cried Fredrick as he recognized an old friend.

"Aye lad, it has been too long," he responded as a brown-flecked owl descended from overhead and perched on his shoulder. He dismounted and took a rope hanging from his saddle, tossing an end to Fredrick and Lamar, aiding them to the crest of the ridge.

The unexpected sight of their friend and ally invigorated both tired pursuers.

Standing at the top, panting and trying to catch his breath, Fredrick admired the view. Below them, shrouded in mists and far away, he could see an ancient, long deserted fort at the base of the valley.

Fredrick looked at Andrej. He was well on in years, older than he remembered. His salt and pepper hair grew wild, merging into filthy rope-like clumps extending down his back. His eyes were bright, and set against deep crow's-feet in a slender, grimy face. His gray-flecked beard and mustache was overgrown and shaggy. His teeth were the color of tree bark. The odor from him was stifling. His avian companion rode on his shoulder and droppings collected where the owl perched, running down both the front and back of his threadbare cloak he wore over modest attire.

The bird watched as the three men talked. Occasionally, he put his head near to Andrej's ear, as if whispering to him. The owl was white, and flecked in dark brown. A beak the color of fine ivory sat between his large golden eyes. Two circles made a figure-eight pattern on his flattened face.

Seeing Andrej brought back to Fredrick pleasant childhood memories. His Father had told him stories of the Bedrich family. Vicious fights, wild hunts, and drunken feasts were the norm for their clan. Mighty warriors all of them, and many who made their home in the Splinterwood feared their name.

"Well young-man," Andrej began, "I expect you track a gang of ogon that crossed the gorge-bridge yesterday? They carry with them a woman. Obviously one they have snared. Who is she?"

"She is Lady Veronica Moresten of Trodenheim. She is to be my wife. You have seen them?" Fredrick paused. His happiness at seeing an old friend melted away to a downcast expression. "Was she alive?"

"She was this morning," answered Andrej. "The ogon struck their camp at the outpost and headed toward the fort early. They move swiftly. I have loitered here where I can watch the valley. My companion Grego keeps track of them from the air. I did not see them cross the bridge, but heard of it through other means. The owl spotted them as they rode west. He told me they held a captive. I followed them to learn what they were up to."

Grego looked at Fredrick as if he understood every word, nodding as if to verify Andrej's story.

"Till now I had no reason to interfere with a band of ogon and a stranger. I found it odd they did not kill her and instead drag her to the fort. I expected someone to arrive looking for her, but I thought whoever came would bring more men."

"It hardly takes an army to best Gnash Mak'Nabb and two of his thugs," said Fredrick confidently.

"Three total, lad?" asked Andrej.

"Yes. Rostov and his soldiers, along with Veronica's father Olan killed many when the ogon attacked, but three escaped. Veronica mentioned that she admired some flowers in a nearby meadow. While I was away fetching them for her as a gift, the fiends ambushed our party. Rostov and my guards were slain in the fighting. I know not if Count Olan lived. He was badly wounded, but insisted that I go after his daughter rather than return him to the castle. Those are the flowers still there in my pack." He gestured toward his horse as he spoke where a linen bound bundle was peeking out of the corner of the saddlebag.

"I saw many more than three. They must have met their clan-mates on the trail during their flight. I'm sorry to hear about Rostov, he was a good man."

A chill gripped Fredrick's heart at Andrej's news. He looked at Lamar. Disappointment and sudden apprehension was written across his face at the news of the larger gang.

Fredrick breathed a deep sigh then said, "We shall take her back despite their efforts. I expect Gnash took her hostage so I will release his brother who has spent many moons in our dungeon. Shattered-Tooth continue to poach on our lands, pilfer caravans, sack houses and murder my people."

"Mak'Nabb and his thugs are a fiendish lot," said Andrej. "I will ride with you. Many years ago, our families fled the old world after the rocks fell from the sky. Your grandfather and mine faced that peril together as they crossed the sea. Now as then, we shall fly toward danger as friends. These ogon should not have taken the woman hostage. They are cowards, with no honor. The trees alone know what they have done to her in the night. The brigands deserve death."

Fredrick understood Andrej's unspoken inference. A repugnance in his heart grew. Under it all, he felt pride in not only Andrej, but also Lamar, who had come all this way with him, never once wavering against the fear both of them bore.

"My friends," he said at last, "every one of them, including Ghronn, will hang from the bridge they ferried the Lady across and committed the murder of her servant. The crows and vermin feast on ogon flesh, and there will be plenty of hanging meat. Song and story of these days will be retold, and no one will

141

doubt my strength when the day comes that I am the Baron at Raddlif."

***

For the rest of the night, after her rescue from the clutches of his rogues, Veronica sat with her back to a tree. The sounds of shouting and stamping feet grew as the band awakened. She heard the snorting and grunting of nearby waboars growing excited by the busy brigands as they prepared to ride.

With her hands bound and in her lap, Veronica could only wait amid the clamor with the sack still over her head. Feeling she had little to lose, she removed the dreaded shroud so she could see what was happening. The bright morning sun burned her eyes as they filled with light. As her vision came back into focus, she could see Gnash standing over her. He said nothing about having taken off the hood, and was near enough she realized he watched her take it off.

"Eat," he commanded. Two long cuts of pork cooked the night before laid on a cloth in his hand. She took one, and Gnash the other. Together, they ate breakfast.

"You ride with me. Do not try to escape. You have nowhere to go, and you cannot out run us."

Veronica nodded her acknowledgment as she nibbled on her cut of cold pork.

"Put out your hands," he said, drawing his dagger and severing the bonds.

"'Remember. My ogon are wild," grumbled Gnash, speaking with a full mouth. "They are away from their mates, so they are restless. Your ways are

142

not ours. Your 'laws' are not *ours!* I lead this gang and I do not wish to kill more of my clans-mates to protect you. Do nothing foolish."

Is he warning me, or advising me? she thought as she looked at him.

His words were coarse, and he spoke in a mocking and fearful tenor, but his bearing told a different story. She sensed confusion, not only in herself, but also in Gnash. His eyes softened. The anger that seethed from them when he first took her away seemed to have cooled, but his determination had not waned. There was no doubt she was still his prisoner, but he was not watching her at every moment, saddling his boar and getting ready to ride in a casual manner.

"Wait here," he commanded as he strode by.

He approached the tree where he had tied his waboar. The beast shook its head pulling at the rope expecting its release. With his back to her, Gnash fidgeted with his clothing with one hand, still gnawing on his shard of pork with the other. As Veronica watched him with curiosity, she saw a stream of urine flow from between Gnash's parted legs. She spun around, turning her back to him in embarrassment. She had no idea how to react, so she waited just as he commanded, listening to the sound of the puddle collecting at Mak'Nabb's feet.

As the pattering sounds subsided, she turned back to find Gnash tugging on the line, freeing his waboar. It pulled against him, grunting and snapping its jaws as it resisted. He thumped it on its snout,

143

cursing at it as he did so and the beast calmed. He put his foot through the stirrup and swung himself up into the thin saddle.

He motioned to Veronica with his hand to come closer, so she approached him.

"Do you have to piss?" he asked. "Get on the other side of the boar away the lads. Be quick! We ride hard today. I will not have you pissing on my ride's back."

Hiding from the ogon in the main camp, she lifted her blood-stained, ragged gown and squatted to relieve herself.

Borhn and Sajj, having seen their leader on his waboar, mounted their own, sitting silently, waiting for orders. Veronica finished and straightened her torn clothes, turning to find Gnash offering a hand to help her up. She took it, feeling the coarseness of his callused flesh. She found it strange that he helped her up instead of making her clamber up on her own. Her thoughts drifted to Fredrick. She pictured him offering up his hand in the same way, but from a graceful strider, not a hideous beast.

With a strong tug, she leaped up onto the grunting creature, holding onto Gnash around the waist.

With no warning, he spurred his waboar and it leaped forth into a fast run. Borhn and Sajj followed as he guided his boar in a circle around the encampment. From his saddle, he took a long black horn, sounding it as he rode. It blew a shrill note that hurt Veronica's ears as she pressed her head against his back, hanging on and cringing in discomfort from the hard and protruding spine of the beast. Sore from the vicious manhandling she endured on the previous day, every muscle in her body was crying out in pain as the two of them moved.

The ogon among the group who had boars fell in, following Gnash as he rode the circle. The rest of them on foot formed a mob in the center. Turning on their heels, the gang cheered as Gnash and his riders circled before stopping and forming a semi-triangular formation behind their leader.

Peeking over Gnash's shoulder, Veronica viewed the gathering and a chill went down her spine. Several slavering and screaming ogon formed an unorganized mob before Mak'Nabb as he began to speak.

His voice was loud and rough, addressing the gang in their native tongue. Though she did not understand the words, she understood the tone of the speech and the reaction it garnished. The mob cheered, brandishing their weapons as Gnash spoke, his language rising and growing more intense as he reached a finishing crescendo.

Raising his horn over his head, soaking in the cheers of his mob, Gnash said finally, "Hang on," and kicked his heels into the sides of the boar. It leaped into a fast run and he deftly dodged the trees of the woods leading the group deeper into the Splinterwood.

Through the morning and into the heat of midday, Veronica rode with Gnash, clutching at him to keep from falling off the waboar. He flew with no concern for comfort as he maneuvered around obstacles in his path.

Nearly at her strength's end, with her head resting against Gnash's back, the beast wheeled around under the two of them. He held up his clawed hand gesturing the horde to a halt, and barked orders for his riders.

"We rest here," he said as he took her by the wrist. "Get down, rest yourself."

He was panting as he spoke, and his body was dripping with perspiration.

She dismounted the boar and stood beside it steadying herself with a hand against the rump of the beast. She found herself in a dell covered with a fine, mossy grass with a small brook cutting through, flowing with water that shimmered like crystals in the midday sun. The mob following Mak'Nabb on foot filtered out of the trees as they caught up to the leading riders. They looked on her with contempt as they stopped; breathing heavily from the day's run through the woods. The gang broke up into groups, sitting on the grass and rocks. Some drank from skins; others took water from the stream, cupping it with their hands and lifting it to their mouths.

"Drink. Refresh yourself," said Gnash as if to snap Veronica out of the exhaustion-induced trance that had overcome her as she stood next to him unsteadily.

She walked toward the running water but after a few steps, her weak and sore legs gave out, and she dropped to the ground below in a heap.

"Sajj! Get off your mount and help her," barked Gnash.

Adroitly, the ogon leaped from his saddle, strutting over to where Veronica laid. As she lifted herself up, expecting aid from him, he struck her across the face with the back of his hand and a bolt of pain coursed through her body.

The force of the blow left her senseless. As her head cleared, she heard fast footsteps and a loud, shouting voice coming closer. Gnash grabbed her by the arm, lifting her to her feet, and steadied her amid Sajj's laughter. The mob, scattered around and watching, laughed along with Sajj.

Gnash spun the laughing ogon to face him then clutched him by both sides of his head. With a vicious snap, he butted him with his forehead. The movement happened so quickly, Sajj did not have time to stop laughing. His laughter ended with the abrupt, crushing impact to his nose, and he dropped to the ground amid the stunned moans of the on-lookers.

"I told you to help her you half-breed!" Gnash roared. "You having trouble understanding me?"

Sajj stood up quickly and attacked in his anger and embarrassment. With two nimble moves, Mak'Nabb blunted his attack sending him back to the floor of the woods for a second time. The moans of the mob rose again as Sajj hit the ground, this time accompanied by a brief burst of chuckles.

"You will not injure her!" Gnash shouted.

Veronica, shocked by Gnash's reaction and rubbing her still throbbing cheek, watched as the two

147

eyed each other with hostility. Sajj wanted to attack again, but Veronica could see that he was too afraid. His face filled with anger and indignation at his defeat. Dark blood ran from his flattened nose and thick lips.

"Get your half-green ass over there and help her. If you hurt her again, I'll break your neck!" said Gnash, pointing in her direction.

Veronica observed the other ogon in the clearing. The entire mob now looked on, muttering to each other with interest. Sajj rose and took her by the shoulders helping to keep her balance as he guided her to the water. She could feel the anger seething in him through the grip he held against her flesh. As the commotion calmed, the band turned away and returned to their food and drink, breaking up into small groups.

Near the brook, the air felt cooler. Parched with thirst, she put her face in the stream and drank deeply. The cool water seeped through her core, its energy refreshing her exhausted mind and body. She washed away the foul blood that stained her breast and neck from the night before.

She brushed her soaked hair from her face with both hands. The excess water poured down and collected on her torn gown, cooling her further.

Her reluctant helper stood over her, glowering angrily.

Gnash sat next to a tree, drinking from a battered leather skin. She stood and approached him, sitting with Gnash while maintaining a respectful distance, but close enough to sense the protection of her kidnapper. She marveled at the irony of it as she struggled to keep her eyes away from meeting with either of them.

With a wave of his hand, Gnash dismissed Sajj who returned to his mount and stood next to it alone. Some of the others, already in small groups, invited him to join them and he shared their drink and food, finally resting in the company of his companions.

For a while, she sat on the ground and listened to the sounds of the woods, afraid to move or speak.

"You are to marry this boy? Fredrick the manling?" Gnash asked after a long silence.

"Yes," she replied.

"Who did he best in combat, or what have you done to earn his respect, that he should win you, and you marry him?"

"Well," said Veronica, as she squinted in confusion at the question, "no one. No one I know of anyway, and earn his respect? I'm not sure I have."

"Then why are you marrying him? Or why has he chosen you?"

"Our fathers arranged it while we were infants."

Mak'Nabb's head flicked at her, his eyes wide with surprise and curious confusion.

"Your fathers agreed you should marry, and you do this? Both of you, agreed to this?"

"I did not agree. I have a duty that I was born into," answered Veronica, not looking at Gnash while holding her forehead against her knees.

"Then why do you not kill him?"

"What?" she cried, offended by the question

and finally meeting his eyes. "Could you do that?"

"If he were to make me marry or otherwise do what I did not want to, yes," explained Gnash. "Mine has been dead for many years. He died in battle against the kopike Red-Hands. Those friends of your manling."

"I'm sorry to hear that," responded Veronica. "But I will not kill my father. I have a duty, and when this is over, I will go through with it. That is if you or your men don't kill me like you did Amma."

"They are not men! They're ogon," said Gnash indignantly, "and I do not wish to kill you. When I killed your servant and friend, you did not cry. There is strength in you that you do not see in yourself. A strength I grow to respect, but you are untrained. Naïve as to the ways of life."

Gnash fell silent. He frowned, looking as if he were pondering a difficult decision. Finally, he drew in a long breath then said, "I regret killing that girl. I was in the throes of the bloodlust that overcome us when ogon join in battle. Her naïve words enraged me further, and my ogon were goading me. I knew what they wanted and I cannot show them weakness. If I thought murdering you both would gain my brother's freedom, I would have, but I know it would not. Nor will slaying your servant. That was pointless. In fact, it will stiffen your manling's resolve. I will not kill you. If you do not wish to marry your boy-baron, I will defeat him and claim you one of my wives. From the Raddlifs I will have either my brother, or revenge! It is for your manling to decide which it will be."

150

Veronica could not believe what she was hearing. The thought of him claiming her as a wife chilled her to the bone, but now he was defending her and treating her with a tepid, awkward sort of kindness.

Is he asking me to forgive him? Is this an apology, or a proposal? she wondered silently as a sense of guilt kindled in her mind at her budding admiration for her captor. *This beast killed Amma, how can I forget that? But without his protection, I'm dead. The others will kill me.*

"We must go." Gnash said, springing to his feet.

Throughout the day, she rode behind Mak'Nabb as he led the mob. Against a setting sun, the group arrived at a great walled fort. The walls connected six towers overgrown by a dense flower-budding ivy. In the fort's interior, Veronica could see the top of a domed edifice. The gang entered through the rust covered main gate. The gate was left open sometime in the distant past and now hung on frozen hinges.

Clinging to Gnash, as he rode the pathway into the fort, she continued taking in the sights surrounding her. She noticed smaller buildings, all of which were in groups of three and formed of the same white stone as the walls protecting them. The edifices, including the largest round one in the center, were in various states of disrepair and covered by stalks of vegetation. Earth collected at their base looking as if the ground would eventually swallow them whole. Patches of ancient pine trees, gray with age, stood as if they were living sentinels over a dead towne.

Set into the front of the central dome, facing toward the fort's main gate, was a wide, ironbound door. Near to it grew a single, vast weeping willow. Veronica pondered how out of place the tree looked. It seemed lonely. The willow was unique and old. Its roots top fed along the ground like an enormous living web of wood. Its green canopy hung like a blanket of leaves obscuring the trunk within.

With his bodyguards in tow and shouting orders to the rest of the gang, Gnash rode to the dome and dismounted, helping her off the beast. She followed him as he stepped to the ironbound double-door and opened it with an ear-piercing screech under great effort. The walls and floor of the dome were fashioned of smoothed stone, and decorated with pictographs of many people engaged in all manners of activity. Some carried pots; others read from books, still others prepared food. It was difficult to see the dome in the gathering darkness. It was decorated with a depiction of a great light, or an ever-present eye. All the people looked like ordinary men and women, small in stature with hair of ebony and olive skin. A portion of the dome, and the wall at the rear of the structure was sundered and collapsing. She could see the darkening blue sky overhead. The cold draft that blew through chilled Veronica and caused her to shiver.

In the center of the floor, sat a massive round fountain through which clean water was still somehow circulating. The ring of freshwater surrounded a tall stone brazier filled with the ashes of a once giant fire. Rusted iron sconces protruded from the walls in various places with the remnants of burned torches still seated within them.

Gnash started a small pilot fire with which he sparked a torch. Some of the dead torches held a flame, and a flickering light filled the area.

"It is here we shall wait," he said. "Tomorrow my messenger rides to the Raddlifs. Then, the Baron will come for you. When he does I will treat for my brother. If he does not," he paused bearing a gloomy expression and turned away. "He'll bring him. It is doubtful he would let his son's bride die for Ghronn."

The ogon foraged what they could for food from around the fort and gathered it in the chamber. Borhn and Sajj sat in a corner away from Veronica drinking and smoking a foul-smelling weed through crude wooden pipes. She noticed Sajj's sour expression and she was glad to keep him at a distance.

Gnash laid on the stone floor and rolled up a small piece of cloth behind his head. "Remember what I told you about running. Stay near me. Sajj is still angry. I am not sure he wouldn't harm you. You might as well rest."

Comforted by his words, she moved closer to Gnash and sat next to the fountain. Her mind was clear now. The fear she felt at the beginning of the ordeal had changed to more of resentment for these creatures. Their leader perplexed her most of all. She found herself confused by him.

He is so strong to lead such a wild group of

beings such as these ogon, she pondered, as she sat quietly on the ground, *but I sense a sentimental streak in him beneath his ferocity.*

"Gnash," she said, surprised at herself for speaking.

"What?" he responded gruffly, not opening his eyes to look at her.

"Why are the Raddlifs' holding Ghronn?" she asked meekly.

"Because he killed a buck and stole food and goods from a Raddlif caravan. During the fight he killed some Newcomers," he said. He laid on his back relaxing with his arm across his eyes not bothering to make eye contact.

Gnash's bold answer surprised her. She expected a story of an innocent ogon falsely accused, or some other equally sad tale of woe. He had all but confessed his guilt and now she was a bargaining pawn for his release.

"You don't deny he did these things?" she asked, bolder than before when she spoke.

"Why should I?" asked Gnash. He sat up and rested on his elbow. His golden eyes flickered in the firelight.

Borhn and Sajj sitting in the corner were talking among themselves, and paying no attention to the two of them.

"So he's guilty?"

"What do you mean?" he replied.

"I mean he did what the Raddlifs say he did. Why are you holding me if you know he broke the law?"

Suddenly, frustration fueled a fire in his eyes.

"The law?" he said angrily. "They live in *our* woods, and if they want to live in it, you must defend your females, and your young. Your food, and your belongings! If they could not defend it, then Ghronn or anyone else may take it. Stealing, is that your word for it?"

Veronica sat in silence, suspecting he was not through speaking.

"We don't know your law," he said as he laid back down. "We don't steal, as you call it, we take what we want. If those who have it can't defend it, they should find someone who can defend it *for* them. He will release Ghronn, and I will avenge the ogon your manling hanged. Though that waits for another day. Now be silent! I have no wish to talk about Raddlif invaders or their law," he finished, covering his eyes again as before.

Veronica sat hugging her knees and looked out the broken ceiling to the darkness outside.

She noticed the silhouette of a bird soaring high above. Soon it descended, entering through the sundered dome, and gliding down, sailing in a lazy circle within the walls.

She watched the bird curiously, as it perched on the top of the fountain in the center of the ruin. The two regarded each other in silence. It was a white owl flecked with brown, inspecting her with sharpened eyes. She sensed something strange about him as they held each other's gaze. The bird looked her straight in the eye deliberately. With growing curiosity, she observed him as it turned its head, looking around the chamber, before turning his attention back to Veronica. He looked at her as though he knew her, and she could not explain the strangeness of her visitor.

"Whoo, Whoo," the owl cooed puffing up, ruffling its feathers and shaking its head.

Gnash laid on the floor. He did not stir, continuing to relax despite the feathered intruder's presence.

Borhn and Sajj, however, who so far had carried a long, whispered conversation, noticed the owl.

Sajj took a few steps forward, then took a stone from the floor and flung it at the visitor.

As the stone hurled through the air, the bird took flight, and it bounced harmlessly off the fountain.

The bodyguards watched as the owl circled twice gathering speed, then flew through the cleaved wall, disappearing into the night.

***

Apprehension beset Fredrick's mind as he and his friends waited patiently for darkness to blanket the ancient fort before advancing. He could tell by the morose expressions of his friends that they shared his feelings.

The trio moved silently, not only out of need of stealth, but because of the nervousness in their hearts for the confrontation they wished to avoid. All three of them knew that a direct fight with the ogon would likely result in their deaths, so they planned a cunning rescue, disappearing into the night before any of their enemies discovered what happened.

Fredrick looked to Andrej who stood behind a tall fir tree. Grego, perched on his shoulder, gazed his way.

"You ready?" whispered Andrej, drawing a knife. Fredrick noticed something different in him now. His bearing was dark and foreboding. His eyes were wide, and far-reaching. As if his sharpened senses were more than human. If Andrej were not already his friend and companion, he would have been frightened by him. The darkness of his manner sobered him to the deadly peril of their plan.

Lamar appeared worried. Fredrick nodded with a sharp drop of his chin trying to calm his friend. He breathed deeply and exhaled, calmed his nerves, then returned Fredrick's reassuring gesture.

The trio moved furtively between the densely packed trees. Andrej, having been in this area often, had given Fredrick a general description of where they would penetrate the ogon's camp. They stopped at the edge of a clearing surrounding the fort's exterior. He guessed that it was fifty yards between the tree line and the wall, giving any archers a clear shot at an incoming attacker. The vicinity was exactly as Andrej had described it. The walls were tall and sturdy. It was not round, consisting of six corners forming a hexagon protecting the interior grounds. He led the group to where the wall had been breached in ages past by an unknown force of great power. Near the broken wall, ancient stones laid where they had fallen when they had been brought low in forgotten times.

As they crept ahead, Fredrick spotted a single ogon. He sat facing the woods, looking out into the forest away from their position. Seeing only one of them troubled him. He knew for sure that others skulked around, unseen in the darkness. There was no doubt now that he and his friends were among the enemy. The feeling was unsettling.

Andrej halted, still as a statue. He turned and gestured, signaling for them to wait. Slowly he crouched, looking out at the ogon who sat on a stone oblivious to the approaching danger.

In a blink of an eye, Andrej had disappeared into the night, sinking into the darkness itself as if it were a pool of still water. He was silent, moving like a phantom through the trees.

For several agonizing minutes, Fredrick's heart pounded in his chest so hard he feared his enemies would hear the drum-like noise.

Suddenly, with barely more than a glint of moonlight against the blade of his knife, Fredrick saw a shadow rise, framed against the night. In an instant the ogon was gone, consumed by the darkness so quickly he did not make a sound.

Another agonizing moment of quiet stillness passed. Out of the darkness, an owl flew toward him, landing on a branch near where he and Lamar waited. He perched on a low limb of a nearby tree, saying one time, "Whooo", before again taking flight. He circled, then flew to where the ogon had been sitting.

Fredrick realized that Grego wanted him to

follow. Slowly and carefully as before, they moved toward the stone. Once there, they found Andrej crouching on one knee, his victim dead on the ground face down beneath him.

Using the fallen stone fragments as cover, the three continued moving to the fort. Fredrick's senses were racing as his heart filled with excitement. His head turned this way and that, checking every subtle sound of the forest for enemies.

Grego rode along on Andrej's shoulder. Suddenly he stopped, taking cover behind a large remnant of the wall. He peeked over the top of the stones and pointed at a fragment in the path ahead.

Fredrick noticed a pungent smell growing bolder as the trio advanced. He glanced up and over their cover of stone, and spotted a stream of smoke rising from among the fragments ahead of them. Someone hid there, and he was smoking.

Andrej gestured to Lamar to prepare his bow. He took an arrow and set it to the bowstring. Fredrick pointed his long-gun toward the smoke, knowing that his guns would only be useful if they were discovered.

With a graceful flap of his wings, Grego took to the air. He circled as the three men watched him in flight, eventually flying to the rising smoke landing on the stone and looking at the figure hidden there.

After a few nerve-racking moments of waiting, a head emerged, silhouetted against the night. He gawked curiously toward the bird while still puffing from his pipe.

Fredrick realized why Andrej had Lamar

prepare his bow. The owl lured his target into view! He pulled back on the string, aimed quickly, and loosed the shaft. The arrow flew passed the bird, skimmed along the stone and plunged into the head of the silhouetted figure. Under the force of the impact, the ogon disappeared, dropping to the ground where he had been sitting only seconds before, enjoying his smoke.

The trio dropped back behind the cover of the stone. Fredrick covered his mouth, stifling a snicker as he reviewed the nimble shot in his mind. Andrej pointed at Lamar, smiling brightly and silently congratulating his handy sharpshooting. Lamar gestured with a salute as he grinned back at them and winked confidently with one eye as if it was just another shot.

Carefully they pressed on, passing through the breach in the perimeter wall, entering the interior. It covered an expansive area. In the center, he spied the dome where he knew from Grego's visit Veronica was captive. Many structures in different sizes, shapes and levels were placed in clusters of three and were in various states of disrepair. Some of them had collapsed over the passing of countless years.

Though the infiltrators had seen enemies around the exterior, no wall guard was visible. At first, he was surprised. But he knew from experience that ogon are savage and wild. Each to his own. He suspected that Gnash did not expect him to attempt a clandestine rescue. Instead, his enemy expected Manfred to return with a retinue of soldiers and bargain with him for her release. Never risking Veronica's safety.

The trio advanced stealthily and soon found themselves near the dome. The rear wall was smashed in line with where the outer wall stood breached. Like the fortification surrounding the fort, the rubble had been left where it lay in shards both large and small. Andrej stayed back to guard, and Lamar positioned himself just outside the breach while Fredrick crept inside.

Torches dimly illuminated the interior. Veronica laid near a fountain in the center of the edifice. He took a moment to look around. Across the chamber, by the large door into the dome itself, he saw Gnash, and another intimidating ogon. Lying next to an empty wine skin and snoring loudly, laid a third brigand. Gnash and his guard played a game using sticks and stones arranged on a square cloth.

Veronica slept on the floor. It frustrated him that she would not see him right away, and he wondered at how she could sleep while held captive. She was too close to Gnash to approach, and too far away to hear his whispers that he feared would give his presence away. His frustration grew as he racked his mind for a way to awaken her quietly.

He stepped back and looked across to Andrej where he had left him. He gestured, pointing toward Veronica. He placed his hands together to form a pillow and laid his head on them then shrugged, hoping Andrej would understand that she was asleep, and he could not rouse her.

Obscured as Andrej was, Fredrick could not make out his reaction to his gestures. He could see only Andrej's dark silhouette as he pointed to the sky. Following his pointing hand, Fredrick spotted Grego's shape as he flew into the building landing on the top of the fountain near to Veronica's position.

"Whoo," cooed the bird, repeatedly as he perched atop the tall fountain.

Annoyed by his presence, the ogon playing at sticks and stones with Gnash stood up, waving his hands to shoo away the intruder, shouting at him in his own language.

Grego ignored him and continued to coo from his perch.

"Borhn! Leave the bird alone, get back over here," said Gnash.

Veronica stirred, awakened by the commotion and the persistent cooing of the owl.

"Now look what you did!" said Gnash sarcastically. "You woke up our guest."

Grego then again took flight. Veronica shook her head, stretched to clear the lingering drowsiness, and noticed the circling bird. She watched him as he soared around the dome. He flew in one last circle, then landed on a large broken stone in front of Fredrick. From his darkened position between the stones where he hid, only Fredrick's face was exposed in the dim light of the ruin.

Veronica looked in his direction at the bird. He could see her eyes go wide with excitement as their eyes met. She gasped involuntarily in surprise and recognition, putting a hand to her mouth. Fredrick quickly gestured her back to silence with a finger to his lips, and returned into the darkness of the shadows, out of sight.

"What?" said Gnash turning his attention away from the game.

Veronica shook her head innocently with a confused expression wiping her nose as if she had sneezed. She sat back down, doing her best to hide her excitement while Gnash eyed her with suspicion.

"Mek' yer play! I wanna beat you again!" said Borhn.

As Gnash turned his attention away, Fredrick saw Veronica sit hugging her knees facing him. He waited, allowing Gnash to return his attention fully back to his game. He then moved into the dim light where Veronica could see his face, gently signaling her to move toward him.

She stood and loitered about the fountain leaning against it. She drew water from it, bringing it to her lips again casually. Gnash looked her way, and Fredrick saw her smile at him. The smile she showed to Gnash looked very sweet, and intimate. A smile he would like to think that she would reserve for him alone. He found it odd, but dismissed it as a ruse on her part to lower his suspicions. As Mak'Nabb played the game, Veronica, dragging her fingers through the water, placed the fountain between her and the distracted ogon. She washed her face patiently, taking her time to lower both ogon's' attentiveness.

Both Gnash and Borhn were enthralled in their

moves, deep in thought and not interested in Veronica.

Fredrick's heart was pounding in his ears as Veronica, noticing that Gnash was not watching her closely, made her way toward her rescuer. She moved quietly, but neither slowly nor quickly, only just enough that she would not gain attention. He continued to hold his finger to his lips to calm her, seeing the excitement etched into her expression. It was obvious that she wanted to cry out and run to him, but to do so would be folly. They would only have moments to make their escape the way they had entered, vanishing into the night to their hidden horses.

Fredrick took her by the hand and pulled her into the cover of the rubble. Without even thinking, their lips met in a warm kiss, and they shared a passionate but fleeting moment concealed in the darkness.

Taking up his long-gun and holding Veronica by the hand, the two slipped out of the back of the dome. Lamar joined them as they flew, following with his bow at the ready.

From between the buildings, they made their way toward the breached outer wall. Fredrick could see it in front of him as it neared, clutching Veronica's hand.

Then, he heard a shrill, loud noise. It was the sound of an ogon war-horn, blaring an alarm!

From the jagged ends of the broken wall, Fredrick could see ogon running toward them, bearing weapons over their heads and charging while one continued to sound a black, curled horn. An arrow passed closely by him from behind, striking the lead ogon and silencing the horn's alarming call. A second shaft passed him on the other side as Veronica shrieked, dropping another enemy.

A third ogon charged brandishing an axe. Rather than fire his long-gun at his attacker, Fredrick parried his attack and countered, using the gun as a cudgel. As the fiend reeled from the impact, Andrej attacked with his knife, killing him quickly.

Hearing the footfalls of reinforcing ogon approaching outside the breached wall, they changed direction. They ran back into the interior of the fort, with enemies pursuing them.

"Toward the main gate! We must lose them in the buildings," cried Andrej as he led them to their secondary escape.

As they flew past the dome, Fredrick saw Gnash stepping through the breach. "How bold manling," he chided, "I didn't expect it of you! You will not get away with it!"

"Go! Run!" commanded Andrej as he drew his sword.

"No! We fight him together!" responded Fredrick, still guilt stricken from leaving Olan and Rostov at the meadow and thirsting for revenge.

"Raddlif, take your woman and run," demanded Andrej. "You will have many more to fight to make your escape. Now go!" He pushed Fredrick by the shoulder to spur him on.

Reluctantly, the Young Baron put his hand on Andrej's forearm and their eyes met in a silent farewell. He turned and ran, fleeing among the shouting voices of the other confused ogon in a frenzy all about them.

The three followed the wall of the dome, turning the corner to find themselves in a small stand of pine trees near a lonely willow. In front of them on their intended escape route, Fredrick spotted a group of ogon oncoming. Borhn led them. He shouted and pointed, whipping them into a rage.

They turned and ran back toward Andrej only to find still more ogon bearing down on them from behind. A feeling of defeat and dread swelled in Fredrick's mind as he realized the beasts had them surrounded.

Aiming carefully, he fired his long-gun between the pines. The loud report of the gun caused the ogon attackers to pause in apprehension as the shot struck one of them, sending him to the ground wailing as his life ebbed.

Lamar shot arrows quickly at the startled attackers. Some of the shafts found their mark, while others sailed by harmlessly.

Fredrick could feel the noose of his enemies tightening. He drew a pistol and fired at the closest screaming, slavering enemy. The shot found its mark, killing him and buying them a precious few seconds. He flipped the pistol to use as a club and withdrew his sword, preparing for the close quarters fight. The ogon were too many, and a desperate sense of despair tormented him as he realized that he and his friends would probably die in their attempt to free his fiancé.

Then, rising steadily, he heard a peculiar noise. Like one he had not heard before, a moaning sounding uproar but deeper and more ominous.

Fredrick and Lamar positioned Veronica behind them for her final defense. She backed up to a pine tree they hoped would cover her back from blades and arrows while they fought the oncoming enemies. They attacked the ogon as they approached. More and more leaped into the fight, screaming a blood-curling war-cry as they did so.

Fredrick swung his weapons furiously. Striking one, then another. He felt a burst of pain as one of his enemy's attacks found its mark. The wound was superficial, but gloom followed, and defeat beleaguered his heart. He could no longer see Lamar, but heard his voice cry out in pain.

The loud moaning sound rose again, but this time, a hollow and deep ripping sound followed. He held the point of his sword in front of him holding several ogon at bay. They heard the noise as well and stopped, looking around in confusion to see what it was. Veronica, though still fearful, had picked up one of the dropped enemy weapons, defending herself from the assaulting ogon, hacking away at the hands of her assailants.

"Fredrick! The trees!" exclaimed Veronica.

He watched in amazement as the pine behind them uprooted itself and walked the ground, sweeping the ogon away with its mighty limbs. Others in the stand pulled themselves free as well, moving swiftly.

The angry pines engaged the ogon with their

great strength, hurling them as if they were children's toys. Some they pierced with sharpened, pike like branches. Another held an ogon by the leg, using him as a flail to beat back the others. The willow, once near the front of the dome, was stamping on them like they were bugs.

The ogon, now afraid and confused by the newly emerging enemy, chopped at the trees with axe and sword.

As Fredrick watched the trees drive the ogon back and away from them, a glimmer of hope returned to him.

Remembering the cry of his friend, he looked for Lamar. He found him lying on the cold ground, clutching at a grievous wound across his shoulder and chest, shivering in pain, and covered in blood.

From behind him, he heard a deep voice say, speaking slowly, "These ogon should not have come here to do their evil! This was once a place of peace, and so it shall remain."

Veronica ran to Fredrick. He held her close to him around her waist, holding out his sword toward the new voice. Emerging from the darkness, he saw an ancient weeping willow approaching. His long dangling branches hung like a giant green cloak. The tree loomed over them. Around it flickered the golden lights of thousands of tiny lightening-flies.

"Who are you? Why are you helping us?" asked Fredrick, his mind racing with the rush of the battle and fear for his friends.

"I am Weep. Lahn sent word through the forest

that these ogon were coming here to disturb this place. The Green-mens do not wish to meddle in the affairs of ogon and men, but we resent them coming here and feared they would murder you. Lahn had said that you were friends to the Green-mens east of the gorge. He crossed the bridge to get word to us that you were—"

"Invader!" shouted a sinister voice, interrupting the still speaking willow.

The Green-Men had scattered the ogon, chasing them throughout the fort and into the forest, but one remained.

"Will you protect Veronica and my wounded friend, Weep? Gnash is mine; I must tend to him myself," he said, stepping forward to face his enemy.

Weep remained silent, but took his canopy and placed it around Veronica and Lamar.

"Yours am I?" said Gnash with a baleful laugh. "We shall see. Who are you to hold Ghronn? To bring *your* justice to *my* people? Andrej learned what it means to face me, and now you will."

It occurred to him that amid the struggle, Andrej had stayed back to fight Gnash to cover their escape. Now he feared for him, not knowing his fate.

"Little One," continued Gnash, turning his ugly gaze to Veronica. "Just when we were becoming friends, you and I. How very rude of your manling to snatch you a way like this. It is bold. I never thought he had it in him."

Veronica remained silent.

"See to Lamar," said Fredrick as the two enemies walked toward each other plying their weapons. With no hesitation, the combat began. Gnash, swinging wildly with his cleaver shaped sword, pushed Fredrick back a few paces as they dueled. Fredrick handled the incoming attacks despite his modest injury, waiting for his opportunity to answer.

In a circle, the two continued their mortal dance. Knowing he had one loaded pistol left, he fought hard, patiently waiting for the opportunity to draw it, and rid the forest of this thief and murderer.

Glancing over Gnash's shoulder, he noticed Lamar was now standing, leaning against Veronica and wincing in pain. Her eyes were wide with concern as she held open the dangling limbs of the willow so she could see clearly. There was still no sign of Andrej.

Both combatants were still trying to gain the upper hand as they both swung their blades at each other, blocking, counter-attacking, and dodging.

In his ferocity, Gnash charged again, but this time he was off balance, and Fredrick knew it. He lowered his body and took Mak'Nabb at the knees, tripping him. The ogon flew forward, landing heavily on his chest a few paces in front of Veronica.

Fearing for her, Lamar drew his knife, placing himself between Veronica and Gnash despite being drenched in sweat, blood and pain.

As Gnash regained his lost footing, Fredrick drew his pistol! In one deft motion, he pulled back the hammer with this thumb. He leveled the barrel a foot from Gnash's face, putting his finger on the trigger to pull it and end the combat and his enemy once and for all.

But suddenly, he heard Veronica shouting.

"Stop, Fredrick! Stop!" she cried, pushing past Lamar and holding out her hands.

Her voice, in that instant, distracted the Young Baron. He looked toward her, and hesitated.

Gnash jumped up! Knocking the pistol aside, he caused it to fire harmlessly into the night. He tackled Fredrick, drawing his own cruel knife and holding Fredrick's head down with the point of his blade beneath his chin.

Fredrick cursed himself. Disappointment plagued him at having come so close to killing his enemy, only to die at the hands of this fiend.

"Gnash! Stop! Both of you please...please..." Veronica pleaded as Lamar held her back from running forward to them.

Mak'Nabb looked away toward Veronica, then returned his frightful gaze to Fredrick. His eyes blazed with a golden rage. Fredrick could feel the tip of the knife biting into his flesh. He was one short upward thrust away from death, and both he and Mak'Nabb knew it.

"This isn't over, manling!" Gnash said, pushing his face so close to Fredrick's that he could feel the heat of his enemy's vile breath wafting against his flesh. "Remember what has happened here. I spared your woman from death, and from the lust of my ogon! I killed my own in her protection! Free Ghronn! Do you hear me? You have back your woman, give me back my brother and this all shall end!"

With that, he released Fredrick and ran, disappearing into the darkness.

Fredrick stood taking Veronica into his arms. He saw several waboars, released in a group, dashing throughout the fort with the other scattered enemies as the trees continued to wander about finishing them off.

As Fredrick held Veronica trying to comfort her, he saw one last ogon stumble out of the dome. He could barely stand, stumbling in his drunkenness. Seeing the surrounding chaos, he drew himself up, and staggered away from the chaos.

The Young Baron turned to follow and finish him, but Veronica pulled Fredrick close. "No," she said. "Stay with me, Fredrick, I need you. Sajj will wait for another time. Leave him be."

Lamar collapsed next to the two of them, and Veronica sat down breathing heavily.

Fredrick sat Lamar up, and leaned him on his shoulder for support, "You will be okay," he said. "We will get you back to the castle. Gavyn will patch you up. Rest yourself."

"Weep," said Fredrick looking up to the towering tree, "The Raddlif family thanks you and the Green-Men of this wood. We stand in your debt."

"Then take your friends and return to your home. Those who come here must come in peace, or they will face us as you have seen!" responded Weep.

"I must find my friend, when I do we shall leave you, but you have my word the Raddlif house will always respect the Green-Men of the

Splinterwood. I shall thank Lahn when next I see him; we are in his debt as well."

With a moan, and what Fredrick thought to be a bow, Weep returned to his place near the front of the dome. One by one, the trees planted themselves back where they started as peacefully as if they had never moved, swaying in the gentle night breeze.

Sore and despondent, Fredrick looked for his friend. He found him behind the dome near the breach in the wall through which he had passed earlier. Andrej did not move as he approached, and it sent a chill down Fredrick's spine. He turned him over to see the ghastly wound where Gnash Mak'Nabb had cut him.

Grief for Andrej and hatred for Gnash gripped his heart. Against Andrej's forehead, Fredrick placed his own. He cried. The emotions of not only the death of his friends, but the entire ordeal overflowed. His Captain and mentor, Rostov, Dead. And what of Olan? Not knowing his fate felt like and open wound in Fredrick's core. The rush of the fight, and the low now that it was over, was too much to bear. Alone in the darkness he wept, thankful that no one could see him except the trees who had saved them, hoping in his pride they would never tell of his moment of weakness.

***

Veronica cradled Lamar in her arms sitting with the giant Green-Man looking down on the two of them. She could see the open gate to the fort in the dimly lit night. To her surprise, Gnash appeared, riding on his beast and stopping in the threshold of the gate before making his escape. His boar moved in a nervous circle underneath him as he stared at her across the distance with a stony, expressionless bearing. After a moment, he spurred the waboar. With a leap, it bolted to a run, disappearing into the Splinterwood.

I'm not frightened of him anymore, she thought as she watched him ride away. *How strange is this whole affair?*

She found it difficult to make sense of the bizarre swirl of emotions she held for Mak'Nabb. He was her captor and Amma's murderer, but also her guardian.

If he killed Fredrick, would I be his fiancée now and not Fredrick's? Would he have given me a choice?

As Fredrick appeared from the darkness she set her contemplations aside. His eyes were red and puffy. He had been crying, but she left it there and did not mention it. Her heart went out to him, but she stayed silent as he rejoined them.

"Andrej? Where is Andrej?" wheezed Lamar through his pain.

Crestfallen, Fredrick answered simply, "He is dead."

Lamar did not reply. He laid with his head in Veronica's lap and grieved at the news.

"Weep," said Fredrick, "I heard what you said, but may we stay here overnight? We will tend to our wounded friend, and leave for home at first light."

174

"We know the ogon misbehave. We did not like them taking the female against her will. You may stay. Stay in peace."

Veronica and Fredrick helped Lamar through the great door into the dome and laid him near the fountain. She tore a piece of cloth from her ruined gown and wet it, squeezing the cool water into Lamar's mouth to quench his thirst. Afterward, she laid the cloth on his head to relax and cool him.

As she attended to Lamar's wound, Fredrick worked sullenly. He stacked what bodies of his enemies he could find. Afterward, he placed Andrej into one of the intact ancient buildings in the fort using the tunics of his felled foes as a shroud, arranging their weapons below his feet. Then he closed the door, sealing it and leaving his friend in his eternal rest. When he returned to the dome, he remained silent for a long and uncomfortable time. She tried to give him his space, but with each passing moment the weight of his silence grew heavier and heavier until she felt compelled to comfort him.

"I'm sorry about your friend," she said meekly, trying to break the burdensome silence.

"His name was Andrej. He was an honorable man. He shouldn't have fallen to that ogon filth!" he said, cursing Gnash under his breath.

"Why did you stop me?" Fredrick asked suddenly, raising his voice in an angry tone. "That fiend should be dead, and next his accursed brother. He took you and held you hostage, but you defended him! Why?"

"Because, Fredrick..." she responded scared to meet his eyes with hers, "he *defended* me." With that, she told him the tale of her ordeal with the ogon. How Gnash stopped his gang from attacking her and slowly became her shield. As she recounted it, she came to feel her story was more of a confession.

She could see that Fredrick was as torn emotionally as she was as he listened quietly to her words. Gnash as her protector, surprised them both, and neither knew exactly what to make of such an inconsistency.

Exhausted, the three of them expired in the dim light of the remaining torches inside the sundered dome. All of them were grateful for the trees outside standing guard. Huddled closely, they finally slept easily.

Chapter 5

*A new continent does not change the fact that the
Blackcrowe family rules those from the land of Annan.
Nothing has changed, except the land we live on.*

-From a letter to his supporters by Cyrus Blackcrowe;
Emperor in Southgate

Veronica awoke to find Fredrick gone, leaving
her with an anxious feeling. Lamar laid wheezing on
his back with his head on a rolled-up tunic as a
makeshift pillow. The morning was cold, and she
hugged her own shoulders, rubbing them to warm
herself against the bite of the chill.

Tending to Lamar, she wished that she had a
blanket with which to cover him fully. His breathing
was regular, but he was in great pain, shivering against
the brisk morning air.

She sat on the edge of the central fountain and
drank some water. Afterward she washed her face,
drying it with the skirt of her ruined gown.

Leaving Lamar to rest, she walked out the
entryway to the fresh morning air. Looking to the
north, over the tops of the jagged trees, loomed
ominous black clouds. A storm was brewing, and she
hoped that it was not making its way south toward
them.

A pang of fear shot through her mind when she
stepped outside and still did not see Fredrick. She
continued to search the area, finding only the old
willow standing in its place. She watched him,
remembering that these trees were unlike any she had

ever seen before.

"The young man searches for the beasts you ride," said a deep voice.

Veronica smiled as she approached the massive tree, looking up to his towering height. "Thank you. I should have known that Fredrick wouldn't leave me alone."

"No," responded the Green-Man. "He has not. He asked me to look after you."

"Weep," she said timidly, "In my homelands, I have never seen a tree who can talk. What are you?"

"What Am I?" he repeated, seeming both surprised and perplexed by the question. "I'm a Green-Man, as are all of my kind. It is not common that men should see us. We prefer to not have much to do with them or ogon, unless they try to chop us down, which makes us angry."

"Are all the trees in the Splinterwood like you? Are they all Green-Men?"

"Oh no, most of the trees of the woods are just trees. Some of the elders have a voice, though their conversations can be a terrible bore. The firs and digger-pines outside the walls need to shout for us to hear them. That brings me sadness. Many things make me gloomy, which is why my branches sag. These ogon made me sad with their mischief, as did your young companion weeping for his fallen friend when he laid him to rest."

He parted the canopy with four of his large boughs like a giant drape to reveal the face hidden behind. His mouth sat crookedly across the higher part of the trunk. His uneven eyes were positioned just above his jagged mouth. To Veronica, they looked like two small wooden cat's eyes as they regarded her. He had many limbs serving him as arms. As he spoke, his top feeding web of roots pulsed and shifted but never left the ground, fixed to his favorite spot, and speaking to her in a matter-of-fact manner.

"What is this place?" she asked.

"When I was a sprout this place was as you see. I grew, but it never changed, only the green stalks clinging to the walls grew larger. There was no one here when I was a sapling, and there will be no one here when I am a stump, and that makes me sad too. Those who built it left long ago. A few trees here remember them. Those few tell stories of how the people would come here and stay for a while, then leave again. One time they left, and they never came back. It is said that they just vanished, and all that remained was their footprints."

"Who were they?" she asked. "Were they men?"

"They were, but they were not like you," answered Weep. "They did not have weapons and did not hunt the animals of the wild for food and sport, or prey upon each other. They brought beasts with them that they raised, and tended gardens within these walls long lost. They looked to the sky with upraised hands, and spoke to it, praising a being who lives there above all else."

"Did they look like the people that are painted on the walls inside?"

"Quite so," Weep explained. "At least that is what the elder trees have told me. I never saw one, and fir trees are prone to exaggerate. Like I said, they can be boring at times, and they know it, so they often embellish their involvement. And you must never listen to the birch trees if they speak; they lie, and will deceive you."

"I'll try to remember that," said Veronica, surprised at Weep's sudden and unexpected revelation about the honesty of birch-trees and wondered if she would ever speak with one.

Excusing herself politely, or at least as politely as she felt she could be to a tree, Veronica wandered back inside and examined the murals under the daylight. It was then she noticed, though it should have been obvious, there were no weapons found among the people in the painting. Those who were not engaged in an activity looked to the light at the top of the dome. Some had raised hands; still others covered their hearts, laying hands on the shoulder of others in a welcoming gesture. The serenity of the mural appealed to her. She envied the people, and the singular purpose that existed between them. To love, and help one another. Curiosity as to their fate burned in her mind. Somehow she knew that whatever happened to them, or wherever they went, they found happiness.

Growing louder from outside, Veronica heard hoofbeats drawing near. She stepped out to find Fredrick riding in, but he had only one horse.

"I could only find Lady, I'm afraid," he said as he flung his leg over the top and dismounted.

"Hopefully the others will find their way back to the castle in time, if they are unharmed. I found Andrej's waboar, but those beasts have only one rider and he was looking for him. They are wild creatures. With Andrej not coming to claim him, I feared he would attack me."

Veronica was glad to see him as he held the bridle of the horse and approached. In the light of the day, she noticed the changes in his face. His beard had grown, and he looked tired. His expression was sullen, lacking the boyish enthusiasm he showed to her at the castle those few nights ago before and during the feast.

"When I woke and you were not here I was afraid for you," she said as the two embraced in front of Weep.

"Not to worry. You had plenty of protection. The road will be long with only one mount. We must get Lamar and ride straight away. Scouts will be out looking for us and we must leave here. There is a storm brewing. If the rain finds us first we will not be found, and must travel all the way on our own."

The mention of search parties comforted Veronica. She thought about her father. His shouts of pain, and the sight of him struggling on the end of a spear were seared into her mind.

"Fredrick," she began in a tone of deep concern, "what happened to father? Did the ogon kill him? I remember seeing him fighting, and speared through the leg. I heard his voice cry out..." She looked away as she started to tremble, unable to finish.

The Young Baron turned her face to his. "I

don't know, and I'm as worried as you. He insisted I come after you right away. The thought of him dying alone in that meadow will haunt me forever, if that has happened, but we need to get back and find out. Count Olan is a strong man. He would not have given up."

Fredrick and Veronica entered the dome to find Lamar rousing from sleep. He was in pain, but was still in a good humor. They refreshed themselves with the water from the fountain, and ate berries foraged while searching for the horses earlier in the morning, but they were bitter, and did little to ease their hunger.

Together they helped Lamar onto Lady, and Veronica rode with him.

After saying their goodbyes to Weep, the three began the journey back to the castle.

It impressed Veronica how easily Fredrick could find trails Lady could travel so Lamar would not have to dismount and walk, wounded as he was. The trip was made longer by going around the Long-Ridge Fredrick climbed on the ride to the fort due to Lamar's condition.

On and on, they trudged through the forest with Fredrick guiding the horse by the reins. Not hooded and in much more pleasant company, she viewed the animals and birds as they traveled. Large cats and skittish rodents would dash into the cover of the bush. One of the cats, one the color of buttery cream, painted with striped legs and proud peaks of fur off its tall ears, dashed up the trunk of a tree. It crouched on a branch, well out of reach, watching them curiously.

"There are so many animals, Fredrick. They seem like they are everywhere."

"We have been lucky so far."

"Lucky?" she asked, frowning in curiosity.

"We have seen no bears, or wolves. The Splinterwood Kodiak is the most dangerous. Most of the time they stay further north, but occasionally wander as far as the gorge. Sometimes, though rarely, one will cross the bridge. The last time that happened, it killed several townes-people before we found it. Even then it escaped us. We believe it went back north. If we see one of them, we must be careful."

"Careful indeed," wheezed Lamar, not sounding at all well to Veronica. "The bears are dangerous, but a thrilling hunt."

The storm followed them like an unwelcome guest through the day as they travelled. Fredrick pushed the group ahead, and though they had only one horse, they made good time.

As evening fell over the woods, exhaustion took hold of Veronica and her companions from the long ride. Her concern for Lamar grew as he leaned heavier and heavier against her back. She felt the heat of his body increasing, and was certain he was feverish.

"We must stop soon. It is getting dark."

"It would be best if we make it to the bridge," said Fredrick. "If Father has not crossed yet, or returns to the castle by night, he must go that way and will find us. We will be there soon."

After a time, the three emerged from the forest

and before them, loomed the mighty gorge. Veronica could see no bridge, only the sheer edge of the cliff, and its drop into the mist shrouded nothingness below. Fredrick handed over the reins. He gestured with this hand to stay put, saying nothing. She noticed his odd, muddled expression, and he stepped to the ledge. She smelled the moisture in the air. Thunder rolled as the storm slowly broke over them.

As Fredrick stood near the gorge, a stone of fear sat in her belly. The cliff was sheer, and visions of him falling, or the ground giving way beneath him, filled her anxious imagination. He turned his head looking left and right, peering into the fading evening light appearing deep in thought. He then turned and walked back, taking Lady by the bridle.

"This way," said Fredrick.

"Are we lost?" she asked.

Fredrick halted, looking at her as if she insulted him using some obscenity or epithet. He glared at her, his brow furled with one eyebrow higher than the other. Finally, after a brief time, he said simply, "No."

It was obvious she angered him. Contritely, Veronica sat back in the saddle staying quiet. Ahead of her, as a cold wind overtook them from the intensifying storm, the bridge appeared through the gathering darkness. As they neared it, Veronica heard a voice speaking out to them from the edge of the clearing near the bridge.

"Hullo, Fredrick," said the voice, "you have returned, and you found your female." He then addressed Veronica. "I'm pleased to see you unhurt. I know your friend died here, and for that I'm sorry. She rests at the top of my branches where she is protected."

Tears dimmed her eyes. Fredrick watched, leaning one foot on a stone. He took off his hat, and wiped the sweat from his forehead with the back of his arm.

Her mind drifted away as she struggled with the sadness in her heart at the mention of Amma. The memory was much to bear, especially in the light of the tangled feelings that had grown for Gnash during her ride with him.

"Are you well," asked Lahn.

She turned away, subtly wiping the moisture from her eyes. "Yes, I'm fine. Veronica, my name is Veronica."

"And a lovely name it is. My name is Lahn. Would you like to see where she rests? I could show you."

Veronica fought mightily to hide her growing emotions. She sniffed as her nose dripped, and she breathed in deeply to gain a voice she struggled to find. "Yes. I would like to see her."

Lahn's wooden lips formed a smile as he reached forward taking Veronica around the waist. She rested her hands on his branches as he lifted her off the horse as easily as a mother lifts her infant baby. Up and up she flew toward the gray shrouded sky. He held her at the top of his canopy in the last of the dim light. At first, she was afraid of what she would find. She did not know if she could bear to look again at the grievous wound that ended Amma's life. She closed her eyes as she rode in Lahn's hands. Then, she drew herself up and looked to her servant and friend's resting place. The branches parted, giving way to the tree's interior. Amma's shrouded body rose to meet her in its cocoon of wood and living leaves. The view from this lofty height was breathtaking, even with the blurriness of vision through her tear-soaked eyes and waning daylight. It made her happy that her friend rested surrounded by such beauty.

"I will protect her as long as I live. On this, you have the word of Lahn, a Green-Man of the Splinterwood."

A booming crash of thunder was all it took to shatter Veronica's veneer of bravery. Dropping her chin to her chest, covering her face with her hands, her emotions overflowed. She cried, sobbing so hard her ribs ached, leaving her struggling for breath and helpless in the branches of the Green-Man.

"Keep...me...here..." struggled Veronica, speaking between gasps. She did not want Fredrick to witness her moment of weakness.

Following the rolling thunderbolt, the sky released its growing anger in a sudden deluge. Veronica was soon soaked, and though she was cold, she found herself happy to be drenched in rainwater that hid the tears streaming from her eyes.

How can I feel this way? she thought, as she struggled against the heavy burden in her heart. *Gnash protected me. He cared for me, but he did this. He put Amma here, but he has said he regrets it. That must count for something, Doesn't it?*

Weak against the clamoring of the storm, she heard Fredrick calling out from below.

"Are you all right?"

His voice strengthened her and drew her thoughts back to him, away from her abductor. She composed herself and dried her face as best she could with wet hands. She looked up to the sky, into the swirl of black clouds overhead, grunting as if she pulled her heavy heart back to her at the end of a great rope.

"Yes, I'm fine. Lahn, thank you, you can put me down."

Gently, as if she were a beloved pet, the Green-Man returned her to the ground. Fredrick smiled, saying nothing as Veronica ran past him, throwing her arms around Lahn.

The tree laughed in his deep voice as she embraced him, and he patted her on the back with shortened, leaf-covered limbs.

"Take this, it will be a keep sake for you to remember me by," said Lahn, extracting the woodsmen's axe imbedded in his leg and presenting it to her. "It is a strange gift, but I have little to give."

She took it and laid her flattened palm against Lahn's wooden lip in a silent display of gratitude.

Fredrick helped Lamar off the horse and tied Lady to a low branch of Lahn's. He made a soft dry spot for him to lay in his sickness and Veronica could see the growing concern in him for his friend.

"You crossed the bridge," said Fredrick. "How are your roots?"

"The ache is terrible, and I doubt I shall cross again," said Lahn. "I'm glad it was not in vain. I would have sent my birds to carry the message, but they are stupid."

Veronica put a hand to her mouth and giggled at the comment.

"It is a long way," Lahn continued, "and they forget things. The trees whispered it one by one across the woods until the last one finally shouted my message over the walls so Weep could hear the message."

As darkness fully blanketed the forest, Fredrick made up a camp with the few resources they had beneath Lahn's canopy. Lamar, sick with fever, was the only one able to sleep. Veronica and Fredrick could do little else than cling to each other for warmth and comfort to pass the cold and miserable night.

***

The swirling clouds overhead blackened the morning sun as the downpour continued. Restless and impatient, Veronica sat next to Lahn. Lamar snored loudly as he slept. His fever was not improving, and though he wore a smile and as pleasant a disposition as he could muster when awake, both she and Fredrick were concerned for him.

Well into the morning, the three of them waited, but the deluge did not subside, and a party from the castle did not arrive. Occasionally, the rain would lighten, just enough for Veronica to hope the storm was ending, but then with a crash of thunder and a streak of lightning, the rain began anew.

Hunger pressed upon them all. Veronica laid her arms across her growling stomach as she blushed from embarrassment.

"You're hungry," said Fredrick.

"I'll be all-right," Veronica responded proudly, trying to sound brave and strong.

"She's hungry," said Lamar, smiling and clutching at his shoulders against the chill that made him shiver.

"Well, we're already wet," said Fredrick. "I shall find food. Surely this rain must end soon. Weather like this isn't uncommon here, but it has been a while since I have seen it last all-night and into the morning."

Fredrick stood, reaching out to her. "Ever take a walk in the rain?"

At first, she giggled, unsure if he was serious. Timidly, she took his hand and he helped her to her feet.

With a tug, he pulled her out into the still falling deluge. "We shall return shortly, Lamar. If we are going to be wet and miserable, let's not be hungry too," said Fredrick as he walked back through the clearing and into the trees with Veronica in tow.

Once at the tree line, Fredrick released her hand and she followed him down a narrow game trail. Her dress snagged on the low branches as she weaved her way along the trail, following Fredrick who passed through at a slow pace so she could keep up.

"We won't be killing any animals, will we?" asked Veronica. She felt ashamed that she sounded weak to the man who had just fought so hard and bore so much pain to win her freedom. "I'm sorry, I just don't want to hurt anything." Her words stammered as he looked at her with sympathy. As their eyes met, Veronica grew nervous and turned away, looking to the drenched ground.

"I know you are still frightened, cold, and soaked to the bone," said Fredrick putting his hands on her shoulders. "There is much to eat in the woods growing right off the trees and vines. Killing is done for you. What has happened in the past days is something I will always regret, and your captors shall pay for their deeds. But for you, it is our family, and the many children we shall have. Come with me, and we'll refresh ourselves and tend to Lamar. We will find water and food. Tomorrow we should be back at the castle."

Veronica fought to retain her balance as Fredrick led her by the hand down an embankment. The grass was tall. All around were wild flowers alive with color, drooping under the weight of the water they collected. Long fingers of moss grew on the trees. She thought about Weep and Lahn wondering if any other Green-Men were watching them.

"Look here!" Fredrick said as he released her hand and moved at a quickened pace to a large section of a fallen stump. It looked as if it had laid in the same place for a hundred years. The wood was cracked, and saturated. The surrounding grass had climbed up its sides, covering a portion of it. He squatted by the stump and she knelt next to him, watching with curiosity.

"There is no need to worry. Look at this." As he finished he turned over the chunk of old wood. The crawling bugs who made their home beneath the wood went into a mad scramble out into the dim daylight. Veronica leaped up squealing at the sight of the sudden infestation. In her mind, they were all coming for her and she started to run away!

With a burst of laughter, Fredrick caught her around the waist and the two followed each other in a circular movement, as if dancing in the falling rain.

"You don't mind killing bugs, do you?" quipped Fredrick, releasing her and walking back to the overturned shard of aged wood. He picked up one of the scrambling bugs displaying it proudly for Veronica. Crawling along his glove was an emerald green beetle. She stared at the insect as it tried in vain to flee.

Fredrick beamed a bright smile at her from behind his hand with his long rain soaked hair obscuring part of his face.

"You are not? You will not eat it?" she said.

"Oh but I am my proper little Lady. Don't your people eat beetles in the mighty city-state of Trodenheim? Surely you don't fear them?"

Veronica snickered, hiding her mouth behind her hands as she struggled to hold back her rising laughter. She did not believe he would eat it, and she tried to imagine how foul tasting such a creature might be. As her disbelief grew, he caught the insect deftly between his finger and his thumb. His eyes went bright over his wide smile. His eyebrows leaped up and down, as if saying *"watch this!"* without speaking a single word.

He placed the bug into his mouth with a quick snap. She heard it crunch as he chewed it up, and imagined the soft, viscous texture of the insect's innards assailing his tongue.

It must be foul. She thought as she watched him for a reaction.

With a swallow, the beetle was gone. He shook his head against the flavor, then wagged his tongue as if to air it out like it was a wet carpet he was trying to dry quickly. Then, he beamed a proud smile as if he enjoyed the bitter snack.

"I feel much better. Here you go," he said as he took another one out of the mud and held it out in presentation.

"No!" exclaimed Veronica, taking steps back away from the offered morsel.

"But you're hungry. It isn't that bad. It's bitter, but try not to focus on that. I need to toughen you up."

She regarded him as he continued beaming his bright smile at her wryly.

"Well, to be honest these green ones are more than a little bitter. Though I'm sure they are an acquired taste," he said, finishing with a chortle.

"Fredrick, how can you eat bugs?" Veronica asked, still holding her hands over her mouth.

"If you're hungry enough you'll eat anything. We eat them when we are on range sometimes to get used to it. You could live on them if you had to, you know, but it would be a sad existence."

Fredrick returned the beetle to the mud as he answered.

"Not to worry though, the cooks will not be laying a plate of green beetles on the table for our dinners at home."

"Lamar will eat them," he said with a laugh as he approached her. "I'll bring him some in my pockets. For you, we'll find some berries that will be more palatable."

Here and there in the glade, large puddles of clean water had collected. Tasting it for himself each time, Fredrick filled the two skins he brought with him. He handed one to Veronica as she knelt beside him.

"Thank you," she said, smiling before drinking. She did not realize how thirsty she was until that moment the cold water hit her chest, and quenched it.

"What was life like for you back in Trodenheim?" asked Fredrick.

The question took her by surprise. She turned it over in her mind for a moment as she pondered it. She never stopped to think about it before, and an answer alluded her.

"I'm sure it's similar to your life, only much colder," she said. "We never see much in the way of hot weather, but that somehow makes the people warmer to one another. Where you were trained to ride, and use weapons, Elga taught me needlework and proper manners, but she is ill tempered, and grumpy. If Father had his way, he would have dismissed her years ago, but Mother would not let him."

"When you arrived at the castle you were so distant," Fredrick said. "Was there someone back home that you are missing? Another noble-suitor?"

"Oh no. I could not spend time with other noble-boys. From time to time, there would be some at the feasts and gathering at our home in the Icekeep, but Father would make me sit as far from them as possible. It's Donal I miss. I do not wish to live so far from him. Our father's devotion to each other is unbreakable and honor is everything to them both. You know what that means for a Lady here in these lands?"

"Yes," he answered, blushing, "I do. They must be… well they cannot..." Fredrick stammered.

I embarrassed him, thought Veronica as she listened to Fredrick trip over the words, surprised at his reaction to her question.

"They must be virgins," Veronica said boldly, "If they are not, the father of the groom may refuse the wedding. The bride will be disgraced, not the intended groom and his family."

The subject of their conversation brought an awkward silence between them. To break it, Fredrick slapped the water up from the puddle at Veronica with a cheerful grin. It was cold as it hit her and ran down her face and chest. She paused in shock, not knowing what to do, so she splashed water back at him as he sat in the grass laughing at her surprised expression.

Water flew back and forth. Veronica jumped up and ran away. She looked back and found Fredrick with a full water-skin in each hand chasing her. She felt like a child again. As if she was playing in a field back home with the few friends she had at the court in Trodenheim.

She dodged him as he drew near to her and she hid behind a tree just inside the glade. She circled it, keeping the tree between them.

Finally, Veronica intentionally slowed, allowing Fredrick to catch her. She heard the hollow thudding sound of the water skins as they hit the ground and his arms closed around her waist. She turned to him, seeing the cheerful and bright smile had changed to a more serious bearing. His expression was a passionate one, starry-eyed.

As the two locked eyes, each in the arms of the other, they both became lost in the moment. Before either of them could protest, they brought together their lips and found themselves in a sensuous kiss. Veronica's knees weakened beneath her from the passion and spontaneity. Fredrick's arms strengthened around her in support. His firm embrace excited her even more. She found herself breathless, in a mix of surprise and desire. The impulsiveness of the moment left her with a steadily growing craving she had never experienced before.

She put her hands to his face, cradling it as they continued kissing. Slowly each one dropped down, first kneeling, then laying in the rain soaked grass as his hands explored her curves.

Lingering in the back of her mind, she knew that she should protest. She should stop him, and they should return to Lamar, who laid wounded and waiting for them, hungry, and feverish. However, a wave of selfish yearning was running wild through her body.

Fredrick put his hands on her. One hand, working its way up her hip, across her abdomen and took her breast in his strong grip. They spilled from her bodice as Fredrick pulled it down from the front. Still they kissed as if they could not stop, each feeding the other with ever-increasing passion. His hand had worked its way back down, working its way between her thighs. Over her ragged gown at first, then diving beneath it. She felt his warmth cradling her between her legs, feeling the pleasurable sensation that started at her core, and burst outward through the rest of her body.

Any confusion she held melted away in the heat of her desire. *I want him. How can this be? But now? Like this?*

She kissed him, her head moving from side to side in a passionate dance following Fredrick's movements.

She started to hear her father's voice in the recesses of her consciousness.

What would he say? What would Baron Manfred do if she were not pure as the tradition calls? There would be no bloody sheet for her to prove her purity. She no longer cared. She was here as was her Young Baron. She wanted him to make their bodies' one. She never thought it would ever happen, but it did.

She closed her eyes and enjoyed the pleasure

his hand was bringing her. As they kissed she felt his tongue run against her lips. She was shocked at first, but it gave way to excitement, and she responded. She opened her own mouth wider and she felt his tongue against hers driving her nearly mad with growing anticipation of his body entering hers.

Then suddenly, Fredrick cried out loudly! It was a cry of pain, not pleasure and he pulled back sitting up straight, kneeling between her legs. She opened her eyes to find Fredrick's once handsome face distorted into a hideous mask of agony! He cursed as he stood up clutching his right hand with his left.

To Veronica's horror, her eyes focused on the source of his pain. A serpent had coiled about his wrist and hand. Its head was between his thumb and his wrist with its sharp fangs buried in Fredrick's flesh. There the snake held on, pumping its deadly venom into him while tightening its grip on his forearm. It was a large snake, as green as the grass in which the two were laying with a gold underbelly. Running the length of its back were black diamond shapes outlined in the same gold as its underside.

"Fredrick!" she shouted impulsively as she sat up kneeling in the wet grass. The heavy rain mercilessly fell upon them both in huge drops. She covered her mouth with one hand while clutching at her still open bodice with the other, suddenly confused and afraid.

"Stay back!" he commanded, trying to pull the head of the snake from his wrist without success. With his uninjured hand, he took his dagger from its sheath, and cut the serpent away. Veronica saw drops of blood run as the blade bit into Fredrick's own flesh as well as the green snake wrapped tightly around his arm.

He dropped the knife, then removed the remaining head of the snake attached to his wrist. She could see the sharp fangs as they slid from Fredrick's flesh. They looked like sewing needles as he tossed the severed head away into the field.

"Help me back to Lamar," said Fredrick. "Try to be calm. The poison is already weakening me. He will know what to do."

Veronica took Fredrick's arm over her shoulders and held him by the uninjured wrist. His weight was heavy against her as she steered him back to the embankment. He could scarcely stand as the venom took hold of his body. The mists were heavy around the dell, and her mind was clouded with fear. The rain soaked forest all appeared the same. Barely able to lift his hand to point, Fredrick directed her toward the bridge.

They stumbled along the narrow trail as Fredrick's weight grew heavier and her heart sank deeper and deeper into despair. Each step was more difficult than the one before, and the rain, ever the rain, continued to fall upon the two of them.

Soon, she could see through the mist to the edge of the clearing and the bridge beyond looming just outside her field of view. Guiding Fredrick, nearly dragging him now, they emerged from the tree line, and she called out to Lamar.

As she looked to where she left him, what she

saw only added to her despair.

A group of ogon surrounded him. Because of her shouting, the entire group turned, glowering at her. Standing behind the group nearest to Lamar, stood a larger one dressed in a black leather tunic and trousers reinforced with steel rings and a leather skullcap to match, scowling at her as were the rest of the band.

She dropped Fredrick, though she did not mean to. Her heart raced in fear, hammering in her chest. Her mind swirled. She heard a crash of thunder and a bolt of lightning split the sky as the scowling figures approached her hastily. She felt her strength drain through her toes as if it were water through a crack in a basin. Her body began to shake uncontrollably as blackness clouded her eyes. She fell, and laid unconscious on the drenched forest floor next to her betrothed.

Chapter 6

Men of the north! Remember who it is we fight. The Blackfeather lays claim to your land, your children and your wives. Remember that when we fight, and we shall gain victory.

–excerpt from his speech to the Army of the North by Olan Moresten

Manfred watched his friend from behind his heavy wooden desk. He dressed casually before breakfast, wearing a wide collard tunic, and dark trousers. Count Olan stood at the only lancet in the dimly lit solar, looking out to the cool morning outside. He had fallen silent, but knowing him as he did, Manfred suspected he was not finished speaking.

Green velvet drapes hung about the lancet tied back by a length of hemp rope. A rug covered the wooden floor and near the entrance were two heavy satin lined armchairs around a small square table. Behind the Baron in the odd-shaped chamber stood two tall bookshelves reaching to the high ceilings. The shelves contained the remaining books brought with them on the crossing that the Raddlif family made from the old world long ago. A few of them were newly bound and blank. He used them to pen a journal of the continuing history of his family and house.

Olan balanced himself against the wall. He wore a simple long white cotton shirt and loose-fitting pants. Under his arm, he supported himself on a wooden crutch, fashioned for him after his return to the castle.

Baron Manfred concealed a silent concern for his friend's injury, but he knew that Olan was strong. He had been injured before and lived to brag about it, all of them etched into his flesh in the form of his runes. The concern was born out of the ogon's bizarre habits in the care of their weaponry. They often sharpened the blades using exotic stones, and peculiar oils and herbs to foul the edges and poison them. The lingering pain caused Gavyn much apprehension, and he was seeing him often.

Manfred's mood was a mixture of relief and unease since his son's return to the castle. With Fredrick alive but unconscious, the relief he felt was bittersweet, and a small comfort.

Olan turned from the lancet to face Manfred, leaning on his crutch. His red, un-kept long hair hung over his rune marked face, underlining his fiery bearing brought forth by his ire.

"A ransom!" he said sharply, "A ransom! Those beasts kidnapped a member of my family and now you expect me to believe that she is safe here?"

"I will deal harshly with those who took her. She *is* safe here."

Olan limped closer to Fredrick, still seated at his desk. "Who is Ghronn?"

"He is Gnash Mak'Nabb's Brother. I will execute him first, and when I capture Gnash he will swing next to him."

"What did this ogon prisoner do?" asked Olan.

"He is a thief and murderer."

"Then why have you not hanged him already?"

"You do not understand the ogon," said Manfred with a stern calmness. "Veronica has returned and my men will find the villain Gnash. The Shattered-Tooth are one of the few tribes in the Splinterwood who are still hostile to our family. They will be dealt with for their insult."

There was a long silence between the two of them. "Has Veronica told you anything further?"

"No. She hasn't. She has said little since her return and is strangely reluctant to speak on the matter. I believe she feels responsible, though it is not so."

"No, it is not her fault. You have my word that I will find these ogon responsible and their punishment will be swift. I lost someone dear to me in this crime as well. Captain Rostov was my friend and best leader. His death cannot go unpunished."

"These 'Shattered-Tooth', as you call them, are you at war with them?"

"No," answered Manfred.

Olan glared at him.

Manfred knew he was expecting an answer more thorough than he received. Each refused to look away and he could see the doubt in Olan's eyes. The feeling twisted like a knife in his guts. His old friend was examining him, and he could sense it.

"No? Nothing else?" Olan asked at last.

"We are not at war with them. These ogon are savages, nothing more."

"Savage or not, this fiend ambushed us and defeated your guards. He is obviously dangerous. I killed several of them myself before they left me there to die rather than finish me. You have never watched your child carried away in the arms of an enemy. If you do not kill this son-of-a-bitch, I will. Even if I must return with my entire army, and burn this whole forest to the ground."

Manfred remained silent choosing to leave the threat hanging in the air. He could not imagine how Olan would have felt watching these monsters abduct his daughter. He hoped that having said his piece, it would be some small comfort to his friend, and deep down he understood his anger. His concern for Olan was genuine, and his words about bringing justice to the perpetrators of this evil deed sincere. He just needed time to prove it.

The Shattered-Tooth sometimes preyed on the outlying farms and homes near the towne, but even the Baron was surprised at Gnash's boldness in taking a noble hostage. Moreover, there was one lingering thought on his mind. Did he know who Veronica was when he took her, or did mere chance play its part in the event? He would never know that until he captured the villain.

As the two men eyed each other in silence, a knock came at the closed door of the solar. Without waiting for an answer, the door opened and Gavyn Wellbrown entered the room holding a leather-bound tome. He approached the Baron, bowing to them both.

"Count, good morning. My Lord, Fredrick has awakened," he said.

Relief washed over Manfred as he heard the words. "Very good, Gavyn, thank you. We shall see him straight away."

"He is still weak," said Gavyn, uneasily.

"Of course he is, but he is on the mend, isn't he?" responded Manfred.

"My Lord. Fredrick…he…" stammered Gavyn.

"He is awake?" demanded Manfred, trying to make sense of Wellbrown's concerned demeanor and broken sentences.

"Yes he is."

"Then I shall see him. Right away."

"I think we should discuss his condition at length before–"

"Not now!" interrupted the Baron. "I will see Fredrick, save your counsel for later."

He strode from the room with Gavyn in tow. Olan followed, hobbling along on his injured leg. In a row, the three men left the solar, crossing the castle through the main foyer and climbing the steps leading to Fredrick's bed-chamber.

As Manfred made his way to his son's room, his speed increased as he tried to hide his excitement, moving with a prideful strut, leaving Olan behind and limping along painfully.

Not only was the Baron relieved that his son was on the mend, he was eager to speak to him and get what answers he could about a group of ogon bold enough to attack an armed Raddlif riding party.

He entered to see his wife sitting at the side of the bed wiping Fredrick's head with a dampened cloth. He sat propped up against the carved wooden headboard. Across his knees was a long tray with a plate from which he was nibbling at his meal of soft eggs, small bits of bacon and buttered bread with a cup of water.

"Father," he said simply as he regarded him entering the chamber. As Manfred's eyes looked upon his boy, fear filled his heart. His arm was wrapped from fingers to shoulders with a white linen bandage. Fredrick's face was gray and pallor, though his expression was one of fatigued happiness. Dark circles formed beneath his eyes running down to his chin on what were once blushing pink cheeks. The darkness appeared to be leaking into his now bluish lips. Though it looked and sounded like him, there was something different in his boy that he could not place.

"Son, I'm glad to see you awake," said Manfred. He took a position next to Kaery who was sitting on a short stool next to the bed placing his hand lovingly on her back. She wiped Fredrick's forehead with a dampened cloth, cooling him in the stuffy chamber.

Olan and Gavyn followed. Manfred noticed that Gavyn was now helping Olan as they stumbled in, closing the door behind him. The two of them stood at the foot of the bed. Olan was smiling and clearly happy to see Fredrick, but Gavyn's bearing was more serious and fretful.

A bright smile came to Fredrick's ashen face again as he saw the Count enter the room holding onto Gavyn's shoulder. Manfred could see the excitement in his expression. Fredrick tried to sit up, wincing in pain before laying back down again. A sudden unexplainable stitch of jealousy crossed Manfred's mind at his son's reaction to seeing Olan. It bothered him that he appeared more excited to see Olan than he.

"How are you feeling," asked Manfred.

"I feel good but still weak, and my arm hurts. I'm hungry, but I'm told I should not overdo it, lest I get a bellyache," he said looking over to his mother and smiling a thin grin.

Kaery giggled. "If you haven't eaten for a while you must start slowly."

"Good advice," responded the Baron.

"I'm so happy to see you alive, Count. To leave you wounded as I did. I thought for sure you would die there and..." his words tapered off.

As he listened to Fredrick, Manfred realized why he reacted the way he had to Olan and felt better about it.

"Lad, I'm proud of you," Olan responded. "You did what a man should do. You protected our families. I will forever be in debt to your bravery."

The two men fell silent, and Manfred noticed that both became misty eyed, then shook it off proudly, hoping no one noticed.

"Now, you must get well, eh Manfred?" said Olan.

"Quite so," he agreed. "Are you able to answer some questions? I am eager to hear what happened. Veronica has been oddly quiet, refusing to speak of it. She mentioned they intended to hold her for Ghronn's release."

206

"It was a Shattered-Tooth gang with Gnash Mak'Nabb leading them," said Fredrick.

"Is he the one that murdered Amma?" asked Olan, his outburst angering the baron, but he did not look at him, continuing to listen to his son's story.

"Yes. We found her body at the bridge with her throat cut."

"Where did they take Veronica?" asked Manfred.

"Deep into the forest. To the old fort beyond the long ridge."

Fredrick then addressed Olan, "it was the most painful thing I have ever done, leaving you there."

"You could not wait for an injured old man. Never think of it again," demanded Olan.

"But I must, for not only were you injured, but I promised to bury Captain Rostov. What happened to his body?"

Manfred put his hand on Fredrick's forehead and moved his hair away from his eyes. "We buried him there in the meadow. I knew you both loved that place, and it seemed a fitting location for his grave. When you're well, we will return, and we can say good-bye together."

For a long while, Fredrick stayed quiet while he handled the feelings from speaking about his dead Captain and friend.

"I wanted to lay him to rest myself, but you have chosen a good place."

There was another brief silence, then Fredrick continued. "Later, we ran into Andrej."

"Bedrich!" burst Manfred in astonishment. "Good fortune for you there. He is an excellent man in a fight."

"He had already spotted the band and was waiting to see who came for her since she was obviously a captive, but he fell in the resulting struggle. Andrej knew the fort well, leading us to a weakness in the wall that we used to attempt a rescue. But we were discovered. I'm not sure if Gnash defeated him or if he fell to strength of numbers. If it were not for the Green-Men that reside there, the ogon would have surely slain us too. I had Gnash at the end of my pistol, but Veronica protected him and he escaped."

"She did what?" roared Olan angrily.

"She protected him, she pleaded for his life and I–"

"Son," interrupted Manfred holding out his hand to stop him, "why? Why would she do that?"

"Because Father, Gnash protected *her*. Some of his thugs tried to rape her while they camped."

Baroness Kaery gasped at Fredrick's words. The silence in the room was ominous. Both families feared something like this could happen to Veronica while in the hands of her captors, but none of them wanted to think about it, much less speak it aloud. They all knew the savagery of some of the ogon in the Splinterwood, and the mayhem that they could sow.

Manfred glanced at Olan. He could see the anger rising on the face of the Count.

"Did the brutes violate her?" asked Olan, his

usually raucous voice was now only little more than a whisper. "She has made no mention of this."

"No, they did not. Gnash himself stopped them. He fought them off and even killed one of his own to shield her from them, severely wounding a second. He continued protecting her through the rest of the time she was with them. The ordeal has resulted in something very strange and hard to explain between those two."

Fredrick paused before continuing his story. "The next morning we left. Our horses had been scattered so we only had one mount between the three of us. A storm had come, and it rained through the night. We only made the bridge before we could go no further."

There was a suspenseful pause as everyone in the room waited for Fredrick to continue but he remained silent.

"And?" asked Manfred

"I'm sorry Father, I remember little after that," he said, looking away.

"How were you bitten?"

"Bitten?" asked Fredrick, seeming to be puzzled by the question.

Manfred looked across to Gavyn in his confusion.

"Your hand was bitten by a grass-adder," wheezed the apothecary. "You don't remember?"

"No. How did I get back here?"

"I regret to say that our men and scouts did not find you, Fredrick," answered Manfred. "It was Torgk, and a group of his companions, almost dead as it were. He patched you up and brought you back. Did you reach under a rock or something?"

"I'm sorry, what do you mean?" asked Fredrick.

"You were bitten on the hand. What were you doing?"

"I don't remember," he answered.

Manfred studied him. He waited patiently for more of an answer that never came, harboring a lingering suspicion that Fredrick was holding something back.

Kaery sat quietly listening. She spun a wet cloth in the air to chill it, then wiped Fredrick's forehead.

Finally, he said, "Well then. Now is the time for you to get well. People here at the castle are growing impatient. If I must listen to Krell complain about his wife for too many more days, I shall have to invite him on a hunt and lose him in the forest for some peace and quiet." The group laughed, then exited the room.

As the last of the nobles departed, Lamar entered the chamber, smiling brightly with his arm slung about his chest. He too, like the rest of them on the mend, was dressed simply, in a loose-fitting shirt and pants.

"Lamar, good to see you up and around," said Manfred. "Fredrick needs rest, so don't stay too long."

"Yes, Baron, I will say my hello and let Fredrick rest."

The Baron started descending the stairs to his solar when he heard the wheezy voice of Gavyn call out to him. "My Baron, please, we must speak," he said urgently.

"Fine. Follow me to my desk," he answered.

The hustle and bustle of the servants was in full swing as they made their way to the solar in silence. Bertrum Krell was standing in the foyer, along with Reginar Archibald and his wife, among some of the other wedding guests, talking and drinking from silver goblets. As they passed, Krell nodded to Baron Raddlif and he nodded back, not bothering to slow down though he was sure Krell wanted to talk. He was curious as to what was bothering Gavyn and was eager to hear it.

As they entered the solar, Wellbrown closed the door behind them and stood silently at the front of the desk.

"All right, old friend, what is it? What is troubling you?"

"Baron..." stammered Gavyn.

The Old Baron waited, trying to be patient. "Out with it!" he barked at last.

"Master Fredrick, in the effort to keep him alive..."

Manfred sensed his highly emotional state. He was having difficulty with the words he wanted to speak.

"In saving his life the ogon have defiled him. Though I do not feel they did so intentionally, they have cursed Fredrick!"

211

Manfred reeled in disbelief. At first, he thought his old friend and aide was somehow going mad. "What lunacy is this? My son is alive; he was asleep many days but he is alive. His arm is injured. It will heal."

"No, it will not My Lord," cried Gavyn. "It will not heal, not completely. It will heal as long as he holds his full vitality, but he will not, he will fade."

"You were with us when we spoke to him just now. He is awake and alert. He is in pain and his color is pale, but an adder bit him. He is a strong lad! He will recover."

"No. He is awake, and he is alive, but I cannot say for how long, nor will he be dead."

Gavyn paused. They held each other's eyes. The Baron saw the tracks of the old man's tears as they ran down his withered cheeks. "He will be neither. He'll fade until he is between the two, separated from both life and death, the peace of neither will be within his reach. It's his blood sire, I have studied it, I..." His words ended as he choked on them.

Manfred stayed silent, walking to the lancet and looking across to the forest outside. The clearing weather he had seen before was fading and the skies again became dim and dark with the cover of clouds. Anger at the old man was growing in him. The confusion in his mind worsened his ire even more.

"How can a man be neither alive nor dead?" he asked. "What nonsense is this, Gavyn? Are you telling me my son is a night-fiend? One of the Restless? How many years have you been with us that you should come to me with this absurdity?"

He glared at Gavyn, who turned away from Manfred's angry face. He stood staring at the desk in front of him holding his hands together at his waist in a dejected pose.

"The ogon gave Fredrick a potion and cast their incantations on him to save his life from the venom," Gavyn replied. "I do not understand the nature of the incantation, but the potion was concocted of nightsbane, mandrake, and other poisonous reagents. There is no way he could have lived through swallowing it. It should have killed him, just as the snakebite should have. His life-force is unnatural."

"He is strong," retorted Manfred. "You are imagining things."

"I'm not My Lord. Torgk told me what he gave him, and how he treated him. It was blood-magic that I do not fully understand. We must call off the marriage, sire. He has some years before he fades entirely. I know not what a child of their union will suffer, or even *if* the child will be affected by the spell."

"The wedding will go on! There must be a Raddlif heir!" shouted the Baron. His demeanor was angry. He could feel his blood coursing swiftly through his body. His face was hot and red with rage.

"They must not My Lord," insisted Gavyn, his tone pleading. "What of Lady Veronica and her future? We must think of her."

Manfred's heart pounded in his chest. He stormed up to Gavyn raising his hand, striking the old man across the face and dropping him to his knees.

Blood ran from his lip where it split from the force of the blow.

"You will be silent!" barked Manfred. "You will not spread these lies to anyone else. Fredrick is on the mend and will be well soon. You will see to it, as you always have." In his fury, he pointed down at the kneeling old man as if he were scolding and unruly child.

"If you utter any word of this to anyone else, I'll hang you from a tower as an example for those who would betray me!" hissed the Baron.

At hearing the threat, Gavyn folded into a ball and wept.

Manfred hesitated as what had occurred coalesced in his mind. Guilt was cooling his fury as he looked at his long-time apothecary and advisor crying at his feet. In his heart, he wanted to comfort him. He desired to pick up his friend and tell him all will be well, and ask his forgiveness for his anger. But, in his pride, fueled by fear for his son, he set the impulse aside, bearing the guilt instead. He needed answers, and strode from the solar, leaving the old man curled up on the floor alone, weeping in his heartbroken sadness.

***

The bedchamber was stuffy and warm as Fredrick wiped his forehead with a cool cloth. His arm ached in a constant pain, wrapped in a tight and uncomfortable cotton bandage that gathered sweat and itched at him terribly. He wanted to remove them, but was unsure if he should.

214

Manfred, Kaery, Olan, and a strangely silent Gavyn Wellbrown were filing out of the chamber in a row to allow him to rest. As they were leaving, Lamar entered, bowing to the nobles as they greeted him.

"Good to see you up and around lad," said the Baron, patting the Steward on the shoulder. "Fredrick needs rest, so do not stay too long."

Lamar entered and took a seat on the stool next to the bed, smiling brightly. He wore only a long, baggy cotton shirt. A sling of linen bandages held his wounded arm.

"Finally awake. It's good to see you after so long," said Lamar.

"So long? How long was I asleep?"

"It's been three days. No one has told you?"

Fredrick reeled at the news. He was disoriented and could feel that his rest was extended, but he was astonished by the count of days once Lamar disclosed it.

"How are you feeling?" asked Lamar.

"My arm is throbbing and I feel strange," Fredrick answered. "I'm tired, but getting stronger. I hope to be up and 'round soon. How about you, how is the shoulder?"

"I want to take this blasted sling off, but Gavyn has insisted another day or two of it."

A welcome breeze passed through, cooling the suffocating bed-chamber. Fredrick looked out to see the day was becoming dark and gray. He did not see the sun, and found the dismal afternoon growing outside depressing.

"What happened to us? What is this about Torgk?" asked Fredrick.

"Shortly after you and Veronica left for food and water, Torgk and his group crossed and approached me. I told them that you would return, and he offered to escort us back to the castle. Then we heard Veronica scream, and both of you collapsed at the edge of the trail. They carried the two of you to Lahn, and that is when we noticed the bleeding wound on your hand. The ogon talked to each other in their own language. Torgk was trying to organize them. I only picked up a few words, but they were all excited about the bite."

Fredrick listened, feeling both curious and awkward as Lamar went on with the story. A sense of helplessness came over him as he learned he was unconscious with Veronica and his wounded friend surrounded by ogon. Even if they were friendly ones.

"One of the Red-Hand picked you up and carried you to the center of the bridge," Lamar continued. "For an ogon, Torgk seemed rather frantic. He was looking around the area at the weeds and plants, pulling some of them up root and all. He took the flowers wrapped in the linen that you had for Veronica, afterward collecting some implements from his own boar. I think it was a bowl, and a knife. Then he joined the others on the bridge where they had laid you out."

"What did you do?" asked Fredrick, fascinated by the story.

"I could do nothing. They placed Veronica

across my lap, so I was more-or-less stuck, between her and the fever. I felt very weak, and it was awkward because as they laid her down, her bodice and gown fell wide open. I had to pull it back up to cover her and tied her gown back up."

Fredrick's face blushed with embarrassment as Lamar recounted the story.

"Fredrick?" asked Lamar, a sly smile crossing his face.

"Things were getting out of hand with Veronica in the meadow, I'm afraid."

"What would Count Olan say? He would be liable to beat you senseless if he knew that."

"Well, he won't know that unless you tell him, will he? Why the bridge though, I don't understand that?"

"Neither do I," said Lamar. "But the ogon gathered around you, with one staying back with me. I half think he was guarding me that I would not approach. The group were there for a while, chanting in their own language. When they returned, Torgk's arm had a grievous gash running down the inside of his forearm from the elbow to the wrist. They put you in front of him on that savage boar he rides while we rode with this companions. Afterward, we made our way through the storm back to the castle."

Fredrick sat quietly pondering all that he had heard.

"What was it they did to me?" he asked at last.

"I don't know. But you were not dead, and I was happy about that," answered Lamar smiling. "You were in a bad way, Fredrick. Do you remember the snakebite?"

He stopped and played back the event in his mind as he tried to answer the question. He remembered the rain clearly, and entering the small dell with Veronica. He recalled exploring her body in the moments before the entire memory was blurred behind a curtain of searing agony.

"I remember being alone with Veronica in the meadow, but then it's nothing but pain," he answered at last.

"The mere sight of the ogon must have been enough to frighten her to unconsciousness," said Lamar. "It was a grass-adder bite. That certainly should have killed you. Veronica described the serpent to Gavyn when he questioned her about the bite. He has not been the same since your return. He is dour and quiet, spending most of his day pouring over old books, looking in on the two of us, then right back to his research. He has let no one else in your bed-chamber. I believe he is afraid of whatever it was Torgk did."

"Help me to remove this bandage," said Fredrick.

"Do you think that wise? The old man will not be happy about that."

"Just take it off!" demanded Fredrick. Concern had welled up in his mind. An uneasy dread grew in his heart as he learned about what happened during his unconsciousness.

"What have you told my Father about what

happened at the bridge?" asked Fredrick.

"There wasn't much to tell beyond a group of chanting ogon that I couldn't understand. I have seen little of Veronica since we returned. Your father questioned me after he spoke to her. I was surprised at some of the things that he did not know, like Gnash killing Amma. She did not tell him that, and that seemed odd, as if she's holding things back. She is probably just upset though.

"Gavyn had his own questions for me, mostly about Torgk. The Count and Baron Manfred have not had much to say since first questioning me. Their focus has been on Veronica, but she was unconscious while the ogon had you on the bridge, so she really knows nothing about that."

The facts of the time he lost while in the throes of the serpent's venom coalesced in Fredrick's mind. He could not place it, but he knew something was different about himself. Something was wrong.

"Remove the bandage. Don't worry about Gavyn, I'll deal with him if he gets upset."

Starting at his shoulder, Lamar unwrapped the bandages. Fredrick watched in growing fear. His arm was little more than bones, wrapped in a protective linen of living, ashen colored flesh. His skeletal fingers were purple at their tips. Starting at the bite, he could see all his veins lined against the gray flesh of his arm. He could move his arm and fingers, but it was painful to do so.

A knock then came from the door and it started to slowly open.

With a nod of his chin, Fredrick silently commanded Lamar to the door to stop whoever was entering. With his uninjured hand, he pulled the blanket up over his forearm, hiding his injury from the arriving unexpected visitor.

He could hear Lamar exchanging words at the door, but in his haste to cover his arm he did not hear what he said.

"The Servant wants your breakfast tray," announced Lamar.

"Come back later!" commanded Fredrick.

Lamar closed the door and returned to bedside.

"Help me to wrap this back up," said Fredrick. "Keep this to yourself. Say nothing. It would not do for how bad my arm looks to get around."

With great care, they restored the bandages to Fredrick's arm.

"You need to rest, My Lord," he said as he finished. "I'll return later."

The two joined hands as they said their good-bye and Lamar left the chamber, closing the door behind him.

Seeing the ashen colored remnant of his arm, frightened Fredrick. The fear that it would not fully heal, and stay crippled, dogged his mind. He laid back in his bed, putting his good hand to his face, whispering to himself trying to calm his dread stricken heart.

Then, from the balcony across the chamber, he heard a strange but familiar sound. It was coming from outside, and Fredrick questioned how that could be with his bed-chamber on the highest floor of the castle.

He heard the noise again, and his curiosity grew. It was a strange sound, like a word, but a word dropping down from the sky.

His interest overcame the weakness and pain in his body, as well as the worry that gripped his mind. He stood up, feeling the cold wooden planks of the floor beneath his bare feet for the first time in days.

One step at a time, cradling his crippled arm, he stumbled over to the balcony standing in the cool breeze of the morning, looking out to the ash-colored clouds in the distance. There, his eyes focused on a winged figure soaring gracefully over the castle.

Down and down it spiraled until at last landing on the carved wooden handrail of the balcony. A welcome excitement grew in his troubled heart at the sight of the bird.

"Whooo…" said the owl as he regarded Fredrick with his golden eyes.

"Good morning, Grego," said Fredrick happily at seeing the companion of his lost friend.

He reached out with this still good hand, petting the bird on the head, feeling its soft feathers against his fingers, feeling thankful he still had one good hand to experience the smoothness of his new companion.

Grego leaned against Fredrick's hand in acceptance. With a leap, and flap of the wings, he jumped up and perched on Fredrick's shoulder. Once there the bird ruffled his feathers, and shook his head as he relaxed on his new perch.

"Whooo…" cooed the owl.

"Indeed, my friend," said Fredrick. "It is good to see you too."

***

The Baron sat upon his black strider, looking down from a small hill. In the distance, several ogon milled about a central cooking pit containing a raging fire with flames licking the sides of a bronze cauldron. He wore a knee-length leather coat. His trousers were brown against black riding boots. A brimmed brown hat protected his head from the deteriorating weather. He bore no weapon.

He rode slowly and alone, following a narrow trail toward the camp.

Soon he arrived. The ogon eyed him suspiciously as he moved through. Unarmed as he was, they stood aside, parting a small path for him. A tall greeter appeared from behind an orange lean-to among a gathering of tents, standing among the group of on-lookers.

Manfred stopped his horse a respectful distance from the figure as he stood tall in the center of his troop. He recognized him immediately. Torgk Ant'Togin approached, still clad in his ring-mail leather raiment. The two of them held each other's gaze for a long moment in silence.

He was uneasy among the group of scowling ogon. His familiarity with the Red-Hands mattered little to ease his discomfort.

"Baron," said Torgk at last, speaking through his thick accent and stubbornly refusing to bow as he greeted him. "What is it brings you down from the castle? I trust Fredrick is on the mend."

"That is what I'm here to discuss, Torgk," responded Raddlif. "Where is Rak? Is he at camp?"

"He is."

"I would speak to the two of you. Alone," said Manfred in a haughty tone.

The tenor of the visitor's speech caused the others standing near to Torgk to begin muttering to one another. Baron Manfred realized that he was terser than necessary, but he did not care. He was still carrying around the anger, fear and concern that plagued him after his conversation with Gavyn before leaving the castle.

A cynical smile came to Torgk's face as he put his hands out, gesturing to quiet the group of on-lookers. He spoke a few words in their language and they broke up, returning to their business around the camp.

"Raddlif, friend to Red-Hand, I will take you to Gan'Sann. Though I warn you, he is tired. Sometimes he sits alone, drinking black-beer. After a time, it turns his mood foul. I suggest you mind your tongue."

Saying nothing, he swung his leg around and dismounted. Torgk motioned, and an ogon came and took the reins of the horse. Manfred followed around the central fire and through the scattered tents and lean-tos to a small isolated area. Next to a huge tree, proud and ancient, sat a single figure in a throne fashioned of wood, bones and skins. He did not look back at them, but it was obvious he sensed them as they approached. He sat staring quietly off into the woods, as if in a trance. For a long moment, he sat motionless, ignoring his guests. Then he regarded them, looking at the Manfred with blood-shot eyes.

"Baron," he greeted, not bothering to stand, "It is a surprise to see you at our camp, but you are welcome all the same."

"I have come to learn what has happened to my son."

"Has happened?" repeated Rak, appearing baffled by the question. "Is the boy not well?"

Torgk frowned in confusion as he stepped up beside the throne and stood next to his Chieftain.

"He is well, Gan'Sann," said Torgk, his arms folded at his chest. He leaned closer and the two spoke in their own tongue. Baron Manfred did not understand the words, but he heard no malice or hostility from either of them. Only an odd confusion revealed itself in their tone and mannerisms as they waved their hands, as if trying to solve a riddle.

Despite the efforts of many, including Gavyn, none of them had fully grasped the languages of the ogon. Each clan had its own dialect, several of them sounding similar, but owning different meanings from innumerable years of clans breaking away or uniting at various times in their long history.

"He is awake and appears to be well," said Manfred, "but our apothecary has expressed concern about what you performed on him to save his life. What did you do, or what did you give him?"

Torgk and Rak regarded each other, then spoke

in a hushed tone again. Manfred felt his temperature rise, as their whispers angered him.

He took a step forward, speaking loudly. "Speak common that we may all understand! What have you done to Fredrick?"

At his sudden outburst, Torgk stepped ahead to meet him, "Careful Newcomer," he said in a menacing tone. "We have honored Fredrick. What we did, is what we do to those few who receive the honor your son has gained, though we rarely wait until someone is near death to give them the rite. But seeing how your son would have died otherwise, I performed the incantation, and honored him."

"What is this rite?" responded Manfred.

"He has been made ceaseless. He is one with the forest. He will not die. Not for many, many ages, or until the Splinterwood itself dies, or I do. Those of us, those in the Red-Hand Clan who bear knowledge judged of value, are hallowed so they may serve through the ages. So that those skills, or the knowledge they possess, will not fade with them. Fredrick is friend to Ogon and Men. He is a friend to the woods as you are. Your son was within minutes of death. Purely by chance, he had forest-orchids in his pack. His friend Lamar explained that he had plucked the flowers to give them to his woman, though that I do not understand since they are dangerous. We find you Newcomers courtship rituals confusing. We took the mandrake that grows off the roots of Lahn the Green-Man and performed the ritual to save him. I gave him the blood required myself. We are brothers now, your son and me. I am proud to have to have him as my blood-brother."

Torgk held out his left arm. Manfred peered at the gash in his flesh. It had been stitched to heal with strands of grass. The cut was long and straight, obviously from a blade, and looked as if it still had many days remaining to heal.

"We have never honored a man so, Baron Manfred," said Rak, pouring a pungent black drink from a flagon into a goblet made of a beast's horn. "You should be proud of your son. He is a brave lad! To have faced Mak'Nabb's group alone was brave beyond measure. Gnash is cunning. I knew his grandfather. His name was Ghnod. He betrayed me, then he and his followers left the Red-Hand. Gnash favors him, he has Ghnod's eyes, and his ferocity. He rides well, as do all his family."

Manfred turned from the two of them and walked a small circle thinking about all he had learned. He knew nothing of what Rak mentioned about defections from the Red-Hand, and at any other time would have been interested to hear more. He began to understand Gavyn's concern. It weakened him, and he felt his knees giving way. The Old Baron reached out and steadied himself against the nearby tree. He stood there a moment leaning against it before drawing himself up.

"He is cursed," said Manfred. "You have cursed him with your bloody evil rituals. He is as Gavyn suggests, he will not live, and he will not die. He will linger between the two."

"A curse, say you? Your son will forever carry the Raddlif name. Is this not the desire of men? Is this not why you have brought the female from the frozen lands far in the north, so that she may produce a son by which to carry it? That is no longer necessary."

"Yes a curse!" shouted Manfred. He held up his head boldly. Anger, disappointment, and resentment beset his mind erupting to the surface as a geyser. "How could you do that to him? How could you do that to my son?"

Rak and Torgk exchanged bewildered glances.

"We do not understand," said Rak, now standing and strutting forward toward the Baron. He frowned and dropped the goblet still filled with drink to the ground. "Do you disrespect this gift we have given your son?"

"Gift?" he answered sarcastically, "He is not one of you. He is a man. You have condemned him! Condemned him to unlife. He is unnatural! If he died, he would have done so with honor. What is he now?"

The two of them stood before each other, both angry and breathing heavily. Manfred, a full head shorter than the ogon Chieftain, stood looking up into his scowling face. "You have doomed him and you call it a gift? You have made him Restless! A Shade! Inhuman! You have made the monster men fear will come for them in the night with the fog."

So quickly Manfred could not avoid it, Rak took him by the throat. Torgk stood still, watching and clenching his fists, leaning forward at the ready. Torgk's bearing was furious, as was the Chief who held him. He choked against the strength of Rak's grip, pulling at the Chieftains forearm futilely trying the break the viselike grasp.

Rak's speech dripped with contempt as he spoke. "The boy has been granted an honor saved for the best of my ogon and you come before me to disrespect it? Is there pain? Is there torment? Of course there is. That is the price of near immortality! Nothing is free! Your son will carry the Raddlif name on for ages and this is how you repay me? By insulting our ways?"

As he finished, the Baron felt the grip around his throat release. He coughed as he caught his breath. He composed himself quickly, and the two stood apart with only inches separating their faces. Manfred could smell the ripe stench of the black-beer riding on his breath against his face.

"Torgk," said Rak at last, calmer than before, "I think it is time we returned to our homes. I do not feel welcome here. There is much to consider. We shall not attend the wedding; upon which we have waited."

Rak turned away from Manfred and seated himself back in his macabre throne.

"Fredrick is still friend to us," said Torgk. "For he has been so honored, and this insult came from you, not the boy. For you nothing, be gone! My Chieftain no longer wishes to see you. Because of our pact he has been merciful, had you been armed, you may not have been so lucky."

Torgk shouted into the crowd and they all

began to run hastily about. One of them brought his black strider to Manfred and handed the reins over to him. He placed his foot into the stirrup and mounted the beast who danced nervously beneath him amid the uproar. With a last unpleasant glance between him and Torgk, he turned the horse and rode back to his castle.

As the camp disappeared behind a hill, Manfred's heart was heavy with an awful sadness. Today, he felt he had lost a friend, as well as his son. He watched as his entire world changed before his very eyes, and a pang of fear ran down his spine. It was the first chill of fear he had felt for many, many years.

***

Veronica sat in a tall, well-padded wooden chair near the hearth in her bed-chamber. She was clad in a long white nightgown, sitting with a piece of fine linen into which she was stitching a pair of horses against a clear blue sky. Her mind wandered as her hands worked at the sewing, pushing the needle through the linen, pulling it tight, and repeating the stitches in a hypnotic rhythm.

Her mother sat nearby in her own matching chair, reading from a book about the history of the Raddlif family, written by Manfred's Great-Grandfather, Fredon.

As Veronica stitched away mindlessly, she reflected over the past few days. Her eyes had opened to Mary's smiling face. She was laying in her bed at the castle, and the confusion that comes with regaining consciousness clouded her mind. She remembered sitting up in a panic as Mary and Elga spoke to her soothingly to calm her suddenly frantic mind. Then Mary recounted the details of their rescue. Ironically, by an ogon hunting party.

Veronica's heart leaped with joy upon finding out her father was alive. Fredrick did not know what had happened to him and did his best not to discuss it over the road back to the castle. When her Father entered the room, limping along on his makeshift crutch, she leaped up and threw her arms around him in her happiness. As she embraced him, and the warmth of his touch met her own, she could finally be sure that she had not lost her Father, and she felt very happy.

Now, it had been a few days since that joyful moment. Fredrick's awakening had taken much of the pressure from the castle, its royalty and guests, but Veronica sensed the subdued atmosphere among the group since her return. The guests not directly involved, spoke in whispers, complaining they were still waiting for the ceremony and wanting to return home.

She had spent her day bouncing back and forth between the courtyard, with its turf and peaceful stone benches among the flowers, and her drafty bed-chamber high in the tower. Mary and she were in the court when they both noticed Baron Manfred come from the castle walking at a quickened pace, mount his horse, then ride away, disappearing beyond the wall.

"Isn't that odd?" asked Mary. "He doesn't have his guards with him. He is riding alone and unarmed. I wonder where he is going."

Veronica was as shocked as everyone else when she first saw Fredrick. His unnatural color concerned everyone, but all anyone would say is, "He was bitten by a grass-adder for tree's sake…" then dismiss it.

Each day since their return, she spent time with Fredrick, but Gavyn never left them alone in the room. The group spoke little, and what was said, was restrained small talk. An awkward atmosphere lingered during their visits, as if each had something that they wanted to say, but could not bring themselves to say it openly.

Later, returning to her room to change her clothes for dinner, she looked out of her lancet as had become her habit each evening. She knew the ogon that had brought them home, whom she had only briefly seen at the reception feast, camped in the woods around the castle. However, tonight she saw the ogon of the Red-Hand had struck their camp, and were moving south, into the forest. The sudden change sparked her curiosity. She could not help but to think how odd it was that they would wait this long for the wedding ceremony only to abruptly leave. It seemed so unexpected to her and she wondered what had changed.

Bored and waiting to become tired enough to sleep, she sat warming herself as she stitched away on her needlepoint.

"Veronica," Mary said at last, "what did you and Fredrick talk about today?"

"We were not together long. He is still tired and weak. Gavyn had just finished changing his bandages before he let the Baroness and me in. He will not let anyone in the chamber when he treats him. He even asked Baroness Raddlif if she could leave him alone with Fredrick. That made her angry. When I arrived at his door she was waiting outside, positively fuming."

"Mothers can be protective. You will find this out soon I hope."

"Where is Father?" Veronica asked.

"Probably playing drinking games somewhere. He has made many friends with the soldiers since his arrival. He gets frustrated with the company of royals. You know your father. He is a simple man in many ways."

As Veronica sat looking at her stitches, seeing how many bad ones she had because of her inattention, she suddenly felt an odd sensation come over her. It was a cold feeling. As if someone was watching her. She looked across to Mary who continued to read her book carelessly next to her. She made a few more stitches, hoping the feeling would pass, but it did not. Her heart raced as her blood ran cold in her veins.

She leaned around the chair looking behind her to the lancet. At first, she saw nothing. Her eyes focused, and she could see two gold jewels, suspended in space, staring back. Slowly, the ugly face into which the eyes were set came into view. She recognized it, and as she did it seemed like some unseen figure shouted his name in her ears.

Gnash! He is here!

The figure startled her, and she jumped up from her chair with a shriek.

"What's the matter, dear?" asked Mary, looking up at her from her book with wide eyes. Her back was to the lancet, where the two jewel-like eyes hovered in the darkness.

Veronica remained quiet as she shook off the sensation of disbelief at what she saw.

How can this be? She pondered as she began holding one hand in the other pretending that she had poked her finger with a needle.

"It is nothing," she lied. "I was careless and I poked my finger."

"Well, it happens," responded Mary, returning to her book.

Veronica stood silent again, holding her hand and looking out toward the lancet. The face was gone but not the feeling.

He is still here.

She could sense his presence.

"Mother, I'm tired. I would like to retire," she said.

"It's early for you. Are you alright? You look like you have just seen a ghost," asked Mary.

"I'm fine. Just tired."

Veronica crossed the chamber and sat on the bed.

"I will have Elga bring you up some warmed milk. It will help you sleep."

"No," said Veronica, trying not to sound

impatient. Her heart was hammering in her chest, but it was excitement not panic. She was confused, and in the blink of an eye, many questions flashed through her mind.

Why am I not crying out for the guards? Why am I lying to mother? Why is he here? Will he take me away again?

Her mind was nearly set aflame, burning with curiosity. She felt a strange tenderness, born of obligation, toward someone who had killed to protect her. It was as if a strong wind had entered her mind and created a tornado of mixed and conflicted emotions.

"I just want to go to sleep and rest," said Veronica, still passively trying to get her mother to leave.

"Alright," answered Mary finally. She stood up holding her book under her shoulder and kissed Veronica on the forehead before striding across the room. With a final warm parting smile, she passed through and closed the door.

Hearing the door shut, she saw the darkened figure moving about outside. Again, the face appeared from the darkness, slithered through the lancet with his large frame and entered the room with Veronica.

"Little One," began Gnash, speaking quietly as he crossed the room toward her, "I'm afraid I did not get to say a proper good-bye, before you were so rudely taken from me." His accent was as heavy as she remembered. Deep and guttural.

Her raging emotions left her speechless,

leaving Veronica responding to the intruder's greeting with only an astonished glare. Her heart pounded heavily, and she felt the arteries in her neck pulsing from her racing blood.

"Surprised to see me?" Gnash continued, grinning a wry smirk. "Well, do not fear. I am not here to finish any jobs, or even take you away again. That would be as you Newcomers say, 'impolite'."

Quieting her mind and stepping up to him, Veronica finally found the strength to speak. "How did you get to the castle grounds?"

"Well it wasn't easy to be sure," responded Gnash. "The Raddlifs have improved at protecting their pathetic walls, but they are never as safe as they think they are. The lone wolf will find a path."

Veronica observed him as he crossed the chamber to the hearth, putting his hands near to the low fire to warm them. He picked up the stitched linen that had fallen to the floor when she jumped from her chair earlier. He looked at it with his golden eyes as the needle swung from the still unused thread.

"Is this how you Newcomers pass their time?" Gnash asked sarcastically, "Stitching string into cloth."

"When I'm bored it gives me something to do," Veronica said, taking another step forward, slowly drawing closer to the intruder. Her fear had passed and was replaced by a forbidden fascination. In the chamber with her stood a creature who had taken on several men, including her father who she thought to be indestructible. When she was rescued, she was relieved to be away from her captor, but wondered if she would see her shield again. Now, here he stood before her; she could smell the stench of him. His presence excited her, she did not understand it, but it did, and she did not bother to deny it to herself.

"Strange," he said, stepping closer.

"Why have you come?" Veronica asked.

"You didn't think I would stay away did you? Your Raddlif lord and his manling still have something that is mine, and I told you, I mean to have it back."

Veronica took another step forward.

She held her head up, her shoulders back. Only Gnash's silhouette was visible against the fire's light as it flooded her eyes.

"You are in my bed-chamber; why do you not take him from the prison if you can get in to the castle?"

"He is deep in their dungeon. Looks like they take fewer chances with him then they do with you. It is dangerous that they do not guard you as closely as they do Ghronn."

Her heart quickened as he approached, stopping only inches away. She looked up at his face. That ugly face, but this time it seemed less so. He took her by the shoulders. She felt the strength in his coarse hands. She closed her eyes, waiting for whatever happened next. She feared how far things could go with the intruder. Behind her closed eyes she saw Fredrick's image, but it was Gnash in her bed-chamber. She was in his power, and it charged every fiber of her womanhood with both fear and exhilaration.

"I bring a message," he said, his breath as warm as she remembered. "Tell your manling to release Ghronn and I will spare him, and everyone here. You, my Little One, will not come to harm no matter what happens, so long as I live. I could have you tonight, I can smell the passion on you. The yearning. But I know your manling would not approve. You tell him that if Ghronn dies, it does not matter whose fault it is. He is responsible. If Ghronn dies I will come back, and I will end *him*! If I cannot end Fredrick, I will end all he holds dear, except for you."

She opened her eyes to see his burning countenance showering down on her like rain.

"Choose what you want to tell him about tonight, Little One, but you tell him."

For another moment, he held her melting body in his stern grasp. That moment felt as if time stopped. She was a different woman now, and she knew it. Her adventure had awakened her, as if she had been asleep when she arrived at this place, and awakened by a frightening nightmare. She was looking up at those eyes, unsure if he would change his mind and take her in those few lingering seconds. Then he turned away, and slithered out the lancet, looking back one last time.

"You tell him!" he said, then he was gone.

She stood motionless, her body still pulsing with excitement. She looked at the fire, then at the needlework on the floor. She smiled. The hammering of her heart slowed as she picked the linen up off the floor. She looked at it one last time, before tossing it into the hearth. As she watched the fire consume it, she realized that this might not be the last she would see of Gnash, and the thought did not frighten her for herself, but scared her greatly for Fredrick.

Veronica's night was long and tortured. As she laid on her side watching the glowing embers of the dying fire, she slipped in and out of a light sleep. Sometimes the sleep brought images of Fredrick's face. Other times, the ugly face of Gnash, but in both dreams, she was happy. When she awakened, the memory of the dream faded before she fell asleep again and the next one came.

As the morning approached, she awakened and laid in bed with her mind racing. She thought about different ways to bring up the subject of Ghronn without attracting too much suspicion as to the presence of the intruder. She deeply feared what could happen if the Old Baron found out that Mak'Nabb had penetrated the castle walls so easily.

As the sun rose and she heard the crowing of the cocks in the towne, it brought with it the usual faces of the servants. Elga entered the room and chose a dress for her, while others brought a flagon of water and cups with a small platter of food.

Hurriedly, she dressed herself. Then, amid the protests of her teacher, she left the room and made her way down to the courtyard where she had been in the previous days before. But today, she had other things to do then smell flowers or wander aimlessly.

Chapter 7

*I was impatient. My native Tharrin conscripts fled and
betrayed me at Blackfeather Pass. I should not have trusted
them. They will be dealt with, as will the Moresten and
Raddlif turncoats, who sowed disaffection among my
subjects.*

–Journal entry of Emperor Cyrus Blackcrowe "the
Blackfeather"

Many days had passed since Fredrick and his
companions returned to the castle. After awakening,
confinement to his stuffy bed-chamber left him
growing impatient until he could stand it no longer.

Gavyn labored over him in an uncharacteristic
silence. His normal jolly air was replaced by a morose
and worried pout. When he asked his old friend if
something was wrong, he would dismiss Fredrick with
a wave of his hand, and remain silent.

Overcome with boredom, and wanting to taste
the fresh morning air, Fredrick stood up, opened his
wardrobe amid the protests of the old Apothecary, and
dressed himself.

With Gavyn close behind, and nagging at him
to return to his bed at once, the Young Baron left the
chamber with a crafty smile, as if he were a
troublesome child, making his way to the foyer, then
out to the bailey to enjoy the morning.

Once outdoors, he found Olan, Mary and
Kaery. To his surprise, Manfred was not with them at
breakfast. The group sat quietly, drinking a hot
sweetened red-wine from small handled cups. There

was a silver flagon on the table with matching platters of assorted fruits and breads.

"I'm sorry, Baroness," pleaded Gavyn. "I have tried to convince Fredrick to return to bed, but he isn't listening."

"He gets that from his father," said Kaery smiling, and then sipping her wine. "You should be taking Gavyn's advice, Freddie, but I'm glad to see you up. I'm sure you must be climbing the walls by now."

"That I 'am," replied Fredrick. He felt weak, but leaving the stifling chamber lifted his spirits. His arm ached, but the pain had lessened since he awakened. It looked to be improving, but it was still gaunt and pale leaving his fingertips a ghastly purple hue. He was careful to wear a loose fitting long-sleeved tunic, and wore a glove to keep it from being seen too closely.

"Bring a chair," said Kaery to no one in particular.

"It's all right, Gavyn. Do you wish to join us?"

"No, My Lady, but thank you," replied the old man, turning away then making his way to the castle with a dejected gait.

"Sit down, lad," said Olan. "You still look pale, but I'm glad to see you up and around. I need to get you married so I can return home to my city, and you can get on the job of making me a grandfather again." As he finished, the Count chuckled, draining his goblet before filling a small plate with fruit.

Fredrick seated himself next to Kaery. She

smiled and patted him on his uninjured hand lovingly as a servant filled the goblet in front of him.

"You and Veronica have been spending time together?" asked Mary.

"Yes," responded Fredrick. "I was hoping to see her this morning. Where is Veronica?"

"She is still in her chambers. She has been preoccupied. She knows you are getting better, and the wedding will be soon. A case of the jitters I think, but she is in a much better place about the marriage then when we arrived at Raddlif. I'm sorry that she treated you the way she did early on, Fredrick. She can be a stubborn girl at times."

"It is forgotten," said Fredrick, sipping the hot wine. "Isn't it odd how things work out? This ordeal has brought us closer together than any of us could have hoped for."

"Did she mention her rather unusual request?" asked Kaery as she peeled a dark red-blood orange.

"Request? I don't understand."

"She approached Manfred and asked for the release of Ghronn Mak'Nabb."

Fredrick's eyes went wide with surprise.

"Release?" he asked, breaking his stunned silence.

"Yes. Quite emphatic about it too," continued Kaery.

Fredrick noticed Count Olan squirming in his chair as his mother recounted the story.

"I'm shocked at her behavior," said Olan. "Her approaching the Baron directly is embarrassing for me, not to mention disappointing. She said nothing of it to anyone before talking to him. I cannot explain it and I've commanded her to stay in her chambers."

He turned over the conversation in his mind, realizing the Countess had failed to mention that Veronica was confined to her room and not simply staying there with the jitters. He was perplexed at the obvious lie from Mary exposed by her husband's frustration.

The sudden request for leniency roused his curiosity. He wondered at her motivations and pondered the strange fascination she had with Gnash he noticed when she told him the story of her days in the clutches of his gang. He could not shake the feeling there was something more to what the two of them shared. They were not friends; they were not enemies. What did that make them? He knew at some point that he would have to confront her about the relationship, but, for now, he needed to bide his time.

"Where is Ghronn now?" asked Fredrick.

"Your Father hanged him and his chain-mate shortly after he learned of Gnash's involvement with Veronica."

"He has already been hanged?" replied Fredrick, astonished by the hasty action of his normally measured father.

"Yes. He was dead before Veronica approached him about a pardon. He decided there was no further use in waiting. Veronica seemed quite troubled when she learned of his death and Manfred has been in a strange mood lately. I have never seen him so angry, or quiet and he will not tell me what is bothering him."

"Good riddance to the ogon scum," said Olan holding up his goblet in salute. "And as for you lad, you should have other things on your mind. We need to get Veronica's mind focused on something else like a husband, and a baby. I hope that cock of yours looks better than the rest of you. You will need it soon."

Kaery giggled, hiding her blushing cheeks behind her hands.

"Olan!" exclaimed Countess Mary in a scolding tone. "You are in the company of the Baroness! Mind your tongue."

Olan regarded Kaery through his bushy eyebrows and beard smiling with upturned eyes.

Fredrick felt his cheeks warming. He was blushing at Olan's comment as well, though the color was hard to see through his pallor complexion. He suspected that the Count enjoyed saying things that would get a reaction out of those around him, and now he was sure of it.

From inside the castle appeared Baron Raddlif walking swiftly. He was dressed in quilted leather armor carrying a wide-brimmed hat and riding crop. Behind him, two guards followed stopping a respectful distance from the group and standing at stiff attention.

"I have business in the forest," said Manfred as he approached the group. "Son, you have come down. Good."

"Good morning, Father," said Fredrick. "Where are you going?" Fredrick could sense the air of urgency surrounding the Baron. He was unarmed, but his guards bore weapons and shields.

"I need to find Gan'Sann."

"Gan'Sann?" asked Kaery. "What for?"

"That is my affair," said Manfred abruptly.

"Is it about him leaving? He may return on his own if you give him time."

"I said it is my affair and I do not wish to speak of it further."

Standing at the edge of the table, Manfred tossed apples off the fruit platter to his waiting guards who caught them and ate. Quietly he gathered food for himself, stuffing some into his tunic while holding an apple between his teeth as he did so.

He stepped back and turned to Fredrick.

"Since you are up I see no further reason for delay," Manfred said in an imposing voice after extracting the apple from his mouth. "I grow impatient and wish to get on with it. Two days. That is what you have. Well or not, you will stand before the apothecary in two days' time and be married."

"Manfred," said Olan. "Why are you taking guards? Let me go with you if you ride to trouble. I will help you."

"No, but thank you, old friend," replied Manfred putting a hand to Olan's shoulder. "I must see Gan'Sann alone."

Olan answered only with silence, but Fredrick could sense the disappointment in his manner.

As Fredrick watched him, Manfred suddenly recognized the concerned expressions etched into everyone's faces.

"Do not be troubled. I shall return," he said with a bearing more somber than usual from his normally proud and lively father. "Enjoy yourselves today, and begin preparations. Soon, we can all get on with our lives."

With that, he turned and strutted away with his guards close at his heels throwing aside the cores of their apples as they marched.

Chapter 8

As I watched you waving good-bye from your carriage on the day you left, the girl I knew was leaving to become a woman. I must get to know you all over again when next we meet.

–from an undelivered letter from Donal Moresten to his sister Veronica

"It is decided," said Mary opening a dark stained wardrobe next to Veronica's bed. "Fredrick is up and around. Baron Manfred saw him and declared the wedding will take place in two days. And lucky you are he did after that absurd request you made of him. We're fortunate he didn't throw us out of the castle and send us back to the Icekeep for that."

Veronica sat in her chair near the cold fireplace flipping through the pages of an old book before her Mother entered. She stayed quiet, and carried on as Mary scrambled around the room collecting clothes and other items, arranging them on the still disheveled bed.

Watching over the top of the book, she saw Mary smile brightly each time she passed.

"I have sent Elga to fetch the castle seam-mistresses. We will get you into your gown and make the final alterations. You look thin since your return. We need to be sure everything is perfect."

Still Veronica sat quiet and unmoving, bored by the book and annoyed by her Mother for disturbing the peace of the early morning.

"What are you doing?" asked Mary, finishing with a smile. "Get up, we have things to do…"

From that moment on, Veronica never experienced a peaceful moment for the rest of the day.

It began with the gown. She climbed into it while surrounded by giggling simply dressed women. Though careful not to, they poked her with needles as they pinched here and pulled there while fitting the garment. She took it off, they would sew on it furiously, then repeat the tedious process.

While she stood on a wooden box with her arms out at her sides, Mary brushed her hair. She arranged it in different ways, each time turning to Elga and asking, "What about this?"

"Dreadful," she responded.

After several attempts met with a snort or a deriding remark Mary slammed the comb on the table and said, "Just go fetch us hot tea you grumpy old crone!"

As she travelled around the castle following various errands, Veronica noticed tables and chairs being arranged in the bailey outside the main foyer on the lawn. At the end of the emerald grass, was a dais of flagstone with tall wooden timbers set with lanterns on both sides. On the dais was a table that a servant was covering with a dark-green lace cloth.

On the stage, the musicians were tuning their instruments. One strummed a thin sounding lute, while another blew a pleasant tune with his flute, playing alongside a melancholy cello.

Fredrick and Veronica met occasionally

through the day as the paths of their preparations crossed. They stopped to talk amid the busy workers. But, before they could say much, the families or servants pulled them away, and set them back on their chores.

The pace of the work was feverish.

In the early evening, Veronica finally returned to her chair to relax. After taking up her book and opening it to read, a knock came at the door, followed by another group of servants invading the chamber. Elga was at the rear, commanding them as if they were a team of dogs pulling her on an invisible sled.

The women swept her up, changed her clothes, and brushed her hair roughly in their haste.

With Veronica ahead of them, they pushed her along the corridors to the dais where Fredrick waited with Lamar. Gavyn stood behind a table while the rest of the families chatted at the foot of the stage.

As she passed by them, she noticed that the Baron was not among the conversing groups, and she found his absence to be odd given his anxious anticipation of the event.

They rehearsed the wedding ceremony in detail. Afterward, the families enjoyed a meal inside the castle's dining hall. With Manfred still absent from the dinner, Olan played host. He spoke at long length about fleeing Annan and the battles in the south to stay free of the boot of the oppressors of the old world. He finished by assuring everyone that nothing shall ever sunder the Raddlif and Moresten families, and the marriage will cement that relationship for all-time.

After the feast Fredrick and Veronica were sealed within their respective chambers with what she learned was called their 'Honor Guard.' It was the guard's job to make sure they both stayed separated before the wedding the next day. In the absence of his father, Lamar assumed the duty of guarding Fredrick. For Veronica, it was Mary and Elga.

As she laid in her bed, nervous but thankful for finally having a moment of peace, she reflected on the rehearsal earlier in the bailey. They ran through it exhaustively, touching on all the different elements of the ritual. Her Father gave a sword to Fredrick, that he was to accept and with which to defend her and his family name. The actual groom's Sword of Protection was not present at the rehearsal. It was a strict tradition that no one would see the weapon until it was presented at the wedding. They would eat two symbolic foods, one bitter and one sweet to represent the different moments in their futures together. Early in the assembly, Gavyn asked if any man dared challenge Fredrick and face the blade given to him by Olan Count of Trodenheim. That moment sent her mind to racing. It unnerved her to think of it, but she pictured Gnash leaping up on the walls and shouting, "I do! I challenge this manling!"

Her thoughts drifted as she laid in the quiet darkness. *When I arrived, I would have welcomed a challenge, or any opportunity to return home. But now? A challenge by a creature regarded as a vicious criminal? Amma's killer. I still cannot go home.* A chill coursed along her spine.

Both Fredrick and Gnash were on her heart, and she could not stop thinking of either of them. She could not explain to herself the feelings she harbored toward Gnash. Her thoughts returned to a statement her father made at the feast after their arrival, 'Love is a choice.' There, alone in the dark, she understood the truth of his words, and what he meant. It was clear a choice was still to be made. These two, man and ogon, fighting over her was exciting. One was handsome the other hideous, but that no longer mattered. Both equally intrigued her. She yearned for attention from them. To one she was betrothed against her will. The other had taken her, also, against her will. She felt as if fate itself used them as instruments to deprive her of the choice of which Olan had spoken, and set her on a course to an unknown future when all that she craved was to return to her home.

She dreamed once of riding out to find Gnash, but wandering the forest alone frightened her. She was shocked by his call in the night, but after he left, she hoped he would appear again in the lancet of the safety of her chamber.

And what of Fredrick? He could have retreated to the castle leaving her in the hands of the villains while calling on the Baron to return with a retinue of men to bargain for her, but he did not. He came alone. Risking his own life, and that of his friends who followed him faithfully. He protected her from Gnash, and Gnash shielded her from his ogon. Both killed in their efforts on her behalf. For Gnash, it was his own people, not his enemies. Now she found both this man, and this monster, inextricably woven together in her heart by an uncanny twist of fate. It became hard for her to separate the differences between them. She cared for them both, wishing that she could see them as friends, rather than bitter enemies. That some manner of peace between them could be found before Mak'Nabb could make good on his threats of revenge. It was that wish that gave her the courage to seek the audience with Baron Manfred that landed her in so much trouble with her own family. She promised herself she would find a way to protect both.

Eventually she drifted off to sleep with the faces of Fredrick and Gnash burned against her closed eyes.

***

The hours leading up to the wedding were no less chaotic than those of the day before. Veronica had spent the past hours in front of a bronze mirror with a team of servants dressing and preparing her for the ceremony.

Presently, she stood alone in the chamber looking at her own blurred reflection on a bronze mirror. She disliked her gown. Gray with an inset of crimson with trumpeted sleeves and a long bell skirt that drug along the floor behind. Her vail hung over her like a canopy, dropping to her waist. Her blurred reflection was oddly symbolic of the thoughts she had as she drifted into sleep the night before. She could see her future no clearer then she could see herself.

The weather outside was threatening and the sun's light was dim through the gathering clouds.

Away in the distance, she could hear rolling thunder. A smell of moisture danced on the passing breeze.

The door flung open and Mary swept into the room with her entourage of servants in tow. They escorted her to the foyer of the castle.

Once there, Olan waited smiling brightly in his pride as she approached. He was dressed in a black leather down coat with matching trousers and boots. Across his chest he wore a wide, gold trimmed crimson sash. A sword with a crimson grip hung from his belt. His hair and beard was as neatly combed as she had ever seen it. In his eyes, she could see tears glistening. He turned away, discreetly wiping the tears on the back of his hand and laughed as he did so. Then he extended his arm, and Veronica placed her arm through his. Together, the two marched to the bailey through the open doors.

The other guests were smiling as she marched by them slowly. On either side of the flagstone dais below Gavyn, stood both families of the bride and groom.

To the right Mary Moresten, dressed in a white gown, waited to be joined by her husband. Her hair was tied up into braids, and at her waist was a crimson sash that matched her husband's.

To the left stood the Baron and Baroness. As was tradition, Kaery Raddlif also wore a white gown with a brooch in the shape of a pine tree encrusted in emeralds that shined even in the dim light of the overcast day. Manfred stood behind his wife. As she glanced at him, she noticed his morose bearing. His appearance was unkempt. A coarse stubble remained on his face, and his raiment appeared as if he had recently returned from a hunt. Against the others, he appeared to be unusually under-dressed.

Standing on the dais, smiling and handsome, Fredrick watched as she approached standing with his arms stiffly at his sides. Though he was smiling, and clearly happy, Veronica noticed his drawn and pale face. Black circles still clouded his bright eyes. He pushed his long and oiled hair straight back on his head. He wore a green vest that hung to his knees held together by a silver clasp in the shape of a pine tree at his belly. Under the vest, he wore a thick tan cotton tunic with a wide collar and long baggy sleeves. His breeches were black, bulging at the sides of his knees, and tucked into a pair of polished riding boots bearing shining steel spurs at his heels, and buckles at the ankles. Leather riding gauntlets covered his hands, and hanging from his belt there was a scabbard that bore no sword.

A bird rode on his shoulder. It was a brown-flecked white owl, and she slowly realized she had seen it once before. In the dome at the fort. The bird viewed her as she and her Father approached, then he flapped his wings, flew up into the air and landed at the top of the timber post nearest to Fredrick. From his perch, the owl watched with interest. His head flicked about, drinking in the faces of the other guests.

Lamar stood as best-man dressed in colors to match. Over the top of his matching garb, the Steward bore his orange striped sash of station.

At the end of the dais, Olan stopped then spoke loudly, presenting the sword to Fredrick. He asked if he would accept it and with it defend their families and their honor. Fredrick accepted it without hesitation.

Count Olan limped up onto the dais and she knew that he must be enduring significant pain in doing so. She tried to convince him to use his crutch, but he was much too proud a man to walk with a stick while being watched by the likes of Bertrum Krell. He presented the sword to Fredrick who placed it into the empty scabbard at his waist. Glowing with happiness, Olan Moresten slapped him hard on the shoulder in satisfaction. He then stepped down, taking his place next to Mary who held her hands out in greeting.

Gavyn Wellbrown began the ceremony. His voice was low, and somber. More somber than she expected from the old man she met in the past who seemed to be such a jolly chap. She dismissed it as his being serious about the moment, and perhaps nervous about his task.

After presenting them both with the bitter root, then the sweet fruit, Gavyn took the cover off the last of three vessels on the table and said, "And last, salt. Salt cures, preserves, and makes pure." He took a pinch of salt in his fingers. "Lady Veronica Moresten, daughter of Olan sovereign of Trodenheim, will you take Fredrick for your husband? To be faithful to him, to bear his children, be his lover, and preserve the name of the family Raddlif until death takes you from him?"

Veronica looked at Fredrick who smiled

brightly behind his sickly face. The words struck her as she listened to them in the moment. It suddenly seemed like an eternity since she arrived in the Splinterwood with her heart set on finding a way out of this marriage. Now, she heard the words, and she hesitated to answer but for reasons she could never have imagined. She had two on her mind. One a man. Handsome, brave, and devoted. The other a monster. Savage, wild, and forbidden. Both wanted her. Now she stood before one, knowing that she could never stand before the other, caring for both, and wanting the best for them. And what of Amma? The thought that she betrayed her memory with her fascination for Gnash weighed heavily on her heart. Keeping things from Fredrick, like Gnash's night visit, beset her mind with guilt. She felt the raging river of emotions rising in her mind would eventually drown her heart, but, at last, she took a deep breath. The time for her choice had come.

"I will," she said proudly. She made sure she said it loud enough for all to hear, making sure no one who would ever write a song or story about this day would ever deny her choice.

"Face me," said Gavyn. As she did, he reached out and sprinkled the salt on her lips, afterward taking up a second pinch and holding it as before.

"Baron-Apparent Fredrick Raddlif, seventh Raddlif Baron and third in the Splinterwood Forest, will you accept Lady Veronica as your wife and lover. To hold her, to love her, to protect and keep her as you will your family name, until death takes you from her?"

"I will," said Fredrick without hesitation.
"Face me."

Wellbrown sprinkled the pinch of salt on
Fredrick's lips.

"And now by the leave of both Baron Manfred
and Count Olan, as well as their families, I pronounce
you husband and wife. The salt on your lips is the
symbol of the healing, cleansing, and preserving
nature of the union of marriage. Fredrick, you may
kiss your bride."

Veronica saw her new spouse beam a smile as
Gavyn fell silent. He took a half step forward and the
two joined hands as the crowd around the tables stood
waiting in anticipation. As their lips met, she felt a
warmth run through her as if she just taken a quick
shot of a strong alcoholic drink. He put his body right
against hers, kissing her deeply. Her knees trembled.
Sensing it through their kiss, Fredrick's hand snapped
to the small of her back, steadying her to the erupting
ovation of the group looking on.

"Save it for the wedding suite!" shouted the
voice of Bertrum Krell among the applause, followed
by the sound of laughter.

"You will not have to wait long for that
grandchild, Olan!" shouted another voice.

"Atta' boy!" responded Olan, as he pulled
Mary close to him. "I might start on my next one
tonight! Aye, Mary?"

The Countess blushed, wiping away tears from
her eyes and slapping Olan playfully on the cheek

while he went on laughing at his own jape.

Fredrick dropped from the stone dais and took Veronica by the waist, helping her down. From there, the two took their place at the wedding table.

Veronica relaxed amid the merry gathering. She tasted the sweet wine and enjoyed it.

The newlyweds sat in silence as they ate their meal together beneath the gray swirl of clouds gathered overhead. They felt that their guests were doing the talking for them. They turned their attentions energetically about the table as the strong wine and ale loosened everyone's spirits. Soon the conversation was so loud it nearly drowned out the musician's happy tunes.

The wedding gifts floated about the table as the guests each took a turn inspecting them. They were all valuable items of clothing, jewelry, and occasionally rare books and trinkets from their individual lands. The most useful of the gifts came from none other than the often aloof, Bertrum Krell. The gray day had already grown cold, and the Lord of Krellton presented Veronica with a dark-green hooded cape. It was well crafted, and trimmed with fur. Down the right breast, embroidered in silver, were the three tokens of Raddlif, Moresten, and then finally the twin chevrons of Krell's own house. She was grateful for the gift, and wrapped it around her shoulders to keep off the oncoming chill.

Soon, the guests sat back in their chairs with full bellies. Only bones and gristle remained on the serving platters among the empty breadbaskets, gravy trenchers, and overturned spice bowls.

At last, the Baron stood at the head of the table, holding out his goblet to his guests. "Friends," he said as a hush fell over the gathering. His voice was downcast. His unkempt appearance made it even more so. "All of you know where this tale begins, and today, chapter one is completed, and Fredrick and Veronica's new life will begin chapter two. Count Olan, will you rise and join me?"

"Aye!" said Olan as he stood up shakily, holding out the flagon of ale in one hand while balancing himself against the table with the other.

"Dear friends," said Manfred, "will you join me in wishing happiness and long life and love to Fredrick and Veronica? May these two have healthy children, and a peaceful life as they carry this family on through this generation, laying the path for the next one." The Baron paused and stared into his drink. He looked to Veronica as if he had something else he wanted to say, but something stopped him. Finally, he collected himself and said only, "as they must do for both our families, so they may endure for all time."

The guests applauded as Manfred finished. Everyone, held up their goblets and toasted the newlyweds. Even Gavyn, who had been so sullen before, lifted his goblet and drank quickly, but still bore a crestfallen air about him.

"Son, will you address our guests?" Manfred continued.

Fredrick stood, "Honored friends, I thank you for coming. On behalf of myself, and my new wife," he paused, sharing a smile with Veronica, "I thank you for the beautiful gifts. I thank you for the loyalty you have shown my Father. I shall aim to earn and keep that trust in his stead when it is my time to rule this forest and these lands." Fredrick raised his goblet above his head in salute then continued, "To you friends, and to the future."

The guests around the table responded in agreement, lifting their cups. Some sipped politely, while others quaffed them down deeply.

The celebration continued through the afternoon despite the worsening weather. As the guests grew tired, the party slowed and small pockets of conversation formed.

Count Olan stumbled around the groups, slapping his friends hard on the back as he arrived. He greeted each of them with a warm belly laugh, saying something most of them could not understand through his slurred speech, then he moved on to the next group.

Finally, rain fell on the bailey, soaking the celebrators in a deluge. Manfred Raddlif cried out, "Friends, the rain is threatening to cut short the celebration." Most of the women were running for cover, but stopped when they heard the Baron's voice. "Shall we escort the lovers to the wedding suite?" he said holding is arms out to his sides to highlight the question. It was clear he had taken his fill of the ale as well.

A great cheer came up from the guests at Manfred's question. The women collected Veronica, and the men gathered Fredrick. The newlyweds found themselves at the head of the tumultuous group, and escorted into the foyer. The crowd moved along the corridors to a chamber high in the tower where the group pushed them, one at a time into the suite then slamming the door behind them.

"I want that grandson right away!" said the drunken Count, slurring his words.

"Don't do anything I wouldn't do, Veronica!" said one of the women whose voice she did not recognize.

"Well that isn't," responded another of the men, followed by the slapping sound of hand on flesh amid the mischievous laughter.

Veronica stood at the door listening. The mirth faded as the footsteps of the guests retreated from the tower. After a time, all that remained was the sound of the rain as it fell outside.

"Are you cold?" asked Fredrick as he approached the still unlit fireplace.

"A little," answered Veronica. Now that she was alone with her new husband, her nervousness returned.

She looked around the room. It was oval, and in its center was a bed covered with dark-green linen. Each post was carved at the top in the shape of different trees of the Splinterwood. A sheer canopy of thin cloth with its corners embroidered with sprigs of ivy surrounded the bed. Intricately sewn tapestries lined the walls with a single lancet facing to the east, looking to where the sun would rise the next morning.

The wooden floor was covered by an oval rug, tan in color, and taking up most of the floor. Drops of falling rain splashed through the lancet, soaking the heavy drapes that hung at it sides and held open by a golden line of string. Oil lamps swung from cleats set into the ceiling, burning with a warm orange glow. A table bearing a flagon and a platter of small cakes, along with silver cups, sat near the lancet for the newlyweds.

Both had expected it to be later before retiring to the bridal suite, but with the rain, the two arrived sooner than anticipated.

"It will be cold in the forest tonight," said Fredrick, "but I love the smell when the rain comes."

Veronica stood just inside the closed door watching her new husband in nervous anticipation of what was to come. He took a lamp from the cleat on the wall and brought it near to the fireplace where strips of cloth waited. He lit an end of one, and placed it onto a carefully stacked pile of wood waiting within the hearth. Rapidly, the fire quickened to a tall flame in the dry wood, warming the chamber and filling it with a soothing light.

Fredrick did not stand once the blaze began. He loitered on one knee, tending the flame with a poker in his uninjured hand, staring into the bright flames and removing his gauntlets.

"Hard to believe this chamber was for storage a few months past, isn't it?" he said finishing with a chuckle. "Father felt my bed-chamber is too small. It took us weeks and twenty cats to get the rats out so we could move the furniture in. But don't worry, the staff cleaned it thoroughly. One day, it will serve as the wedding suite for our children."

He is nervous, she thought as she listened quietly. His nervousness made her own more bearable.

Finally, Fredrick turned to face his bride.

"I'm not sure why I'm telling you that," he said, with an anxious smile.

She smiled, remained silent, and crossed the room to approach him. The two of them stood face-to-face. Veronica looked up to meet his eyes. They were so close together each could feel the other's breath on their faces. Gently, Fredrick kissed her. She felt her temperature rising, as if the fire he had lit in the hearth had suddenly taken hold of her as well through his kiss. He put his arms around her, but favored his wounded arm in doing so. Using his uninjured hand, he unfastened the buttons of the gown while they kissed.

Her excitement and expectation grew, slowly overtaking her tension. She felt her body changing as Fredrick's touch aroused her. His hands were coarse, and the injured one, cold. They were hands of a man who knew weapons, tools and labor.

Step by slow step, the two made their way closer to the bed. Veronica's gown hung around her loosely. With a shrug of the shoulders, it fell to the chamber floor, leaving only her transparent, diaphanous silk underclothes that caressed her curves closely.

Fredrick pulled the canopy-drape to one side and loosened his own clothing as she watched him.

Her chest heaved as she breathed, waiting to unleash her growing excitement on her new husband.

Embracing each other, they laid on the bed. She glanced through the lancet at the still falling rain and receding light of the day. At last, she closed her eyes and the two of them, united in their lives together, joined in flesh and blood.

***

Veronica's eyes opened slowly, finding herself next to Fredrick. Both laid naked in the warm and comfortable bed. She could still feel the results of their passion about her body. Having been her first time with a man, the sensation felt at first painful, despite Fredrick's slow tenderness, but later pleasurable, and now a lingering pleasant sensation remained.

Turning in the bed, she noticed that it was still dark over the forest. The falling rain had stopped, leaving the sill of the lancet wet and dripping.

For a few moments, she laid still in contemplation of the day she had experienced. She smiled as she thought back to the ceremony, the food, the music, the words spoken to each other, and the drink from which her head still swooned. She listened to Fredrick who slept deeply. His breathing was deep and regular.

The hearth in the fireplace was cold and dying, no longer the blaze that raged during the passion she and Fredrick shared. Her mind wandered back, remembering how Fredrick had held her and how it felt to have him within her most intimate embrace.

Occasionally while the two made love she opened her eyes. She remembered seeing the fire in the hearth. The tall flames spilled from it, licking the stones at the top of the fireplace as it raged, growing hotter and higher. The flames grew with the excitement both she and Fredrick experienced. Though it was Veronica's first, it became clear it was not Fredrick's, despite whatever impressions his family was under.

Hunger gnawed at her belly as she laid in the bed peering out to the darkness beyond the lancet. The still lingering clouds darkened the moonlight, and the blackness outside seemed as if she could reach out and drag her fingers along it as she would a smooth silken drape.

Her cast-off gown still lay in a pile where it had fallen. Drawing back the covers carefully to not wake Fredrick, Veronica rose out of bed and put on her gown. The garment hung loosely around her as she walked across the chamber to the plate on the table.

Into the cup, she poured some wine from the flagon. She never liked the wine before, but now the taste seemed more palatable. She sipped it lightly. On the plate sat various fruits and small pastries. She took one of the cakes and ate it. Its texture was flakey, the center filled with sweetened apples.

As she washed the apples over her tongue, savoring their sweet flavor, a strange feeling swept over her. The hairs on the back of her neck stiffened. She scanned the room, looking for the source of the peculiar sensation.

What is that? Was it movement?

She stood still, peering into the darkness, wondering if whatever disturbed her was only her imagination. At first, she saw nothing. Still, a sense of inquisitiveness came into her mind with a spark of fear growing into flame. At first, she wanted to run, to wake Fredrick. She looked to him as he slept. She took a single step toward him before stopping herself. Although fear coursed through her veins, she did not want to wake him. A curious boldness surfaced above the fear as she waited for the sensation to come again.

She heard a sound coming from outside the lancet.

That's it. It's a scraping noise, she thought as she turned toward it leaning forward and straining to listen.

The sound was subtle, almost natural, but loud enough to hear it. The sound was familiar, like a dog who tries to run on stone but slips and does not gain footing, leaving its claws to drag along the surface. She walked to the lancet and looked out. At first, she saw nothing in the thick and lingering blackness. Then, slowly and stealthily, a shadow moved. A streak of lightning lit up the sky and she caught a glimpse of a drenched figure clinging to the stones of the wall illuminated by the flash.

"Woman, it is done then?" whispered the darkness.

Her fear turned into a forbidden excitement. Veronica quickly composed herself to not gasp or cry out and wake Fredrick. For if she did, she would doom the figure on the wall. Once she heard the whisper, she knew who clung there in the dark.

"Yes," she answered in a soundless whisper.

"Do you know the tower above this chamber?"

Veronica nodded. It was the same tower that Fredrick had taken her to on the night of their feast.

"Go there. Do not wake your manling," said the hushed voice.

Falling silent, the figure climbed the sheer face of the castle and disappeared.

Excitement gripped Veronica's heart. Clutching at her gown to keep it from falling away, she walked lightly. She was unsure of the time and did not know if guests were still milling around the corridors celebrating. She stopped at the door and listened, hearing nothing outside. Quietly, she turned the knob and slipped out.

Through the corridors she crept like a thief who had stolen the property of a king. Carefully, she checked her corners before passing to remain unseen. Her heart hammered in her chest and she realized that she was perspiring from the heated emotions driving her mind. The cold drafts of the castle met the moisture on Veronica's face and neck, sending chills down her spine, and she had to fight to keep her teeth from chattering.

She followed the winding stairs to the tower roof. At the top, Gnash had opened the trapdoor, and she climbed through to find him at the edge near the battlements. He was but a lithe shadow under the returning rain. He wore only a tight pair of leather trousers and his feet were bare. He breathed deeply from his climbing, and his soaked hair clung to his head.

"Why have you come?" she asked.

Gnash smiled wryly at her before he answered, "Why have I come? The question is, why have *you* come, Little One?"

The unasked question, 'why have you not called the guards?' hung in the air between them. With no answer to offer, Veronica remained silent. *Why do I protect this creature that the family calls a 'fiend'?*

After the silence between the two of them passed, Gnash said, "To answer your question, I have come to bid you farewell, and tell you I regret what must happen here. At least, to you, Little One. When I took you, I fully intended to ransom you and likely, kill you. To make you an example of what happens when someone attacks my friends and family. I did not let my ogon have you because murder is one thing, rape is another. I will not have it said by the manling that I am a rapist. You are strong, though I don't believe you understand that strength in yourself. You have earned my respect, and my protection. I had thoughts to take you as a wife. To offer you a place in my clan, and I would not have you soiled by others who had no intention for you beyond their own pleasure. Your manling's boldness in coming to your rescue has made this even more difficult. If it were not for you, he would have defeated me when we faced each other in combat. Even he too has earned a measure of respect I cannot deny for his bravery and skill."

"What will happen? What are you saying, Gnash?" she asked, calling him by name to soften his heart, sensing the worsening threat that lingered and feeling concern for both Fredrick and he.

"Your 'Baron'," said Gnash snidely, "has hanged Ghronn and left his body to rot. He hanged him because I took you. Do not fear, I hold you blameless in his death, which is why I regret that you should be involved in my revenge. I told you I will have vengeance, or my Brother. With Ghronn dead, only revenge remains." He was angry now and his voice grew louder. Veronica feared he would be heard, but now, with these threats, and feelings that she was powerless to stop him, she wondered if it was not for the best if he were.

"Gnash," she said softly. "Don't do this. Give me time. Let me speak for you. One day Fredrick will be Baron. He did not execute your Brother. His father did. He was injured and had no part of it. With time, I can heal this rift between the two of you. There can be peace."

"He is an invader, just as his father and his grandfather were. He no longer has his friends among the Red Hand. The manling's Father has angered that drunken coward Gan'Sann, and it will be to his doom that he did. Even now he rides into the forest with his men to gain knowledge and salvage the pact, but he is failing." Gnash went silent and approached Veronica.

He stood close to her and she saw his face through the dim moonlight. The darkness softened it and it did not appear so ugly to her now. With the back of his hand, he touched her cheek. His hand was still warm despite the chilling wind.

"Return to your land, Little One. Go with your father and return to your home. He is a brave man, and a good warrior. I had to spear him myself to stop him, and still I missed, only wounding him."

It was Gnash! Gnash nearly killed my father. Why do I feel this way? Was his protection so valuable? Why do I not call out? Veronica's thoughts raged like a fire in her mind, separate from her words she spoke. She could not understand her own heart, and the sensation was like nothing else she had ever experienced.

"I cannot," she responded, her voice wavering from the cold and her gathering emotions.

"I do not want you to watch me destroy this manling of yours, but I will," he replied, his tone just short of pleading. "Everything here, I will raze. I will purge the invaders from the forest. Just as we should have before the other clans convinced my people there was value in their presence."

"Please don't, Gnash. Please," pleaded Veronica. "Let me speak with him. You can have peace with his family. You can! The Baron is old and set in his ways. I have forgiven you what happened to Amma, because of what you did to protect me. Because you did not kill me as well. Can you not forgive Fredrick? For me Gnash, put aside your anger. It is duty; it is duty that has driven all of us to this pain. For once, let us do something for ourselves, and forgive. End the pain–"

As Veronica spoke, Gnash held up his hand, interrupting her. "You do not understand. He is not who you think he is anymore. The Red-Hands have performed their blood-magic on him. No good can come of it."

Veronica paused as confusion swept through her mind. "What are you saying?" she asked after a long silence. "What magic?"

"The manling is cursed. Ogon should not cast incantations on men, but they did. My own people will not perform blood-rites. It is forbidden, but the Red-Hands are conjurers, they are evil."

When she heard Gnash refer to the Red-Hands as evil, she marveled at the irony. She wondered if the Red-Hand felt that way about themselves, and knew the Raddlifs did not see them in that light at all.

Could it be they chose the wrong side years ago, and never realized it? Is there even a right side to choose in this forest?

"I do not know if the curse will affect the cub you have produced tonight," said Gnash.

"A child? How do you know that?"

"You have already conceived it; I can smell it on you."

Veronica felt exposed. *Can he read my mind, and my body?* she wondered, fearing that it might be so.

"What did the Red-Hands do?" she asked, as concern for Fredrick overrode her other feelings.

"Though he is still angry with me, Lahn the

green-man told me what happened at the bridge," said Gnash. "I'm not a conjurer, and do not understand such things, but their ways are unnatural, no good can come of it. Torgk has been the guardian of three Red-Hand Chieftains. He is kept alive by unnatural means, but he is ogon, not a man. I suspect it is the same with Fredrick now, and since it affects him, it could affect your cub as well. Torgk has no offspring."

Veronica turned from Gnash and walked to the edge of the wall as a bolt of golden lightning rent the sky overhead. The thunder that followed was loud, rolling along the clouds as it died into the storm. The rain poured heavily as Veronica stood at the battlements. Tears ran down her face as she fought to hold back her emotions.

The two stood apart in silence. Then, Veronica perceived Fredrick's voice calling out from below.

Fearing for her husband, his enemy standing on the tower, she turned back toward the intruder. Gnash was still there, standing in the downpour with his golden gaze fixed on her. The footsteps grew louder. They were heavy and rapid. Fredrick was running up the corridor, and soon would be ascending the winding steps to the tower.

"If you ever wish to find me, come to the bridge on the first day of Treeswake. What your people call spring," said Gnash. He held his hand out to Veronica as though he were asking her to come with him. She stood motionless, overwhelmed by what was transpiring. Then, Gnash turned away, and with a deft leap, he jumped over the battlements and climbed down the way he came, leaving her alone on the tower.

"Veronica?" said Fredrick, as he emerged through the trapdoor. "What are you doing out here? You'll catch your death in this rain."

She stayed silent. Unmoving. She felt as if she had just awakened and was puzzled as to whether this was real or just a dream.

Fredrick put his arms around her as the downpour soaked them both. She clutched at his arms around her chest as if he suddenly anchored her to reality. She loved him now, and she knew her place.

"Hold me, Fredrick."

"What is wrong, why are you up here?"

"We came up here once before, do you remember?" asked Veronica. "I told you I did not want you, or this marriage. I regret saying that. I came here to put those selfish feelings behind me, and hope that you can forgive me."

Veronica heard her own spoken half-truth. She had come to the tower to see an ogon that was the enemy of her husband. Now, he was gone, having delivered his grim message. When she found herself in Fredrick's arms she wanted to put all her harsh words behind her, despite what her original purpose was in coming to this place. Though her confession about her regrets were not true when she came here, they became true as she took comfort in her husband's embrace. She knew in her heart, that she was Fredrick's wife to whatever end it led. Her love for him had taken root, just as her father said it would. She was determined to stand by him, despite Gnash's

272

warning and threats. Suddenly and poignantly, she understood duty, and the sometimes-dreadful cost of it. They stood in the furious rain, and she wished that the falling water could wash away the fear she felt for the future they faced together.

"Those words are forgotten," said Fredrick. "You are my wife now. All that I have and all that I am, are yours. Come down. I'll rebuild the fire and we'll take off these wet clothes."

The two of them descended back into the castle. On a whim, Veronica turned and looked at the spot over which Gnash had leaped for his final descent. There she noticed a silhouette flying high, framed against the furious lightning in the sky. It drew closer and landed on the battlements. She could not see its face, but she knew she had seen the figure before and realized it was an owl. The one who visited her in the dome, and had been recently riding upon Fredrick's shoulder.

"Whooo," said the bird before it flew away again into the night sky.

An uncomfortable remorseful feeling washed over her as she watched the bird soar away. She asked herself quietly if it had been near the entire time she spoke with Gnash.

Was the Owl listening? What did it hear?

She dismissed it, and followed her husband into the tower, retreating to their wedding chamber.

Lying in bed with Fredrick, listening to him breathe and trying to relax her tortured mind, the excitement of her rendezvous lingered in her hammering heart.

I must find a way to heal them, she thought silently as she laid with her hand on Fredrick's chest.

I will. I must.

Making up her mind to heal the rift between the two-who-would-be-enemies in her heart no matter the cost, she slowly relaxed, and fell into a peaceful sleep at her husband's side.